TALES OF THE BLACK WIDOWERS

- A victim has so many possessions that he doesn't know what was stolen from him

- A girl sees a fire, three thousand miles away—a half hour before it starts

- A crook gets his Ph.D. through an unusually ingenious plan for cheating

- A conspiracy in Uncle Sam's Army involves Yankee Doodle

These are just some of the tantalizing problems that confront and confound the members of the Black Widowers Club.

"Appealing five-finger exercises."
—*Kirkus Reviews*

ISAAC ASIMOV

TALES
of the
BLACK WIDOWERS

A FAWCETT CREST BOOK

Fawcett Publications, Inc., Greenwich, Connecticut

TALES OF THE BLACK WIDOWERS

THIS BOOK CONTAINS THE COMPLETE TEXT OF
THE ORIGINAL HARDCOVER EDITION.

A Fawcett Crest Book reprinted by arrangement with
Doubleday and Company, Inc.

ISBN 0-449-22944-0

Printed in the United States of America

10 9 8 7 6 5 4 3 2

To Ellery Queen's Mystery Magazine

to David Ford

and to the Trap-Door Spiders

for reasons detailed in the introduction

Special Note

The erudite copy reader points out that since the stories that follow were written for separate publication in a magazine originally, I identify the continuing characters each time, and do it repetitiously. He pointed out several of the more nauseating examples of this and, with reverence for his exalted position, I corrected the matter in accordance with his suggestions. There undoubtedly remain some dozens of repetitions that could bear revision, but I hate to introduce too many changes from the pristine originals. Would you forgive me, then, for permitting them to stay?

Contents

Introduction

Because I have a friendly and personal writing style, readers have a tendency to write to me in a friendly and personal way, asking all kinds of friendly and personal questions. And because I really am what my writing style, such as it is, portrays me to be, I answer those letters. And since I don't have a secretary or any form of assistant whatever, it takes a lot of the time I should be devoting to writing.

It is only natural, then, that I have taken to writing introductions to my books in an attempt to answer some of the anticipated questions in advance, thus forestalling some of the letters.

For instance, because I write in many fields, I frequently get questions such as these:

"Why do you, a lowly science fiction writer, think you can write a two-volume work on Shakespeare?"

"Why do you, a Shakespearean scholar, choose to write science fiction thrillers?"

"What gives you, a biochemist, the nerve to write books on history?"

"What makes you, a mere historian, think you know anything about science?"

And so on, and so on.

It seems certain, then, that I will be asked, either with amusement or with exasperation, why I am writing mystery stories.

Here goes, then.

I started my writing career in science fiction, and I still write science fiction when I can, for it remains my first and chief literary love. However, I am interested in many things and among them has been the mystery. I have been reading mysteries almost as long as I have been reading science fiction. I remember risking my life when, as a ten-year-old, I pilfered forbidden copies of *The Shadow* from under my father's pillow when he was taking his afternoon nap. (I asked him why *he* read it if I was forbidden, and he said he needed it in order to learn English, whereas I had the advantage of school. What a rotten reason I thought that was.)

In writing science fiction, then, I frequently introduced the mystery motif. Two of my novels, *The Caves of Steel* (Doubleday, 1953) and *The Naked Sun* (Doubleday, 1957), are full-fledged murder mysteries for all that they are science fiction as well. I have written enough shorter science fiction mysteries of one sort or another to make it possible to publish a collection of them as *Asimov's Mysteries* (Doubleday, 1968).

I also wrote a "straight" mystery novel, *The Death Dealers* (Avon, 1958),* which was eventually reissued in 1968 by Walker & Company under my own title of *A Whiff of Death*. This, however, dealt entirely with science and scientists and its atmosphere was still that of the science fiction novel, as was true of two mystery short stories I sold to mystery magazines.

Increasingly, I felt the itch to write mysteries that had nothing to do with science. One thing that held me back, though, was the fact that the mystery had evolved in the last quarter-century and my tastes had not. Mysteries these days are heavily drenched in liquor, injected with drugs, marinated in sex, and roasted in sadism, whereas my detective ideal is Hercule Poirot and his little gray cells.

But then, back in 1971, I received a letter from that gorgeous blond young lady, Eleanor Sullivan, who is managing editor of *Ellery Queen's Mystery Magazine* (or *EQMM* for short), asking if I would consider writing a short story for the magazine. Of course, I jubilantly agreed, because I thought that if they *asked* for one, they couldn't possibly have the cruelty to reject it once written,

---

* Well, it was rejected by Doubleday, if you must know.

and that meant I could safely write my own kind of story —very cerebral.

I began revolving plot possibilities in my head rather anxiously, for I wanted something with a reasonable twist to it and Agatha Christie, all by herself, had already used virtually all possible twists.

While the wheels were slowly turning in the recesses of my mind, I happened to be visiting the actor David Ford (who was in both the Broadway and Hollywood versions of *1776*). His apartment is filled with all kinds of interesting oddities, and he told me that he was convinced once that someone had taken something from his apartment but he could never be sure because he couldn't tell whether anything was missing.

I laughed and all the wheels in my head, heaving a collective sigh of relief, stopped turning. I had my twist.

I then needed a background against which to display the twist and here we have something else.

Back in the early 1940's, legend has it, someone got married to a lady who found her husband's friends unacceptable, and vice versa. In order to avoid breaking off a valued relationship, those friends organized a club without officers or bylaws for the sole purpose of having a dinner once a month. It would be a stag organization so that the husband in question could be invited to join and his wife legitimately requested not to attend. (Nowadays, with Women's Lib so powerful, this might not have worked.)

The organization was named the Trap-Door Spiders (or TDS, for short) probably because the members felt themselves to be hiding.

Thirty years have passed since the TDS was organized but it still exists. It is still stag, though the member whose marriage inspired the organization is long since divorced. (As a concession to male non-chauvinism, a cocktail party was given on February 3 1973, at which the TDS wives could meet one another—and this may become an annual custom.)

Once a month, the TDS meets, always on a Friday night, almost always in Manhattan, sometimes in a restaurant, sometimes in a member's apartment. Each meeting is co-hosted by two volunteers who bear all the expenses for the occasion and who may each bring a guest. The average attendance is twelve. There are drinks and conversation from 6:30 to 7:30 P.M.; food and conversation from 7:30 to 8:30 P.M.; and just conversation thereafter.

After the meal each guest is grilled on his interests, his profession, his hobbies, his views, and the results are almost always interesting, often fascinating.

The chief among the general eccentricities of the TDS are these: (1) Every member is addressed as "Doctor" by the others, the title going along with the membership, and (2) each member is supposed to try to arrange for a mention of the TDS in his obituary.

I had been a guest myself on two different occasions, and when I moved to New York in 1970, I was elected to membership.

Well, then, thought I, why not tell my mystery story against the background of the meeting of an organization something like the TDS? My club would be called the Black Widowers and I would cut it in half to make it manageable—six people and one host.

Naturally, there are differences. The members of the TDS have never, in real life, attempted to solve mysteries and none of them is as idiosyncratic as the members of the Black Widowers. In fact, the members of the TDS are, one and all, lovable people and there is a mutual affection that is touching to see. Therefore, please be assured that the characters and events in the stories in this book are my own invention and are not to be equated with anyone or anything in the TDS, except insofar as they may seem intelligent or lovable.

In particular, Henry, the waiter, is my own invention and has no analogue, however remote, in the TDS.

So, having my plot and my background, I wrote a story

I named "The Chuckle." It was accepted by *EQMM*, which renamed it "The Acquisitive Chuckle."†

After the first sale, there was no stopping me, of course. I began to write one Black Widower tale after another and in little more than a year I had written eight and sold each of them to *EQMM*.

The trouble was that, even though I was holding myself back, and not writing as many as I wanted to write, I was still producing them faster than *EQMM* could publish them.

I finally broke under the strain of not-writing, so I wrote three more, at my natural rate of production, and decided not to plague the magazine with them. Then I wrote a fourth and sold it to them. That brought the total to twelve, with enough wordage for a book. My loyal publishers, Doubleday & Company, had been waiting patiently in the wings ever since the first story, so I am now putting them together as *Tales of the Black Widowers*—and here you are.

Any questions?‡

---

† *EQMM* invariably changes my titles. This doesn't bother me, because I always look forward to book publication, in which I can change the titles back to what they should be. Sometimes I don't, as, on rare occasions, an editorial change of title meets my approval. For instance, I really think "The Acquisitive Chuckle" is better than "The Chuckle," so I am keeping that.

‡ I hope not.

1

The Acquisitive Chuckle

Hanley Bartram was the guest, that night, of the Black Widowers, who monthly met in their quiet haunt and vowed death to any female who intruded—for that one night per month, at any rate.

The number of attendees varied: five members were present on this occasion.

Geoffrey Avalon was host for the evening. He was tall, with a neatly trimmed mustache and a smallish beard, more white than black now, but with hair nearly as black as ever.

As host, it was his duty to deliver the ritual toast that marked the beginning of the dinner proper. Loudly, and with gusto, he said, "To Old King Cole of sacred memory. May his pipe be forever lit, his bowl forever full, his fiddlers forever in health, and may we all be as merry as he all our lives long."

Each cried, "Amen," touched his lips to drink, and sat down. Avalon put his drink to the side of his plate. It was his second and was now exactly half full. It would remain there throughout the dinner and was not to be touched again. He was a patent lawyer and he carried over into his social life the minutiae of his work. One and a half drinks was precisely what he allowed himself on these occasions.

Thomas Trumbull came storming up the stairs at the last minute, with the usual cry of "Henry, a scotch and soda for a dying man."

Henry, the waiter at these functions for several years now (and with no last name that any Black Widower had ever heard used), had the scotch and soda in readiness. He was sixtyish but his face was unwrinkled and staid.

His voice seemed to recede into the distance even as he spoke. "Right here, Mr. Trumbull."

Trumbull spotted Bartram at once and said to Avalon in an aside, "Your guest?"

"He asked to come," said Avalon, in as near a whisper as he could manage. "Nice fellow. You'll like him."

The dinner itself went as miscellaneously as the Black Widowers' affairs usually did. Emmanuel Rubin, who had the other beard—a thin and scraggly one under a mouth with widely spaced teeth—had broken out of a writer's block and was avidly giving the details of the story he had finished. James Drake, with a rectangular face, a mustache but no beard, was interrupting with memories of other stories, tangentially related. Drake was only an organic chemist but he had an encyclopedic knowledge of pulp fiction.

Trumbull, as a code expert, considered himself to be in the inner councils of government and took it into his head to be outraged at Mario Gonzalo's political pronouncements. "God damn it," he yelled, in one of his less vituperative moods, "why don't you stick to your idiotic collages and your burlap bags and leave world affairs to your betters?"

Trumbull had not recovered from Gonzalo's one-man art show earlier that year, and Gonzalo, understanding this, laughed good-naturedly, and said, "Show me my betters. Name one."

Bartram, short and plump, with hair that curled in ringlets, clung firmly to his role as guest. He listened to everyone, smiled at everyone, and said little.

Eventually the time came when Henry poured the coffee and began to place the desserts before each guest with practiced legerdemain. It was at this moment that the traditional grilling of the guest was supposed to begin.

The initial questioner, almost by tradition (on those occasions when he was present), was Thomas Trumbull. His swarthy face, wrinkled into a perennial discontent, looked angry as he began with the invariable opening question: "Mr. Bartram, how do you justify your existence?"

Bartram smiled. He spoke with precision as he said, "I have never tried. My clients, on those occasions when I give satisfaction, find my existence justified."

"Your clients?" said Rubin. "What is it you do, Mr. Bartram?"

"I am a private investigator."

"Good," said James Drake. "I don't think we've ever had one before. Manny, you can get some of the data correct for a change when you write your tough-guy crap."

"Not from me," said Bartram quickly.

Trumbull scowled. "If you don't mind, gentlemen, as the appointed grillster, please leave this to me. Mr. Bartram, you speak of the occasions upon which you give satisfaction. Do you always give satisfaction?"

"There are times when the matter can be debated," said Bartram. "In fact, I would like to speak to you this evening concerning an occasion that was particularly questionable. It may even be that one of you might be useful in that connection. It was with that in mind that I asked my good friend Jeff Avalon to invite me to a meeting, once I learned the details of the organization. He obliged and I am delighted."

"Are you ready now to discuss this dubious satisfaction you gave or did not give, as the case may be?"

"Yes, if you will allow me."

Trumbull looked at the others for signs of dissent. Gonzalo's prominent eyes were fixed on Bartram as he said, "May we interrupt?" Quickly, and with an admirable economy of strokes, he was doodling a caricature of Bartram on the back of his menu card. It would join the others which memorialized guests and which marched in brave array across the walls.

"Within reason," said Bartram. He paused to sip at his coffee and then said, "The story begins with Anderson, to whom I shall refer only in that fashion. He was an acquisitor."

"An inquisitor?" asked Gonzalo, frowning.

"An *acquisitor*. He gained things, he earned them, he bought them, he picked them up, he collected them. The world moved in one direction with respect to him; it moved toward him; never away. He had a house into which this flood of material, of varying value, came to rest and never moved again. Through the years, it grew steadily thicker and amazingly heterogeneous. He also had a business partner, whom I shall call only Jackson."

Trumbull interrupted, frowning, not because there was anything to frown about, but because he always frowned. He said, "Is this a true story?"

"I tell only true stories," said Bartram slowly and precisely. "I lack the imagination to lie."

"Is it confidential?"

"I shall not tell the story in such a way as to make it easily recognized, but were it to be recognized, it would be confidential."

"I follow the subjunctive," said Trumbull, "but I wish to assure you that what is said within the walls of this room is never repeated, nor referred to, however tangentially, outside its walls. Henry understands this, too."

Henry, who was refilling two of the coffeecups, smiled a little and bent his head in agreement.

Bartram smiled also and went on, "Jackson had a disease, too. He was honest; unavoidably and deeply honest. The characteristic permeated his soul as though, from an early age, he had been marinated in integrity.

"To a man like Anderson, it was most useful to have honest Jackson as partner, for their business, which I carefully do not describe in detail, required contact with the public. Such contact was not for Anderson, for his acquisitiveness stood in the way. With each object he acquired, another little crease of slyness entered his face, until it seemed a spider's web that frightened all flies at sight. It was Jackson, the pure and the honest, who was the front man, and to whom all widows hastened with their mites, and orphans with their farthings.

"On the other hand, Jackson found Anderson a necessity, too, for Jackson, with all his honesty, perhaps because of it, had no knack for making one dollar become two. Left to himself, he would, entirely without meaning to, lose every cent entrusted to him and would then quickly be forced to kill himself as a dubious form of restitution. Anderson's hands were to money, however, as fertilizer is to roses, and he and Jackson were, together, a winning combination.

"Yet no paradise continues forever, and a besetting characteristic, left to itself, will deepen, widen, and grow more extreme. Jackson's honesty grew to such colossal proportions that Anderson, for all his shrewdness, was occasionally backed to the wall and forced into monetary loss. Similarly, Anderson's acquisitiveness burrowed to such infernal depths that Jackson, for all his morality, found himself occasionally twisted into questionable practices.

"Naturally, as Anderson disliked losing money, and Jackson abhorred losing character, a coolness grew between the two. In such a situation the advantage clearly lay on the side of Anderson, who placed no reasonable limits on his actions, whereas Jackson felt himself bound by a code of ethics.

"Slyly, Anderson worked and maneuvered until, eventually, poor honest Jackson found himself forced to sell out his end of the partnership under the most disadvantageous possible conditions.

"Anderson's acquisitiveness, we might say, had reached a climax, for he acquired sole control of the business. It was his intention to retire now, leaving its everyday running to employees, and concerning himself no further than was required to pocket its profits. Jackson, on the other hand, was left with nothing more than his honesty, and while honesty is an admirable characteristic, it has small direct value in a hockshop.

"It was at this point, gentlemen, that I entered the picture. . . . Ah, Henry, thank you."

The glasses of brandy were being passed about.

"You did not know these people to begin with?" asked Rubin, his sharp eyes blinking.

"Not at all," said Bartram, sniffing delicately at the brandy and just touching it to his upper lip, "though I think one of you in this room did. It was some years ago.

"I first met Anderson when he entered my office in a

white heat. 'I want you to find what I've lost,' he said. I have dealt with many cases of theft in my career and so I said, naturally, 'Just what is it you have lost?' And he answered, 'Damn it, man, that's what I've just asked you to find out.'

"The story came out rather raggedly. Anderson and Jackson had quarreled with surprising intensity. Jackson was outraged, as only an honest man can be when he finds that his integrity is no shield against the conniving of others. He swore revenge, and Anderson shrugged that off with a laugh."

"Beware the wrath of a patient man," quoted Avalon, with the air of precision research he brought to even his least portentous statements.

"So I have heard," said Bartram, "though I have never had occasion to test the maxim. Nor, apparently, had Anderson, for he had no fear of Jackson. As he explained, Jackson was so psychotically honest and so insanely law-abiding that there was no chance of his slipping into wrongdoing. Or so Anderson thought. It did not even occur to him to ask Jackson to return the office key; something all the more curious since the office was located in Anderson's house, in among the knickknackery.

"Anderson recalled this omission a few days after the quarrel, for, returning from an early evening appointment, he found Jackson in his house. Jackson carried his old attaché case, which he was just closing as Anderson entered; closing with startled haste, it seemed to Anderson.

"Anderson frowned and said, inevitably, 'What are you doing here?'

" 'Returning some papers which were in my possession and which now belong to you,' said Jackson, 'and returning the key to the office.' With this remark, he handed over the key, indicated papers on the desk, and pushed the combination lock on his battered attaché case with fingers that Anderson could swear trembled a little. Jackson looked about the room with what appeared to Anderson to be a curious, almost a secretively satisfied, smile and said, 'I will now leave.' He proceeded to do so.

"It was not until Anderson heard the motor of Jackson's car whirring into action and then retreating into the distance that he could rouse himself from a kind of stupor that had paralyzed him. He knew he had been robbed, and the next day he came to me."

Drake pursed his lips, twirled his half-empty brandy glass, and said, "Why not to the police?"

"There was a complication," said Bartram. "Anderson did not know what had been taken. When the certainty of theft dawned on him, he naturally rushed to the safe. Its contents were secure. He ransacked his desk. Nothing seemed to be missing. He went from room to room. Everything seemed to be intact as far as he could tell."

"Wasn't he certain?" asked Gonzalo.

"He couldn't be. The house was inordinately crowded with every variety of object and he didn't remember all his possessions. He told me, for instance, that at one time he collected antique watches. He had them in a small drawer in his study; six of them. All six were there, but he was nagged by the faint memory of seven. For the life of him, he could not remember definitely. In fact, it was worse than that, for one of the six present seemed strange to him. Could it be that he had had only six but that a less valuable one had been substituted for a more valuable one? Something of this sort repeated itself a dozen times over in every hideaway and with every sort of oddment. So he came to me—"

"Wait a while," said Trumbull, bringing his hand down hard on the table. "What made him so certain that Jackson had taken anything at all?"

"Ah," said Bartram, "that is the fascinating part of the story. The closing of the attaché case, and Jackson's secretive smile as he looked about the room, served in themselves to rouse Anderson's suspicions, but as the door closed behind him, Jackson chuckled. It was not an ordinary chuckle. . . . But I'll let Anderson tell it in his own words, as nearly as I remember them.

" 'Bartram,' he said, 'I have heard that chuckle innumerable times in my life. I have chuckled that way myself a thousand times. It is a characteristic chuckle, an unmis-

takable one, an unmaskable one. It is the acquisitive
chuckle; it is the chuckle of a man who has just obtained
something he wants very much at the expense of someone
else. If any man in all the world knows that chuckle and
can recognize it, even behind a closed door, that man is
myself. I cannot be mistaken. Jackson had taken something of mine and was glorying in it!'

"There was no arguing with the man on this point. He
virtually slavered at the thought of having been victimized
and, indeed, I had to believe him. I had to suppose that
for all Jackson's pathological honesty, he had been lured,
by the once-in-a-lifetime snapping of patience, into
theft. Helping lure him must have been his knowledge of
Anderson. He must have known Anderson's intent hold
on even the least valued of his belongings, and realized
that the hurt would extend far deeper and far beyond the
value of the object taken, however great that value might
have been."

Rubin said, "Maybe it was the attaché case he took."

"No, no, that was Jackson's. He'd owned it for years.
So there you have the problem. Anderson wanted me to
find out what had been taken, for until he could identify a
stolen object and show that the object was, or had been,
in the possession of Jackson, he could not prosecute—and
he was most intent on prosecution. My task, then, was to
look through his house and tell him what was missing."

"How would that be possible, if he himself couldn't
tell?" growled Trumbull.

"I pointed that out to him," said Bartram, "but he was
wild and unreasoning. He offered me a great deal of
money, win or lose; a very handsome fee, indeed, and he
put down a sizable portion of it as a retainer. It was clear
he resented beyond measure the deliberate insult to his
acquisitiveness. The thought that an amateur non-acquis-
itor like Jackson should dare beard him in this most
sacred of his passions had driven him, on this one point,
mad, and he was prepared to go to any expense to keep
the other's victory from being final.

"I am myself quite human. I accepted the retainer and
the fee. After all, I reasoned, I had my methods. I took

up the question of insurance lists first. All were outdated, but they served to eliminate the furniture and all the larger items as possible victims of Jackson's thievery, for everything on the lists was still in the house."

Avalon interrupted. "They were eliminated anyway, since the stolen object would have had to fit into the attaché case."

"Provided that it was indeed the attaché case that was used to transport the item out of the house," pointed out Bartram patiently. "It might easily have been a decoy. Prior to Anderson's return, Jackson could have had a moving van at the door and taken out the grand piano had he so chosen, and then snapped the attaché case in Anderson's face to mislead him.

"But never mind that. It wasn't likely. I took him around the house room by room, following a systematic procedure of considering the floor, walls, and ceiling, studying all the shelves, opening every door, considering every piece of furniture, going through every closet. Nor did I neglect the attic and the basement. Never before had Anderson been forced to consider every item of his vast and amorphous collection in order that somewhere, somehow, some item would jog his memory of some companion item that was *not* there.

"It was an enormous house, a heterogeneous one, an endless one. It took us days, and poor Anderson grew more befuddled each day.

"I next tackled it from the other end. It was obvious that Jackson had deliberately taken something unnoticeable, perhaps small; certainly something that Anderson would not easily miss and therefore not something to which he was greatly attached. On the other hand, it made sense to suppose that it was something Jackson would want to take away, and which he would find valuable. Indeed, his deed would give him most satisfaction if Anderson, too, found it valuable—once he realized what it was that was gone. What, then, could it be?"

"A small painting," said Gonzalo eagerly, "which Jackson knew to be an authentic Cézanne, but which Anderson thought was junk."

"A stamp from Anderson's collection," said Rubin, "which Jackson noted had a rare mistake in the engraving." He had once written a story which had hinged on this precise point.

"A book," said Trumbull, "which contained some hidden family secret with which, in due time, Jackson could blackmail Anderson."

"A photograph," said Avalon dramatically, "that Anderson had forgotten but which contained the likeness of an old sweetheart which, eventually, he would give a fortune to buy back."

"I don't know what business they were in," said Drake thoughtfully, "but it might have been the kind where some unvalued gimcrack might actually be of great value to a competitor and drive Anderson to bankruptcy. I remember one case where a formula for a hydrazo-intermediate—"

"Oddly enough," said Bartram, breaking in firmly, "I thought of each of these possibilities, and I went over each with Anderson. It was clear that he had no taste in art and such pieces as he had were really junk, and no mistake. He did not collect stamps, and though he had many books and could not tell for certain whether one was gone, he swore he had no hidden family secrets anywhere that were worth the skipped beat of a blackmailer's heart. Nor had he ever had any old sweethearts, since in his younger days he had confined himself to professional ladies whose photographs he did not prize. As for his business secrets, they were of the sort that would interest the government far more than any competitor, and everything of that sort had been kept far from Jackson's honest eyes in the first place and were still in the safe (or long in the fire) in the second. I thought of other possibilities, but, one by one, they were knocked down.

"Of course, Jackson might betray himself. He might blossom out into sudden wealth, and in ferreting out the source of the wealth, we might learn the identity of the stolen object.

"Anderson suggested that himself and paid lavishly to have a twenty-four-hour watch put on Jackson. It was useless. The man kept a dull way of life and behaved precisely as you would expect someone minus his life savings to behave. He lived parsimoniously, and, eventually, took a menial job, where his honesty and his calm demeanor stood him in good stead.

"Finally, I had but one alternative left—"

"Wait, wait," said Gonzalo, "let me guess, let me guess." He tossed off what was left of his brandy, signaled Henry for another, and said, "You asked Jackson!"

"I was strongly tempted to," said Bartram ruefully, "but that would scarcely have been feasible. It doesn't do in my profession to even hint at an accusation without evidence of any sort. Licenses are too fragile. And in any case, he would simply deny theft, if accused, and be put on his guard against any self-incrimination."

"Well, then . . . ," said Gonzalo blankly, and petered out.

The other four furrowed brows one and all, but only silence followed.

Bartram, having waited politely, said, "You won't guess, gentlemen, for you are not in the profession. You know only what you read in romances and so you think gentlemen like myself have unlimited numbers of alternatives and invariably solve all cases. I, myself, being in the profession, know otherwise. Gentlemen, the one alternative I had left was to confess failure.

"Anderson paid me, however, I'll give him that much credit. By the time I said my goodbyes to him, he had lost some ten pounds. There was a vacant look in his eyes and, as he shook hands with me, they moved round and round the room he was in, still looking, still looking. He muttered, 'I tell you I couldn't possibly mistake that chuckle. He took something from me. He took something from me.'

"I saw him on two or three occasions thereafter. He never stopped looking; he never found the missing object. He went rather downhill. The events I have described took place nearly five years ago, and last month, he died."

There was a short silence. Avalon said, "Without ever finding the missing object?"

"Without ever finding it."

Trumbull said, with disapproval, "Are you coming to us to help you with the problem now?"

"In a way, yes. The occasion is too good to miss. Anderson is dead and whatever is said within these walls will go no farther, we all agree, so that I may now ask what I could not ask before. . . . Henry, may I have a light?"

Henry, who had been listening with a kind of absent-minded deference, produced a book of matches and lit Bartram's cigarette.

"Let me introduce you, Henry, to those you so efficiently serve. . . . Gentlemen, may I introduce to you, Henry Jackson."

There was a moment of clear shock and Drake said, "*The* Jackson."

"Exactly," said Bartram. "I knew he was working here and when I heard it was at this club that you met for your monthly meetings, I had to beg, rather shamelessly, for an invitation. It was only here that I could find the gentleman with the acquisitive chuckle, and do so under conditions of both bonhomie and discretion."

Henry smiled and bent his head.

Bartram said, "There were times during the course of the investigation when I could not help but wonder, Henry, whether Anderson might not have been wrong and whether there might possibly have been no theft at all. Always, however, I returned to the matter of the acquisitive chuckle, and I trusted Anderson's judgment."

"You did right to do so," said Jackson softly, "for I *did* steal something from my one-time partner, the gentleman you have referred to as Anderson. I never regretted the act for one moment."

"It was something of value, I presume."

"It was of the greatest value and no day passed without my thinking of the theft and rejoicing in the fact that the wicked man no longer had what I had taken away."

"And you deliberately roused his suspicions in order that you might experience the greater joy."

"Yes, sir."

"And you did not fear being caught?"

"Not for one moment, sir."

"By God," roared Avalon suddenly, his voice soaring to breakneck loudness. "I say it again. Beware the wrath of a patient man. I am a patient man, and I am tired of this endless cross-examination. Beware my wrath, Henry. What was it you carried off in your attaché case?"

"Why, nothing, sir," said Henry. "It was empty."

"Heaven help me! Where did you put whatever it was you took from him?"

"I didn't have to put it anywhere, sir."

"Well, then, what did you take?"

"Only his peace of mind, sir," said Henry gently.

Afterword

This story first appeared in the January 1972 issue of *Ellery Queen's Mystery Magazine*.

It taught me an object lesson, too, in this matter of chains of logical deduction. I've often thought that the ease with which story detectives weave their inexorable webs of logic was too pat; that in real life there would always be large holes.

Sometimes, the holes appear even in the stories. After "The Acquisitive Chuckle" had appeared, a reader wrote to tell me that I had neglected to specify that Jackson's attaché case was really his own, and that it might well have been the attaché case that he had stolen. That had never occurred to me and so, of course, it didn't occur to any of the characters in the story.

For the book, therefore, I added a couple of lines to take care of that possibility. (That shows you, by the way, that readers aren't merely replete with troublesome questions, as the Introduction would seem to imply. Sometimes they are very useful, and I appreciate those occasions greatly.)

2

Ph as in Phony

The meeting of the Black Widowers was marred, but only slightly, by the restlessness of James Drake.

It was a shame that this had to be so, for the dinner was unusually good, even allowing for the loving care with which the Milano Restaurant took care of its special group every month. And if the veal *cordon bleu* needed anything to add the final bit of luster, it was Henry's meticulous service, which had plates on the table where no plate had been before, yet without any person present able to catch it en route.

It was Thomas Trumbull's turn to host, something he did with a savagery to which no one paid the slightest bit of attention; a savagery made particularly bitter by the fact that, as host, he did not think it fit to come charging in just one second before the pre-dinner drinks had completed their twice-around (three times for Rubin, who never showed the effects).

Trumbull exercised host's privilege and had brought a guest for the grilling. The guest was tall, almost as tall as Geoffrey Avalon, the Black Widowers' patent-attorney member. He was lean, almost as lean as Geoffrey Avalon. He was clean-shaven, though, and lacked the solemnity of Avalon. Indeed, his face was round and his cheeks plump, in a manner so out of keeping with the rest of his body that one might have thought him the product of a head transplant. He was Arnold Stacey, by name.

"Arnold Stacey, Ph.D.," Trumbull had introduced him.

"Ah," said Avalon, with the air of portentousness he automatically brought to his most trivial statement, "Doctor Doctor Stacey."

"Doctor Doctor?" murmured Stacey, his lips parting as

though getting ready for a smile at the pleasantry sure to follow.

"It is a rule of the Black Widowers," said Trumbull impatiently, "that all members are doctors by virtue of membership. A doctor for any other reason is—"

"A doctor doctor," finished Stacey. And he smiled.

"You can count honorary doctorates, too," said Rubin, his wide-spaced teeth gleaming over a beard as straggly as Avalon's was crisp, "but then I would have to be called Doctor Doctor Doctor—"

Mario Gonzalo was mounting the stairs just then, bringing with him a faint whiff of turpentine as though he had come straight from his artist's studio. (Trumbull maintained you couldn't draw that conclusion; that Gonzalo placed a drop of turpentine behind each ear before any social engagement.)

Gonzalo was in time to catch Emmanuel Rubin's statement and said, before he had quite reached the top step, "What honorary doctorates did you ever receive, Manny? *Dis*honorary doctorates, I'm ready to believe."

Rubin's face froze as it usually did when he was attacked without warning, but that was merely the short pause necessary to gather his forces. He said, "I can list them for you. In 1938, when I was only fifteen, it so happens I was a revivalist preacher and I received a D.D. from—"

"*No,* for God's sake," said Trumbull, "don't give us the list. We accept it all."

"You're fighting out of your weight, Mario," said Avalon with wooden amiability. "You know Rubin can never be spotted in an inconsistency when he starts talking about his early life."

'Sure," said Gonzalo, "that's why his stories are so lousy. They're all autobiographical. No poetry."

"I have written poetry," began Rubin, and then Drake came in. Usually, he was the first person there; this time, the last.

"Train was late," he said quietly, shucking his coat. Since he had to come in from New Jersey to attend, the only surprise was that it didn't happen oftener.

"Introduce me to the guest," Drake added, as he turned to take the drink Henry held out for him. Henry knew which he preferred, of course.

Avalon said, "Doctor Doctor Arnold Stacey . . . Doctor Doctor James Drake."

"Greetings," said Drake, holding up his glass in salute. 'What's the nature of the lesser doctorate, Doctor Stacey?"

"Ph.D. in chemistry. Doctor Doctor, and call me Arnold."

Drake's small grizzled mustache seemed to bristle. "Ditto," he said. "My Ph.D. is in chemistry, too."

They looked at each other, warily, for a moment. Then Drake said, "Industry? Government? Academic?"

"I teach. Assistant professor at Berry University."

"Where?"

"Berry University. It's not a large school. It's in——"

"I know where it is," said Drake. "I did graduate work there. Considerably before your time, though. Did you get your degree at Berry before you joined the faculty?"

"No, I——"

"Let's sit down, for God's sake," roared Trumbull. "There's more drinking and less eating going on here all the time." He was standing at the host's seat, with his glass raised, glowering at the others as each took his seat. "Sit down! Sit down!" And then he intoned the ritual toast to Old King Cole in singsong while Gonzalo blandly kept time with a hard roll, which he broke and buttered when the last syllable was done.

"What's this?" said Rubin suddenly, staring down at his dish in dismay.

"Pâté de la maison, sir," said Henry softly.

"That's what I thought. Chopped liver. Damn it, Henry, I ask you, as a pathologically honest man, is this fit to eat?"

"The matter is quite subjective, sir. It depends on the personal taste of the diner."

Avalon pounded the table. "Point of order! I object to Manny's use of the adjectival phrase 'pathologically honest.' Violation of confidence!"

Rubin colored slightly. "Hold on, Jeff. I don't violate any confidence. That happens to be my opinion of Henry quite independently of what happened last month."

"Ruling from the chair," said Avalon stubbornly.

Trumbull said, "Shut up both of you. It is the ruling of the chair that Henry may be recognized by all Black Widowers as that rare phenomenon, a completey honest man. No reason need be given. It can be taken as a matter of common knowledge."

Henry smiled gently. "Shall I take away the *pâté*, sir?"

"Would *you* eat it, Henry?" asked Rubin.

"With pleasure, sir."

"Then I'll eat it, too." And he did so, with every sign of barely controlled nausea.

Trumbull leaned over to Drake and said in a voice that was low for him, "What the hell's bothering you?"

Drake started slightly and said, "Nothing. What's bothering *you?*"

"You are," said Trumbull. "I've never seen a roll taken apart into so many pieces in my life."

The conversation grew general after that, centering chiefly on Rubin's aggrieved contention that honesty lacked survival value and that all the forces of natural selection combined to eliminate it as a human trait. He did well defending his thesis till Gonzalo asked him if he attributed his own success as a writer ("such as it is," said Gonzalo) to plagiarism. When Rubin met the point head on and tried to prove, by close reasoning, that plagiarism was fundamentally different from other forms of dishonesty and might be treated independently, he was hooted down.

Then, between main course and dessert, Drake left for the men's room and Trumbull followed him.

Trumbull said, "Do you know this guy Stacey, Jim?"

Drake shook his head. "No. Not at all."

"Well, what's wrong, then? I admit you're not an animated phonograph needle like Rubin but you haven't said a word all dinner, damn it. And you keep looking at Stacey."

Drake said, "Do me a favor, Tom. Let me question him after dinner."

Trumbull shrugged. "Sure."

Over the coffee, Trumbull said, "The time has come for the grilling of the guest. Under ordinary circumstances, I, as the possessor of the only logical mind at the table, would begin. On this occasion, I pass to Doctor Doctor Drake since he is of the same professional persuasion as our honored guest."

"Doctor Doctor Stacey," began Drake heavily, "how do you justify your existence?"

"Less and less as time goes on," said Stacey, unperturbed.

"What the hell does that mean?" broke in Trumbull.

"*I'm* asking the questions," said Drake with unaccustomed firmness.

"I don't mind answering," said Stacey. "Since the universities seem to be in deeper trouble each year, and as I do nothing about it, my own function as a university appendage seems continually less defensible, that's all."

Drake ignored that. He said, "You teach at the school where I earned my master's degree. Have you ever heard of me?"

Stacey hesitated. "I'm sorry, Jim. There are a lot of chemists I haven't heard of. No offense intended."

"I'm not sensitive. I never heard of you, either. What I mean is: Have you ever heard of me at Berry U.? As a student there?"

"No, I haven't."

"I'm not surprised. But there was another student at Berry at the same time as myself. He went on for his doctorate at Berry. His name was Faron, FA-R-O-N; Lance Faron. Did you ever hear of him?"

"Lance Faron?" Stacey frowned.

"Lance may have been short for Lancelot; Lancelot Faron. I don't know. We always called him Lance."

Finally Stacey shook his head. "No, the name isn't familiar."

Drake said, "But you have heard of David St. George?"

"Professor St. George? Certainly. He died the same year I joined the faculty. I can't say I know him, but I've certainly heard of him."

Trumbull said, "Hell and damnation, Jim. What kind of questions are these? Is this old-grad week?"

Drake, who had drifted off into thought, scrambled out of it and said, "Wait, Tom. I'm getting at something, and I don't want to ask questions. I want to tell a story first. My God, this has been bothering me for years and I never thought of putting it up to all of you till now that our guest—"

"I vote the story," shouted Gonzalo.

"On condition," said Avalon, "it not be construed as setting a precedent."

"Chair decides the precedents," said Trumbull at once. "Go ahead, Drake. Only, for God's sake, don't take all night."

"It's simple enough," said Drake, "and it's about Lance Faron, which is his real name, and I'm going to slander him, so you'll have to understand, Arnold, that everything said within these walls is strictly confidential."

"That's been explained to me," said Stacey.

"Go on," shouted Trumbull. "You *will* take all night. I know it."

Drake said, "The thing about Lance is that I don't think he ever intended to be a chemist. His family was rich enough—well, I'll tell you. When he was doing graduate work, he had his lab outfitted with a cork floor at his own expense."

"Why a cork floor?" Gonzalo wanted to know.

"If you'd ever dropped a beaker on a tile floor, you wouldn't ask," said Drake. "He majored in chemistry as an undergraduate because he had to major in something and then he went on to do graduate work in the same field because World War II was on in Europe, the draft was beginning—it was 1940—and graduate work in chemistry would look good to the draft board. And it did; he never got into the Army as far as I know. But that was perfectly legitimate; I never got into uniform, either, and I point no fingers."

Avalon, who had been an army officer, looked austere, but said, "Perfectly legitimate."

Drake said, "He wasn't serious about it—about chemistry, I mean. He had no natural aptitude for it and he never worked, particularly. He was satisfied to get no more than a B minus and it was about all he was good for. Nothing wrong with that, I suppose, and it was good enough to sweat out a master's degree for himself—which doesn't amount to much in chemistry. The grades weren't good enough to qualify him for research toward the doctorate, however.

"That was the whole point. We all—the rest of us who were in graduate chemistry that year—assumed he would only go as far as the master's. Then he'd get some sort of job that would keep his draft exemption going; we figured his father would help out there—"

"Were the rest of you jealous of him?" asked Rubin. "Because that kind of guy—"

"We weren't jealous of *him*," said Drake. "Sure, we envied the situation. Hell, those were the days before government grants fell about us like snowflakes. Every college semester, I lived a suspense story called 'Do I Dig Up the Tuition Or Do I Drop Out?' All of us would have liked to be rich. But Lance was a likable guy. He didn't parade the situation and would lend us a few bucks when we were in a hole and do it unostentatiously. And he was perfectly willing to admit he wasn't a brain.

"We even helped him. Gus Blue tutored him in physical organic—for a fee. Of course, he wasn't always scrupulous. There was one preparation he was supposed to have synthesized in lab, and we knew that he bought a sample at a chemical supply house and turned it in as his own. At least, we were pretty sure he did, but it didn't bother us."

Rubin said, "Why not? That was dishonest, wasn't it?"

"Because it wouldn't do him any good," said Drake in

annoyance. "It just meant another B minus at best. But the reason I bring it up is that we all knew he was capable of cheating."

"You mean the rest of you wouldn't have?" interposed Stacey. There was a touch of cynicism in his voice.

Drake lifted his eyebrows, then dropped them again. "I wouldn't guarantee any of us if we were really pushed. The point is, we weren't. We all had a fighting chance to get through without the risk of cheating, and none of us did. As far as I know. Certainly, I didn't.

"But then there came a time when Lance made up his mind to go on for his Ph.D. It was at a smoker. The war jobs were just beginning to open up and there were a few recruiters on campus. It meant money and complete security from the draft, but Ph.D.'s meant a lot to us and there was some question as to whether we'd come back to school once we got away from class for any reason.

"Someone (not I) said he wished he were in Lance's shoes. Lance had no choice to make. He would take the job.

" 'I don't know,' said Lance, maybe just to be contrary. 'I think I'll stay right here and go on for the Ph.D.'

"He may have been joking. I'm sure he was joking. Anyway, we all thought he was, and we laughed. But we were all a little high and it became one of those laughs without reason, you know. If one of us started to die down, he would catch someone else's eyes and start off again. It wasn't that funny. It wasn't funny at all. But we laughed till we were half suffocated. And Lance turned red, and then white.

"I remember I tried to say, 'Lance, we're not laughing at you,' but I couldn't. I was choking and sputtering. And Lance walked out on us.

"After that, he was going for his Ph.D. He wouldn't talk about it but he signed all the necessary forms and that seemed to satisfy him. After a while, the situation was as before. He was friendly.

"I said to him, 'Listen, Lance, you'll be disappointed. You can't get faculty approval for doctoral research with not a single A on your record. You just can't.'

"He said, 'Why not? I've talked to the committee. I told them I'd take chemical kinetics under St. George, and that I'd make an A in that. I said I'd let them see what I could do.'

"That made less than no sense to me. That was funnier than the remark we laughed at. You'd have to know St. George. You ought to know what I mean, Arnold."

Stacey nodded, "He gave a stiff course in kinetics. One or two of the brightest would get an A minus; B's and C's otherwise."

Drake shrugged. "There are some professors who take pride in that. It's a kind of professorial version of Captain Bligh. But he was a good chemist; probably the best Berry has ever had. He was the only member of the faculty to achieve national prominence after the war. If Lance could take his course and get a high mark, that would be bound to be impressive. Even with C's in everything else, the argument would be: 'Well, he hasn't worked much because he hasn't had to, but when he finally decided to buckle down, he showed fire-cracking ability.'

"He and I took chemical kinetics together and I was running and sweating and snorting every day of that course. But Lance sat in the seat next to me and never stopped smiling. He took notes carefully, and I know he studied them, because when I found him in the library it was always chemical kinetics he was working on. It went down to the wire like that. St. George didn't give quizzes. He let everything hang on the discussion periods and on the final examination, which lasted three hours—a *full* three hours.

"In the last week of the course, there were no lectures and the students had their last chance to pull themselves together before finals week. Lance was still smiling. His work in the other courses had been usual Lance quality, but that didn't bother him. We would say, 'How are you doing in kinetics, Lance?' and he would say, 'No sweat!' and sound *cheerful*, damn it.

"Then came the day of the finals—" Drake paused, and his lips tightened.

"Well?" said Trumbull.

Drake said, his voice a little lower, "Lance Faron passed. He did more than pass. He got a 96. No one had ever gotten over 90 before in one of St. George's finals. I doubt somehow that anyone ever did afterward."

"I never heard of anyone getting it in recent times," said Stacey.

"What did you get?" asked Gonzalo.

"I got 82," said Drake. "And except for Lance's, it was the best mark in the class. Except for Lance's."

"What happened to the fellow?" asked Avalon.

"He went on for his Ph.D., of course. The faculty qualified him without trouble and the story was that St. George himself went to bat for him.

"I left after that," Drake went on. "I worked on isotope separation during the war and eventually shifted to Wisconsin for my doctoral research. But I would hear about Lance sometimes from old friends. The last I heard he was down in Maryland somewhere, running a private lab of his own. About ten years ago, I remember I looked up his name in *Chemical Abstracts* and found the record of a few papers he turned out. Run of the mill. Typically Lance."

"He's still independently wealthy?" asked Trumbull.

"I suppose so."

Trumbull leaned back. "If that's your story, Jim, then what the hell is biting you?"

Drake looked about the table, first at one and then at another. Then he brought his fist down so that the coffee-cups jumped and clattered. "Because he *cheated*, damn his hide. That was not a legitimate final exam and as long as he has his Ph.D., mine is cheapened by that much— and yours, too," he said to Stacey.

Stacey murmured, "Phony doctor."

"What?" said Drake, a little wildly.

"Nothing," said Stacey, "I was just thinking of a colleague who did a stint at a medical school where the students regarded the M.D. as the only legitimate doctor's degree in the universe. To them, a Ph.D. stood for 'phony doctor.' "

Drake snorted.

"Actually," began Rubin, with the typical air of argumentativeness he could put into even a casual connective, "if you—"

Avalon cut in from his impressive height, "Well, see here, Jim, if he cheated, how did he get through?"

"Because there was nothing to show he cheated."

"Did it ever occur to you," said Gonzalo, "that maybe he didn't cheat? Maybe it was really true that when he buckled down, he had fire-cracking ability."

"No," said Drake, with another coffeecup-rattling fist on the table. "That's impossible. He never showed the ability before and he never showed it afterward. Besides he had that *confidence* all through the course. He had the confidence that could only mean he had worked out a foolproof plan to get his A."

Trumbull said heavily, "All right, say he did. He got his Ph.D. but he didn't do so well. From what you say, he's just off in a corner somewhere, poking along. You know damn well, Jim, that lots of guys get through to all kinds of professional positions, even without cheating, who have all their brains in their elbows, and so what. Why get mad at one particular guy, cheating or not? You know why I think you're off your rocker on the subject, Jim? What gripes you is that you don't know how he did it. If you could figure it out, why you'd forget the whole thing."

Henry interrupted, "More brandy for anyone, gentlemen?"

Five delicate little glasses were raised in air. Avalon, who measured out his allowance with an eye dropper, kept his down.

Drake said, "Well, then, Tom, you tell me. How did he do it? You're the code expert."

"But there's no code involved. I don't know. Maybe he—he—managed to get someone else to do the test for him and handed in someone else's paper."

"In someone else's handwriting?" said Drake scornfully. "Besides, I thought of it. We all thought of it. You don't suppose I was the only one who thought Lance cheated, do you? We all did. When that 96 went up on that bulletin board, after we got our breath back—and that took a while—we demanded to see his paper. He handed it over without trouble and we all went over it. It was a near-perfect job, but it was in his handwriting and with his turns of phrase. I wasn't impressed by the few errors he made. I thought at the time he threw them in just in order not to have a perfect paper."

"All right," said Gonzalo, "someone else did the test and your friend copied it over in his own words."

"Impossible. There was no one in the class but the students and St. George's assistant. The assistant opened the sealed test papers just before the test started. No one could have written a paper for Lance and another for himself, even if you could imagine no one else seeing it done. Besides, there wasn't anyone in the class capable of turning out a 96-level paper."

Avalon said, "If you were doing it right there, it would be impossible. But suppose someone managed to get a copy of the questions well before the test and then swatted away at the textbooks till he worked out perfect answers. Couldn't Lance have done that somehow?"

"No, he couldn't," said Drake flatly. "You're not suggesting anything we didn't think of then, take my word for it. The university had had a cheating scandal ten years before or so and the whole procedure had been tightened up. St. George followed standard procedure. He worked out the questions and turned it in to his secretary the day before the test. She mimeographed the necessary number of copies in St. George's presence. He proofread them, then destroyed the mimeograph and the original. The question papers were packaged and sealed and placed in the school safe. The safe was opened just before the test and the papers handed to St. George's assistant. There was no chance of Lance seeing the questions."

"Maybe not just then," said Avalon. "But even if the professor had the questions mimeographed the day before the test, how long might he have had the questions in his possession? He might have used a set of questions used on a previous—"

"No," interrupted Drake. "We carefully studied all previous test papers prepared by St. George as a matter of course before the final exam. Do you think we were fools? There were no duplications."

"All right. But even if he prepared an entirely new test, he might have prepared it at the beginning of the semester for all you know. Lance might somehow have seen the questions early in the semester. It would be a lot easier to work out answers to a fixed number of questions in the course of the semester than to try to learn the entire subject matter."

"I think you've got something there, Jeff," said Gonzalo.

"He's got crud there," said Drake, "because that's not the way St. George worked it. Every question in that final exam turned on some particular point that some particular student goofed up on in class. One of them, and the most subtle, covered a point that I had missed in the last week of lectures. I pointed out what I thought was a mistake in a derivation, and St. George—well, never mind. The point is that the tests had to be prepared after the last lectures."

Arnold Stacey broke in, "Did St. George *always* do that? If he did, he would have been handing a hell of a lot to the kids."

"You mean the students would have been waiting for questions covering errors made in the discussion periods?"

"More than that. The students would have deliberately pulled boners on those parts of the subject they actually knew well in order to lure St. George into placing twenty points' worth on it."

Drake said, "I can't answer that. We weren't in his previous classes, so we don't know whether his previous tests followed the same line."

"Previous classes would have passed on the news, wouldn't they? At least if classes in the forties were anything like classes now."

"They would have," admitted Drake, "and they didn't. He did it that way that year, anyway."

"Say, Jim," said Gonzalo, "how did Lance do in the dicsussion periods?"

"He kept quiet; played it safe. We all took it for granted he'd do that. We weren't surprised."

Gonzalo said, "What about the department secretary? Couldn't Lance have wheedled her into telling him the questions?"

Drake said grimly, "You don't know the secretary. Besides, he couldn't have. He couldn't have suborned the secretary, or broken into the safe, or pulled any trick at all. From the nature of the questions, we could tell the exam had been constructed in the last week before it had been taken, and during that last week he couldn't have done a thing."

"Are you sure?" asked Trumbull.

"Oh, you bet! It bugged us all that he was so confident. The rest of us were sea green with the fear of flunking and he *smiled*. He kept smiling. On the day of the last lecture, someone said, 'He's going to steal the question sheet.' Actually, *I* said it, but the others agreed and we decided to—to—well, we kept an eye on him."

"You mean you never let him out of your sight?" demanded Avalon. "Did you watch at night in shifts? Did you follow him into the john?"

"Damn near. He was Burroughs' roommate and Burroughs was a light sleeper and swore he knew every time Lance turned over."

"Burroughs might have been drugged one night," said Rubin.

"He might have, but he didn't think so, and no one else thought so. Lance just didn't act suspicious in any way; he didn't even act annoyed at being watched."

"Did he know he was being watched?" said Rubin.

"He probably did. Every time he went somewhere he would grin and say, 'Who's coming along?' "

"Where did he go?"

"Just the normal places. He ate, drank, slept, eliminated. He went to the school library to study, or sat in his room. He went to the post office, the bank, a shoestore. We followed him on every errand all up and down Berry's main street. Besides—"

"Besides, what?" said Trumbull.

"Besides, even if he had gotten hold of the question paper, it could only have been in those few days before the test, maybe only the night before. He would have had to sweat out the answers, being Lance. It would have taken him days of solid work over the books. If he could have answered them just by getting a look at them, he wouldn't have had to cheat; he would have gotten a look at them in the opening minutes of the test period."

Rubin said sardonically, "It seems to me, Jim, that you've painted yourself into a corner. Your man couldn't possibly have cheated."

"That's the whole point," cried Drake. "He *must* have cheated and he did it so cleverly no one could catch him. No one could even figure out how. Tom's right. *That's* what gripes me."

And then Henry coughed and said, "If I may offer a word, gentlemen?"

Every face went up as though some invisible puppeteer had pulled the strings.

"Yes, Henry?" said Trumbull.

"It seems to me, gentlemen, that you are too much at home with petty dishonesty to understand it very well."

"Why, Henry, you hurt me cruelly," said Avalon with a smile, but his dark eyebrows curled down over his eyes.

"I mean no disrespect, gentlemen, but Mr. Rubin maintained that dishonesty has value. Mr. Trumbull thinks that Dr. Drake is only annoyed because the cheating was clever enough to escape detection and not because it existed at all, and perhaps all of you agree to that."

Gonzalo said, "I think you're hinting, Henry, that you're so honest that you're more sensitive to dishonesty than we are and can understand it better."

Henry said, "I would almost think so, sir, in view of

the fact that not one of you has commented on a glaring improbability in Dr. Drake's story that seems to me to explain everything."

"What's that?" asked Drake.

"Why, Professor St. George's attitude, sir. Here is a professor who takes pride in flunking many of his students, and who never has anyone get above the 80's on the final examination. And then a student who is thoroughly mediocre—and I gather that everyone in the department, both faculty and students, knew of the mediocrity—gets a 96 and the professor accepts that and even backs him before the qualifying committee. Surely he would have been the first to suspect dishonesty. And most indignantly, too."

There was a silence. Stacey looked thoughtful.

Drake said, "Maybe he couldn't admit that he could be cheated *from,* if you know what I mean."

Henry said, "You find excuses, sir. In any situation in which a professor asks questions and a student answers them, one always feels somehow that if there is dishonesty, it is always the student's dishonesty.. *Why?* What if it were the professor who were dishonest?"

Drake said, "What would he get out of that?"

"What does one usually get? Money, I suspect, sir. The situation as you described it is that of a student who was quite well off financially, and a professor who had the kind of salary a professor had in those days before the government grants began to come. Suppose the student had offered a few thousand dollars—"

"For what? To hand in a fake mark? We saw Lance's answer paper, and it was legitimate. To let Lance see the questions before having them mimeographed? It wouldn't have done Lance any good."

"Look at it in reverse, sir. Suppose the student had offered those few thousand dollars to let him, the student, show the professor the questions."

Again the invisible puppeteer worked and there was a chorus of "What?"s in various degrees of intonation.

"Suppose, sir," Henry went on patiently, "that it was Mr. Lance Faron who wrote the questions, one by one in the course of the semester, polishing them as he went along. He polished them as the semester proceeded, working hard. As Mr. Avalon said, it is easier to get a few specific points straight than to learn the entire subject matter of a course. He included one question from the last week's lectures, inadvertently making you all sure the test had been created entirely in the last week. It also meant that he turned out a test that was quite different from St. George's usual variety. Previous tests in the course had not turned on students' difficulties. Nor did later ones, if I may judge from Dr. Stacey's surprise. Then at the end of the course, with the test paper completed, he would have mailed it to the professor."

"Mailed it?" said Gonzalo.

"I believe Dr. Drake said the young man visited the post office. He might have mailed it. Professor St. George would have received the questions with, perhaps, part of the payment in reasonably small bills. He would then have written it over in his own handwriting, or typed it, and passed it on to his secretary. From then on all would be normal. And, of course, the professor would have had to back the student thereafter all the way."

"Why not?" said Gonzalo enthusiastically. "Good God, it makes sense."

Drake said slowly, "I've got to admit that's a possibility that never occurred to any of us. . . . But, of course, we'll never know."

Stacey broke in loudly. "I've hardly said a word all evening, though I was told I'd be grilled."

"Sorry about that," said Trumbull. "This meathead, Drake, had a story to tell because you came from Berry."

"Well, then, because I come from Berry, let me add something. Professor St. George died the year I came, as I said, and I didn't know him. But I know many people who did know him and I've heard many stories about him."

"You mean he was known to be dishonest?" asked Drake.

"No one said that. But he was known to be unscrupulous and I've heard some unsavory hints about how he maneuvered government grants into yielding him an income. When I heard your story about Lance, Jim, I must admit I didn't think St. George would be involved in quite that way. But now that Henry has taken the trouble to think the unthinkable from the mountain height of his own honesty—why, I believe he's right."

Trumbull said, "Then that's that. Jim, after thirty years, you can forget the whole thing."

"Except—except"—a half smile came over Drake's face and then he broke into a laugh—"I *am* dishonest because I can't help thinking that if Lance had the questions all along, the bastard might have passed on a hint or two to the rest of us."

"After you had all laughed at him, sir?" asked Henry quietly, as he began to clear the table.

Afterword

This story first appeared in the July 1972 issue of *Ellery Queen's Mystery Magazine,* under the title "The Phony Ph.D."

The reason for the title change was clear. *EQMM* runs a series of excellent stories by Lawrence Treat with titles such as "H as in Homicide," "C as in Cutthroat," and so on. Naturally, the magazine wanted to reserve such titles to Mr. Treat.

Here in the book, however, I hope Mr. Treat won't mind if I go back to "Ph as in Phony," since that seems to me to be perfect. I promise I won't use that type of title again.

This story, incidentally, betrayed me into a bit of vanity of a type unusual for me. (Certain other types are usual.) A Professor Porter of the University of Oregon wrote to point out certain infelicities in the story in connection with qualifying for research toward the doctorate. He signed it with a "Ph.D." after his signature to indicate that he was qualified to discuss the matter.

And he was, for he was entirely right and I have adjusted the version of the story as presented here to meet his objections. However, in answering the letter, I was so anxious not to have him think I was myself unqualified that I placed a "Ph.D." after my signature, too. The initials were legitimate, for I obtained it in chemistry at Columbia in 1948, but I think it's the only time I used it in anything but official scholarly communications.

3

Truth to Tell

When Roger Halsted made his appearance at the head of the stairs on the day of the monthly meeting of the Black Widowers, the only others yet present were Avalon and Rubin. They greeted him with jubilation.

Emmanuel Rubin said, "Well, you've finally managed to stir yourself up to the point of meeting your old friends, have you?" He trotted over and held out his hands, his straggly beard stretching to match his broad grin. "Where've you been the last two meetings?"

"Hello, Roger," said Geoffrey Avalon, smiling from his stiff height. "Pleased to see you."

Halsted shucked his coat. "Damned cold outside. Henry, bring—"

But Henry, the only waiter the Black Widowers ever had or ever would have, had the drink waiting. "I'm glad to see you again, sir."

Halsted took it with a nod of thanks. "Twice running something came up. . . . Say, you know what I've decided to do?"

"Give up mathematics and make an honest living?" asked Rubin.

Halsted sighed. "Teaching math at a junior high school is about as honest a living as one can find. That's why it pays so little."

"In that case," said Avalon, swirling his drink gently, "why is free-lance writing so dishonest a racket?"

"Free-lance writing is *not* dishonest," said free-lance Rubin, rising to the bait at once, "as long as you make no use of an agent—"

"What have you decided to do, Roger?" interrupted Avalon blandly.

"It's just this project I dreamed up," said Halsted. His forehead rose white and high, showing no signs of the hairline that had been there perhaps ten years ago, though the hair was still copious enough at the top and around the sides. "I'm going to rewrite the *Iliad* and the *Odyssey* in limericks, one for each of the forty-eight books they contain."

Avalon nodded. "Any of it written?"

"I've got the first book of the *Iliad* taken care of. It goes like this:

> *"Agamemnon, the top-ranking Greek,*
> *To Achilles in anger did speak.*
> *They argued a lot,*
> *Then Achilles grew hot,*
> *And went stamping away in a pique."*

"Not bad," said Avalon. "In fact, quite good. It gets across the essence of the first book in full. Of course, the proper name of the hero of the *Iliad* is Achilleus, with the 'ch' sound as in—"

"That would throw off the meter," said Halsted.

"Besides," said Rubin, "everyone would think the extra 'u' was a mistake and that's all they'll see in the limerick."

Mario Gonzalo came racing up the stairs. He was host for that session and he said, "Anyone else here?"

"Nobody here but us old folks," said Avalon agreeably.

"My guest is on his way up. Real interesting guy. Henry will like him because he never tells a lie."

Henry lifted his eyebrows as he produced Mario's drink.

"Don't tell me you're bringing George Washington!" said Halsted.

"Roger! A pleasure to see you again. . . . By the way, Jim Drake won't be here with us today. He sent back the card saying there was some family shindig he had to attend. The guest I'm bringing is a fellow named Sand— John Sand. I've known him on and off for years. Crazy guy. Horse-race buff who never tells a lie. I've heard him not telling lies. It's about the only virtue he has." And Gonzalo winked.

Avalon nodded portentously. "Good for those who can. As one grows older, however—"

"And I think it will be an interesting session," added Gonzalo hurriedly, visibly avoiding Avalon's non-libidinous confidences. "I was telling him about the club, and that for the last two times we had mysteries on our hands—"

"Mysteries?" said Halsted with sudden interest.

Gonzalo said, "You're a member of the club in good standing, so we can tell you. But get Henry to do it. He was a principal both times."

"Henry?" Halsted looked over his shoulder in mild surprise. "Are they getting you involved in our idiocies?"

"I assure you, Mr. Halsted, I tried not to be," said Henry.

"Tried not to be!" said Rubin hotly. "Listen, Henry was the Sherlock of the session last time. He—"

"The point is," said Avalon, "that you may have talked too much, Mario. What did you tell your friend about us?"

"What do you mean, talk too much? I'm not Manny. I carefully told Sand that there could be no details because we were priests at the confessional, one and all, as far as anything in this room is concerned, and he said he wished he were a member because he had a difficulty that was driving him wild, and I said he could come the next time because it was my turn to host and he could be my guest and—here he is!"

A slim man, his neck swathed in a thick scarf, was mounting the stairs. The slimness was accentuated when he took off his coat. Under the scarf, his tie gleamed bloody red and seemed to lend color to a thin and pallid face. He seemed thirtyish.

"John Sand," said Mario, introducing him all round in a pageant that was interrupted by Thomas Trumbull's heavy tread on the steps and the loud cry of "Henry, a scotch and soda for a dying man."

Rubin said, "Tom, you can come early if you relax and stop trying so hard to be late."

"The later I come," said Trumbull, "the less I have to hear of your Goddamn stupid remarks. Ever think of that?" Then he was introduced, too, and all sat down.

Since the menu for that meeting had been so incautiously devised as to begin with artichokes, Rubin had launched into a dissertation on the preparation of the only proper sauce for it. Then, when Trumbull had said disgustedly that the only proper preparation for artichokes involved a large garbage can, Rubin said, "Sure, *if* you don't have the right sauce—"

Sand ate uneasily and left at least a third of an excellent steak untouched. Halsted, who had a tendency to plumpness, eyed the remains enviously. His own plate was the first one cleaned. Only a scraped bone and some fat were left.

Sand seemed to grow aware of Halsted's eyes and said to him, "Frankly, I'm too worried to have much appetite. Would you care for the rest of this?"

"Me? No, thank you," said Halsted glumly.

Sand smiled. "May I be frank?"

"Of course, If you've been listening to the conversation around the table, you'll realize frankness is the order of the evening."

"Good, because I would be anyway. It's my—fetish. You're lying, Mr. Halsted. Of course you want the rest of my steak, and you'd eat it, too, if you thought no one would notice. That's perfectly obvious. Social convention requires you to lie, however. You don't want to seem greedy and you don't want to seem to ignore the elements of hygiene by eating something contaminated by the saliva of a stranger."

Halsted frowned. "And what if the situation were reversed?"

"And I was hungry for more steak?"

"Yes."

"Well, I might not want to eat yours for hygienic reasons, but I would admit I wanted it. Almost all lying is the result of a desire for self-protection or out of respect for social convention. To myself, though, it seems that a lie is rarely a useful defense and I am not at all interested in social convention."

Rubin said, "Actually, a lie *is* a useful defense if it is a thorough-going one. The trouble with most lies is that they don't go far enough."

"Been reading *Mein Kampf* lately?" said Gonzalo.

Rubin's eyebrows went up. "You think *Hitler* was the first to use the technique of the big lie? You can go back to Napoleon III; you can go back to Julius Caesar. Have you ever read his *Commentaries?*"

Henry was bringing the baba au rhum and pouring the coffee delicately, and Avalon said, "Let's get to our honored guest."

Gonzalo said, "As host and chairman of this session, I'm going to call off the grilling. Our guest has a problem and I direct him to favor us with it." He was drawing a quick caricature of Sand on the back of the menu card, with a thin, sad face accentuated into that of a distorted bloodhound.

Sand cleared his throat, "I understand everything said in this room is in confidence, but—"

Trumbull followed the glance, and growled, "Don't worry about Henry. Henry is the best of us all. If you want to doubt someone's discretion, doubt someone else."

"Thank you, sir," murmured Henry, setting up the brandy glasses on the sideboard.

Sand said, "The trouble, gentlemen, is that I am suspected of a crime."

"What kind of crime?" demanded Trumbull at once. It was his job, ordinarily, to grill the guests and the look in his eye was that of someone with no intention of missing the grillage.

"Theft," said Sand. "There is a sum of money and a wad of negotiable bonds missing from a safe in my company. I'm one of those who have the combination, and I had the opportunity to get to it unobserved. I also had a motive because I've had some bad luck at the races and needed some cash badly. So it doesn't look good for me."

Gonzalo said eagerly, "But he didn't do it. That's the point. He didn't do it."

Avalon twirled the half-drink he was not going to finish and said, "I think in the interest of coherence we ought to allow Mr. Sand to tell his story."

"Yes," said Trumbull, "how do *you* know he didn't do it, Mario?"

"That's the whole point, damn it. He *says* he didn't do it," said Gonzalo, "and that's good enough. Not for a court maybe, but it's good enough for me and for anyone who knows him. I've heard him admit enough rotten things—"

"Suppose I ask him myself, okay?" said Trumbull. "Did you take the stuff, Mr. Sand?"

Sand paused. His blue eyes flicked from face to face, then he said, "Gentlemen, I am telling the truth. I did not take the cash or the bonds. That is only my unsupported word, but anyone who knows me will tell you that I can be relied on."

Halsted passed his hand over his forehead upward, as though trying to clear away doubts. "Mr. Sand," he said, 'you seem to have a position of some trust. You can get into a safe with assets in it. Yet you play the horses."

"Lots of people do."

"And lose."

"I didn't quite plan it that way."

"But don't you risk losing your job?"

"My advantage is, sir, that I am employed by my uncle, who is aware of my weakness, but who also knows I don't lie. He knew I had the means and opportunity, and he knew I had debts. He also knew I had recently paid off my gambling debts. I told him so. The circumstantial evidence looked bad. But then he asked me directly whether I was responsible for the loss and I told him exactly what I told you: I did not take the cash or the bonds. Since he knows me well, he believes me."

"How did you come to pay off your debts?" said Avalon.

"Because a long shot came through. That happens, too, sometimes. That happened shortly before the theft was discovered and I paid off the bookies. That's true, too, and I told this to my uncle."

"But then you had no motive," said Gonzalo.

"I can't say that. The theft might have been carried out as long as two weeks before the discovery. No one looked in that particular drawer in the safe for that period of time—except the thief, of course. It could be argued that after I took the assets the horse came through and made the theft unnecessary—too late."

"It might be argued," said Halsted, "that you took the money in order to place a large bet on the horse that came in."

"The bet wasn't that large, and I had other sources, but it could be argued so, yes."

Trumbull broke in, "But if you still have your job, as I suppose you do, and if your uncle isn't prosecuting you, as I assume he isn't . . . Has he gone to the police at all?"

"No, he can absorb the loss and he feels the police will only try to pin it on me. He knows that what I have told him is true."

"Then what's the problem, for God's sake?"

"Because there's no one else who can have done it. My uncle can't think of any other way of accounting for the theft. Nor can I. And as long as he can't, there will always be the residuum of uneasiness, of suspicion. He will always keep his eye on me. He will always be reluctant to trust me. I'll keep my job, but I'll never be promoted; and I may be made uncomfortable enough to be forced into resignation. If I do, I can't count on a wholehearted recommendation, and from an uncle, a halfhearted one would be fatal."

Rubin was frowning. "So you came here, Mr. Sand, because Gonzalo said we solved mysteries. You want us to tell you who really took the stuff."

Sand shrugged. "Maybe not. I don't even know if I can give you enough information. It's not as though you're detectives who can make inquiries. If you could tell me just how it *might* have been done—even if it's farfetched, that would help. If I could go to my uncle and say, 'Uncle, it might have been done this way, mightn't it?' Even if we couldn't be sure, even if we couldn't ever get the assets back, it would at least spread the suspicion. He wouldn't have the eternal nagging thought that I was the only *possible* guilty party."

"Well," said Avalon, "we can try to be logical, I suppose. How about the other people who work with you and your uncle? Would any of them need money badly?"

Sand shook his head. "Enough to risk the possible consequences of being caught? I don't know. One of them might be in debt, or one might be undergoing blackmail, or one might be greedy, or just have the opportunity and act on impulse. If I were a detective I could go about asking questions, or I could track down documents, or whatever it is they do. As it is—"

"Of course," said Avalon, "we can't do that either. . . . Now you had both means and opportunity, but did anyone else?"

"At least three people could have gotten to the safe more easily than I and gotten away with it more easily, but not one of them had the combination, and the safe wasn't broken into; that's certain. There are two people besides my uncle and myself who have the combination, but one had been hospitalized over the period in question and the other is such an old and reliable member of the firm that to suspect him seems unthinkable."

"Aha," said Mario Gonzalo, "there's our man right there."

"You've been reading too many Agatha Christies," said Rubin at once. "The fact of the matter is that in almost every crime on record, the most suspicious person is indeed the criminal."

"That's beside the point," said Halsted, "and too dull besides. What we have here is a pure exercise in logic. Let's have Mr. Sand tell us everything he knows about every member of the firm, and we can all try to see if there's any way in which we can work out motive, means, and opportunity for some one person."

"Oh, hell," said Trumbull, "who says it has to be one

person? So someone's in a hospital. Big deal. The telephone exists. He phones the combination to a confederate."

"All right, all right," said Halsted hastily, "we're bound to think up all sorts of possibilities and some may be more plausible than others. After we've thrashed them out, Mr. Sand can choose the most plausible and use it, too—"

"May I speak, sir?" Henry spoke so quickly, and at a sound level so much higher than his usual murmur, that everyone turned to face him.

Henry said, softly once more, "Although not a Black Widower—"

"Not so," said Rubin. "You *know* you're a Black Widower. In fact, you're the only one who's never missed a meeting."

"Then may I point out, gentlemen, that if Mr. Sand carries your conclusions, whatever they may be, to his uncle, he will be carrying the proceedings of this meeting beyond the walls of this room."

There was an uncomfortable silence. Halsted said, "In the interest of saving the ruin of an innocent person's life, surely—"

Henry shook his head gently. "But it would be at the cost of spreading suspicion to one or more other people, who might also be innocent."

Avalon said, "Henry's got something there. We seem stymied."

"Unless," said Henry, "we can come to some definite conclusion that will satisfy the club and will not involve the outside world."

"What do you have in mind, Henry?" asked Trumbull.

"If I may explain . . . I was interested to meet someone who, as Mr. Gonzalo said before dinner, never tells a lie."

"Now come, Henry," said Rubin, "you're pathologically honest yourself. You know you are. That's been settled."

"That may be so," said Henry, "but I tell lies."

"Do you doubt Sand? Do you think he's lying?" said Rubin.

"I assure you—" began Sand, almost in anguish.

"No," said Henry, "I believe that every word Mr. Sand has said is true. He didn't take the money or the bonds. He is, however, the logical one against whom suspicion may rest. His career may be ruined. His career, on the other hand, may *not* be ruined if some reasonable alternative can be found, even if that does not actually lead to a solution. And, since he can think of no reasonable alternatives himself, he wants us to help him find some for him. I am convinced, gentlemen, that this is all true."

Sand nodded. "Well, thank you."

"And yet," said Henry, "what is truth? For instance, Mr. Trumbull, I think that your habit of perpetually arriving late with a cry of 'Scotch and soda for a dying man' is rude, unnecessary, and, worse yet, has grown boring. I suspect others here feel the same."

Trumbull flushed, but Henry went on firmly. "Yet if, under ordinary circumstances, I were asked if I disapproved of it, I would say I did not. Strictly speaking, that would be a lie, but I like you for other reasons, Mr. Trumbull, that far outweigh this trick of yours, so the telling of the strict truth, which would imply a dislike for you, would end by actually being a great lie. Therefore I lie to express a truth—my liking for you."

Trumbull muttered, "I'm not sure I like your way of liking, Henry."

Henry said, "Or consider Mr. Halsted's limerick on the first book of the *Iliad*. Mr. Avalon quite rightly said that Achilleus is the correct name of the hero, or even Akhilleus with a 'k,' I suppose, to suggest the correct sound. But then Mr. Rubin pointed out that the truth would seem like a mistake and ruin the effect of the limerick. Again, truth creates a problem.

"Mr. Sand said that all lies arise out of a desire for self-protection or out of respect for social convention. But we cannot always ignore self-protection and social convention. If we cannot lie, we must make the truth lie for us."

Gonzalo said, "You're not making sense, Henry."

"I think I am, Mr. Gonzalo. Few people listen to exact

words, and many a literal truth tells a lie by implication. Who should know that better than a person who carefully always tells the literal truth?"

Sand's pale cheeks were less pale, or his red tie was reflecting light upward more efficiently. He said, "What the hell are you implying?"

"I would like to ask you a question, Mr. Sand. If the club is willing, of course."

"I don't care if they are or not," said Sand, glowering at Henry. "If you take that tone, I might not choose to answer."

"You may not have to," said Henry. "The point is that each time you deny having committed the crime, you deny it in precisely the same form of words. I couldn't help but notice since I made up my mind to listen to your exact words as soon as I heard that you never lied. Each time, you said, 'I didn't take the cash or the bonds.' "

"And that is perfectly true," said Sand loudly.

"I'm sure it is, or you wouldn't have said so," said Henry. "Now this is the question I would like to ask you. Did you, by any chance, take the cash *and* the bonds?"

There was a short silence. Then Sand rose and said, "I'll take my coat now. Goodbye. I remind you all that nothing that goes on here can be repeated outside."

When Sand was gone, Trumbull said, "Well, I'll be damned!"

To which Henry replied, "Perhaps not, Mr. Trumbull. Don't despair."

Afterword

This story first appeared in the October 1972 issue of *Ellery Queen's Mystery Magazine,* under the title "The Man Who Never Told a Lie." I think the magazine title is pedestrian, so I changed it back to my original one.

I wrote this story on February 14, 1972. I remember that, not because I have a phenomenal memory, but because it was written in the hospital the day before my one and (so far) only operation. Larry Ashmead, my Doubleday editor, visited me that day and I gave him the manuscript and asked him to see that it was delivered to the *EQMM* offices by messenger.

I also told him to explain that I was in the hospital, as I ordinarily deliver the manuscripts myself so that I can flirt with the beauteous Eleanor (to say nothing of the vivacious Constance DiRienzo, who is the executive editorial secretary).

Larry did as requested, of course, and I got the news that the story was taken while I was still in the hospital recovering. Since then I have wondered (when I had nothing better to do) if the story was accepted out of sympathy for my poor, suffering self, but I guess not. It was tapped for a best-of-the-year mystery anthology put out by Dutton, so I guess it's okay.

Oh, and that accounts for the fact that this story is the shortest in the book. I had to get it done before the surgeon took his scalpel from between his teeth, whetted it on his thigh, and got to work.

4

Go, Little Book!

"My wife," said Emmanuel Rubin, with a tremor of indignation shaking his sparse chin beard, "has bought another bull."

Discussion of women and, particularly, of wives, was considered out of bounds at the staunchly masculine monthly meetings of the deliberately named Black Widowers, but habits die hard. Mario Gonzalo, who was sketching the guest of the meeting, said, "In *your* mini-apartment?"

"It's a perfectly good apartment," said Rubin indignantly. "It just *looks* small. And it wouldn't look all that small if she didn't have bulls in it made of wood, of porcelain, of tile, of bronze, and of felt. She has them from a foot across to an inch across. She has them on the wall, on the shelves, on the floor, and suspended from the ceiling—"

Avalon, from his austere height, swirled his drink slowly and said, "She requires a symbol of virility, I presume."

"When she has *me?*" said Rubin.

"*Because* she has you," said Gonzalo, and took the drink pressed upon him by the Black Widowers' perennial and indispensable waiter, Henry—then hurried to his seat to avoid Rubin's explosive reply.

At the other end of the table, James Drake said to Roger Halsted, "A, B—" and paused, lengthily.

"What?" said Halsted, his high, white forehead flushing and wrinkling as his eyebrows moved upward.

"Long time, no C," said Drake, coughing at his own cigarette smoke, which he frequently did.

Halsted looked disgusted. "I think I'll make it longer next time. I was here last month, but you weren't."

"Family!" said Drake briefly. "What's this I hear about you rewriting the *Iliad* into limericks?"

"One for each book," said Halsted, with obvious self-satisfaction. "The *Odyssey*, too."

"Jeff Avalon recited the limerick to the first book as soon as he saw me."

"I've written one for the second. Would you like to hear it?"

"No," said Drake.

"It goes like this:

> *"Agamemnon's dream strategy slips,*
> *The morale of his troops quickly dips.*
> *First Thersites complains,*
> *But Odysseus restrains,*
> *And we next have the Cat'log of Ships."*

Drake received it stolidly. He said, "You have one too many syllables in the last line."

"Can't help it," said Halsted with unusual heat. "It's impossible to do the second book without mentioning the Catalog of Ships and that phrase has three unaccented syllables in a row. I leave one out by elision and say Cat'log with an apostrophe. That makes it all fifteen perfect anapests."

Drake shook his head. "Wouldn't satisfy a purist."

Thomas Trumbull, scowling malevolently, said, "I hope, Henry, that you noticed I came early today, even though I'm not the host."

"I did notice, Mr. Trumbull," said Henry, smiling urbanely.

"The least you can do is give the act public approval after what you said about me last time."

"I approve, sir, but it would be wrong to make an issue of it. That would give the impression that it was hard for you to arrive on time and no one would expect to have you repeat the feat next time. If we all ignore it, it will seem as though we take it for granted that you can do it, and then you will have no trouble repeating."

"Give me my scotch and soda, Henry, and spare me the dialectic."

As a matter of fact, it was Rubin who was the host and his guest was one of his publishers, a round-faced, smooth-cheeked gentleman with a good-humored smile on his face. His name was Ronald Klein.

Like most guests, he found it difficult to hop onto the merry-go-round of talk, and he finally plunged in the direction of the one man at the table he knew.

"Manny," he said, "did I hear you say Jane had bought another bull?"

"That's right," said Rubin. "A cow, actually, because it's sitting on a crescent moon, but it's hard to tell for sure. The makers of these things rarely go into careful anatomical detail."

Avalon, who had been wielding his knife and fork in workmanlike fashion over the stuffed veal, paused to say, "Collector's mania is something that seizes almost every gentleman of leisure It has many delights; the excitement of the search, the ecstasy of the acquisition, the joy of later contemplation. You can do it with anything. I collect stamps myself."

"Stamps," said Rubin at once, "are the very worst thing you can collect. They are thoroughly artificial. Vest-pocket nations put out issues designed deliberately to fetch high sums. Mistakes, misprints, and so on create false values. The whole thing is in the hands of entrepreneurs and financiers. If you've got to collect, collect things with no value."

Gonzalo said, "A friend of mind collects his own books. So far, he has published a hundred and eighteen and carefully gets copies of every edition, American and foreign, hard-cover and paperback, book-club and condensed. He's got a whole roomful of them and says he is the only person in the world with a complete collection of his works and that it will be worth a tremendous sum someday "

"After he's dead," said Drake briefly.

"I think he's planning to fake death, sell the collection for a million dollars, then come back to life and continue writing under a pseudonym."

At this point, Klein made his way back on the merry-go-round. "I met a fellow yesterday," he said, "who collects matchbooks."

"I collected matchbooks when I was a kid," said Gonzalo. "I used to go searching all the curbs and alleys for—"

But Trumbull, who had been eating in unwonted silence, suddenly raised his voice to a shout. "God damn it, you bunch of hack talkers, our guest has said something. Mr.—uh—Klein, what was that you said?"

Klein looked startled. "I said I met a fellow yesterday who collects matchbooks."

"That could be interesting," said Halsted agreeably, "if—"

"Shut *up,*" roared Trumbull. "I want to hear about this." His creased, bronzed face turned to Klein. "What's the guy's name? The collector."

"I'm not sure I remember," said Klein. "I just met him at lunch yesterday; never saw him before that. There were six of us at the table, and he got to talking about his matchbooks. Listen, I thought he was crazy at first, but by the time he got through, I decided to start a collection of my own."

"Did he have grayish sideburns, with a little red in it?" asked Trumbull.

"Why, yes, as a matter of fact. Do you know him?"

"Umm," said Trumbull. "Hey, Manny, I know you're the host, and I don't want to overstep your prerogatives . . ."

"But you're going to," said Rubin. "Is that it?"

"No, I'm not, damn it," said Trumbull hotly. "I'm asking your permission. I would like to have our guest tell us all about his lunch yesterday with this matchbook collector."

Rubin said, "You mean instead of his being put on the grill? We never put anyone on the grill any more!"

"This could be important."

Rubin thought about it, with a look of some dissatisfaction on his face, then said, "Okay, but after the dessert. . . . What have we got for dessert today, Henry?"

"Zabaglione, sir, to go with the Italian motif of tonight's meal."

"Calories, calories," groaned Avalon softly.

Halsted's teaspoon clinked as he stirred the sugar in his coffee and elaborately ignored Rubin's flat ukase that anyone who added anything at all to good coffee was a barbarian. He said, "Do we humor Tom now and get our guest to tell us about matchbooks?"

Klein looked about the table and said with a small laugh, "I'm willing to do it, but I don't know that it's interesting—"

"I say it's interesting," said Trumbull.

"All right. I won't fight it. I started the whole thing, as a matter of fact. We were at the Cock and Bull on Fifty-third Street—"

"Jane insisted on eating there one time because of the name," said Rubin. "Not so hot."

Trumbull said, "I'll strangle you, Manny. What's all this talk about your wife today? If you miss her, go home."

"You're the only one I know, Tom, who would make any man miss any wife."

"Please go on, Mr. Klein," said Trumbull.

Klein began again. "Okay. I started it, as I said, by lighting a cigarette, while we were waiting for the menu, and then getting uncomfortable about it. I don't know how it is, but it seems there's a lot less smoking at meals these days. At this table, for instance, Mr. Drake is the only one smoking. I guess he doesn't mind—"

"I don't," muttered Drake.

"I did, though, so after a few puffs I stubbed out the cigarette. Only I was embarrassed, so I fiddled with the matchbook I had lit the cigarette with; you know, the ones restaurants always supply at every table."

"Advertising themselves," said Drake. "Yes."

"And this fellow . . . I have his name now—Ottiwell. I don't know his first name."

"Frederick," growled Trumbull, with glum satisfaction.

"Then you *do* know him."

"I *do* know him. But go on."

"I was still holding the matchbook in my hand, and Ottiwell reached for it and asked if he could see it. So I passed it to him. He looked at it and he said something like 'Moderately interesting. Not particularly imaginative in design. I've got it.' Or something like that. I don't remember the exact words."

Halsted said reflectively, "That's an interesting point, Mr. Klein. At least you know you don't remember the exact words. In all these first-person narratives, the fellow telling the story always remembers every word everyone has said, and in the right order. It never carries conviction with me."

"It's just a convention," said Avalon seriously as he sipped at his coffee, "but I admit third-person is more convenient. When you use first-person, you know that the narrator will survive all the deadly perils into which he will be—"

"I wrote a first-person narrative once," said Rubin, "in which the narrator dies."

"That happens in the western song, 'El Paso,' too," said Gonzalo.

"In 'The Murder of Roger'—" began Avalon.

And Trumbull rose and banged his fist on the table. "So help me, you bunch of idiots, I will *kill* the next guy who talks. Don't you *believe* me when I tell you this thing is important? . . . Go *on,* Mr. Klein."

Klein looked more than a little uncomfortable. "I don't see its importance myself, Mr. Trumbull. There's not even much to it. This Ottiwell took to telling us about matchbooks. Apparently, there's a whole thing about it to people who are involved in it. There are all kinds of factors that increase the value: not only beauty and rarity but also whether the matches are intact and whether the friction strip is unmarked. He talked about difference in design, in location of the friction strip, in type and quantity of printing, whether the inside of the cover is blank or not, and so on. He went on and on, and that's about it.

Except that he made it sound so interesting it captured me, as I said."

"Did he invite you to visit his place and see his collection?"

"No," said Klein, "he didn't."

"I've been there," said Trumbull, and having said that, he sat back in his chair with a look of deepest dissatisfaction covering it thickly.

There was a silence and, as Henry distributed the small brandy glasses, Avalon said, with a touch of annoyance, "If the threat of murder has been lifted, Tom, may I ask what the collector's place was like?"

Trumbull seemed to return, as from a distance. "What? Oh . . . It's weird. He started collecting when he was a kid. For all I know he got his first samples out of gutters and alleys like Gonzalo did, but at some point it turned serious.

"He's a bachelor. He doesn't work. He doesn't have to. He's inherited some money and has invested shrewdly, so all he lives for are those damned matchbooks. I think they own his house and keep him on as a caretaker.

"He's got exhibits of prize items on the wall; framed, if you please. He's got them in folders and cases, everywhere. His whole basement is given over to filing cabinets in which they're catalogued by type and alphabet. You wouldn't believe how many tens of thousands of different matchbooks have been manufactured the world over, with how many different legends, and with how many different peculiarities, and I think he's got them all.

"He's got skinny matchbooks that hold two matches apiece; some as long as your arm that hold a hundred and fifty. He's got matches shaped like beer bottles, others shaped like baseball bats or bowling pins. He's got blank matchbooks with nothing on the cover; he's got matchbooks with musical scores on them. Damn it, he's got a whole folder of pornographic matchbooks."

"That I'd like to see," said Gonzalo.

"Why?" said Trumbull. "It's the same stuff you can see anywhere else, except that on a matchbook it's handier to burn and get rid of."

"You've got the soul of a censor," said Gonzalo.

"I prefer the real thing," said Trumbull.

"Maybe at one time you could," said Gonzalo.

"What do you want to do? Play verbal ping-pong? We have something serious under discussion."

"What's so serious about a bunch of matchbooks?" demanded Gonzalo.

"I'll tell you." Trumbull looked up and down the table. "Listen, you bunch of meatheads, what's said in here is *always* confidential."

"We all know that," said Avalon dryly. "If anyone's forgotten, it's you, or you wouldn't have to remind us."

"Mr. Klein will also have to—"

Rubin interrupted at once. "Mr. Klein understands exactly. He knows that nothing that ever goes on in this room is ever, under any circumstances, to be referred to outside. I'll vouch for him."

"Okay. All right," said Trumbull. "So now I'll tell you as little as I can. So help me God, I wouldn't have told you anything except for Klein's luncheon yesterday. It just irritates me. I've had this chewing holes in me for months now; over a year, in fact; and having it come up—"

"Look," said Drake flatly. "Either tell us or don't tell us."

Trumbull rubbed his eyes angrily. He said, "There's an information leak."

"What kind? Where?" said Gonzalo.

"Never *mind*. I'm specifically not saying it's the government. I'm specifically not saying foreign agents are involved, you understand. Maybe it's industrial espionage; maybe it's the theft of the New York Mets' baseball signals; maybe it's cheating on a test, as in the problem Drake brought up a couple of months ago. Let's just call it an information leak, all right?"

"All right," said Rubin. "And who's involved? This guy Ottiwell?"

"We're pretty sure."

"Then reel him in."

Trumbull said, "We have no proof. All we can do is try to block any information from getting to him, and we don't even want to do that—entirely."

"Why not?"

"Because it's not *who* the guy is. It's *how* he does it. If we pull him in and don't know the method he's using, then someone will take his place. People are cheap. It's the *modus operandi* we want."

"Do you have any ideas on the subject?" asked Halsted, blinking slowly.

"It's the matchbooks. What else? It's got to be. All our evidence points to Ottiwell as the leak and he's a crazy guy who collects matchbooks. There's got to be a connection."

"You mean he started collecting matchbooks so he could—"

"No, he's been collecting them all his life. There's no doubt about it. That collection he has right now took thirty years a-building. But once he had his collection, when he was somehow recruited into the business of transmitting information, he naturally worked out a scheme that involved his matchbooks."

"What scheme?" broke in Rubin impatiently.

"That's what I don't know. But it's there. In a way, the matchbooks are perfect for the task. They carry messages already and, properly chosen, they need no tampering. For instance, the restaurant you were in yesterday, Klein, the Cock and Bull. Its matchbooks surely said 'Cock and Bull' on the covers."

"Sounds reasonable. I didn't look."

"I'm sure of it. Well, now, if you want to cancel out a previous message, you put one of those things in the mail, or just tear off half the cover, and mail it. Aren't you saying the previous message was just a cock-and-bull story?"

Gonzalo said, "That's pure bull . . . Sorry, Manny, didn't mean to raise a sore point . . . But look, Tom, anyone who mails a matchbook cover, let alone a matchbook, is asking for it. You spot something funny at once."

"Not if there's a plausible reason to mail matchbooks."

"Like what?"

"Matchbook nuts do it. They correspond and they *trade*. They send matchbooks back and forth. Maybe one guy needs a Cock and Bull to flesh out an animal collection he's building up and returns a spare girlie picture for someone who's specializing in that kind of art."

"And Ottiwell trades?" asked Avalon.

"Sure he does."

"And you never managed to pick up anything he put into the mail?"

A look of contempt came across Trumbull's face. "Of course, we did. A number of times. We'd pick it up, go over it with a fine-tooth comb, then send it on."

"And by so doing," said Rubin, looking off into the distance, "interfering with the United States mails. That's an easy thing to do when it's only a matter of the New York Mets' baseball signals."

"Oh, for God's sake," said Trumbull, "don't be a jackass for, say, fifteen minutes, Manny, just for the novelty of it. You know my field is in codes and ciphers. You know I'm consulted by the government and have my contacts there. Naturally they're interested. They would be even if the leak involved only a case of over-the-fence gossip, and I'm not saying it's any more than that."

"Why?" said Rubin. "Are we that far gone in Big Brotherism?"

"It's simple if you'll stop to think. Any system for transmitting information that can't be broken—whatever the information is—is top-flight dangerous. If it works and is being used for something utterly unimportant, it can be later used to deal with something vital. The government doesn't want any system of transmitting information to remain unbroken, unless it's under its own control. That's *got* to make sense to you."

"All right," said Drake, "so you studied the matchbooks this Ottiwell puts in the mail. What did you get?"

"Nothing," grunted Trumbull. "There was nothing we could make out of it. We studied those damned advertising items on each cover and came up with nothing."

"You mean you looked to see if initial letters of the items spelled a word or something?" said Klein with interest.

"If it were a six-year-old sending it, yes, that's what we would have tried. No, we worked a lot more subtly than that and came up with nothing."

"Well," said Avalon heavily, "if you can't find anything in any of the printed matter of any of the matchbooks he mails—maybe it's a false lead."

"You mean maybe it's not the matchbooks at all?"

"That's right," said Avalon. "It could be all misdirection. This man has the matchbooks handy and he's a bona fide collector, so he makes his collection look as prominent as possible to attract all the attention it can. He shows it to anyone who wants to see it. . . . How did *you* get to see it, Tom?"

"He invited me. I cultivated his friendship."

"And he responded," said Rubin. "There's a man who deserves everything he gets. Don't cultivate *my* friendship, Tom."

"I never have. . . . Look, Jeff, I know what you mean. He talked to Klein yesterday about the matchbooks; he'd talk to anyone. He'd show his collection to anyone willing to go out to Queens. That's why I asked if he invited Klein up to his place. With all that talking, all that self-advertisement, all that glitter and shine, it wouldn't surprise you, I suppose, if he then used some device that had nothing at all to do with the matchbooks. Right?"

"Right," said Avalon.

"Wrong," said Trumbull. "I just don't believe it. He's the real thing. He's *really* a matchbook nut with nothing else in his life. He has no ideological reason to run the terrible risk he's actually running. He isn't committed to the side for which he's working; whether it is national, industrial, or local—and I'm not saying which. He lacks any interest in that. It's only the matchbooks. He's worked out a way of using his damned matchbooks in a new way and that's the glory of it as far as he's concerned."

"Listen," said Drake, coming out of a reverie. "How many matchbooks does he mail off at a time?"

"Who can say? The cases we've intercepted have never been more than eight. And he doesn't really mail them often. I have to admit that."

"All right. How much information can he get across in a few matchbooks? He can't use the messages literally and directly. If he tries to do the Cock and Bull bit to cancel a message, my kid nephew could spot him, let alone you. So it's something subtle and maybe each matchbook can work out to one word, or maybe only one letter. What can you do with that?"

"Plenty," said Trumbull indignantly. "What do you think is needed in these cases? An encyclopedia? Whoever is looking for information, you simp, has it almost all to begin with. There's just some key point missing and that's what's needed.

"For instance, suppose we're back in World War II. Germany has rumors that something big is going on in the United States. A message arrives with only two words on it: 'atom bomb.' What more does Germany need? Sure, no atom bomb existed at the time, but any German with a high-school education would get the idea from those two words and any German physicist would get a damned good idea. Then a second message arrives saying: 'Oak Ridge, Tenn.' That would be a total of twenty individual letters in the two messages taken together and it could have changed the history of the world."

"You mean this guy, Ottiwell, is putting across information like *that?*" demanded Gonzalo, in awe.

"*No!* I told you he wasn't," said Trumbull, annoyed. "He isn't important at all in that way. Do you think I would be talking to all of you about it if he were? It's just that the *modus operandi* could be used for that as well as for anything else, and that's why we have to break it. Besides, there's my reputation. I say he's using the matchbooks and I can't show how. You think I like that?"

Gonzalo said, "Maybe there's secret writing on the inside of the matchbooks?"

"We tested for that routinely, but not a chance. If that's it, why bother using matchbooks? It could be done in ordinary letters and attract a lot less attention. It's a matter of psychology. If Ottiwell is going to use matchbooks, he's going to use a system that can be used only on matchbooks, and that means he's using only the messages that are on them already—somehow."

Klein interrupted. "Imagine starting all this by mentioning yesterday's lunch. Do you have, maybe, a list of matchbooks he sent off? If you have a photostat, we could all look at it—"

"And work out the code that I couldn't? Right?" said Trumbull. "You know ever since Conan Doyle pitted Sherlock Holmes against the Scotland Yard bunglers, there seems to be a notion going around that the professional can't do anything. I assure you, if I can't do it—"

Avalon said, "Well, now, how about Henry?"

Henry, who had been listening gravely, with a look of interest on his unlined, sixtyish face, smiled briefly and shook his head.

But a look of deep thought came over Trumbull's face. "Henry," he said. "I forgot about Henry. You're right, Jeff. He's the smartest man here, which would ordinarily be a compliment, if you weren't all a pack of prize imbeciles.

"Henry," he said, "you're the honest man. You can see the dishonesty of the world without having it blurred by your own larcenous yearnings. Do you agree with me? Do you think this Ottiwell, if he were going to engage in this kind of work, would do so only by using his matchbooks in a way that would make them uniquely useful, or not?"

"As a matter of fact, Mr. Trumbull," said Henry, collecting the dishes that remained, "I do. I agree with you."

Trumbull smiled. "Here we have the word of a man who knows what he's talking about."

"Because he agrees with you," said Rubin.

"I don't entirely agree with Mr. Trumbull, to be sure," said Henry.

"Aha," said Rubin. "Now what do you think, Tom?"

"What I always think," said Trumbull. "That your silence is the best part of you."

"May I—make a little speech?" said Henry.

"Wait a while," said Rubin. "I'm still the host, and I'm taking over. I decide on procedures, and I decide that Henry makes a little speech and that the rest of us all keep quiet except to answer Henry's questions or to ask questions of our own that are right to the point. I have in mind particularly Tom-Tom the drumbeat as a candidate for quiet."

"Thank you, Mr. Rubin," said Henry. "I listen to you gentlemen, on the occasion of all your monthly meetings, with the greatest interest. It is obvious to me that all of you get enormous pleasure, in an innocent way, out of flailing at each other with words. You can't very well flail at a guest, however, so you all have a tendency to ignore the guest and to fail to listen to him when he speaks."

"Have we done that?" asked Avalon.

"Yes, and, it seems to me, Mr. Avalon, you may have missed a most important point in consequence. Since it is not my place to talk—ordinarily—I listen to all of you impartially, the guest included, and I seem to have heard what the rest of you did not. May I have permission, Mr. Rubin, to ask Mr. Klein a few questions? The answers may prove to be of no help, but there is a small chance—"

"Well, sure," said Rubin. "He should be grilled anyway. Go ahead."

"It wouldn't be a grilling," objected Henry softly. "Mr. Klein?"

"Yes, Henry," said Klein, a rather pleased flush crossing his face at being the undoubted center of attention.

"It's just this, Mr. Klein. When you began to tell, rather briefly, the story of your lunch yesterday, you said something like—and I can't repeat the exact words either—you thought he was crazy, but he made everything sound so interesting that by the time he was through, you decided to start a collection of matchbooks of your own."

"That's right," said Klein, nodding. "Sort of silly, I suppose. I certainly wouldn't do anything at all like his deal. I don't mean the spying; I mean this huge collection of his—"

"Yes," said Henry, "but the impression I got was that you were driven to an impulse of collecting right on the spot. Did you by any chance pick up a Cock and Bull matchbook at the conclusion of the lunch?"

"That's right," said Klein. "It's a little embarrassing, now that I think of it, but I did."

"From which table, sir?"

"From our own."

"You mean you took the matchbook you had been holding and had passed on to Ottiwell? It was put back on the table eventually and you picked it up?"

"Yes," said Klein, suddenly defensive. "Nothing wrong with that, is there? They're there for the diners, aren't they?"

"Absolutely, sir. We have matchbooks on this table, which you're all welcome to. But, Mr. Klein, what did you do with the matchbook when you picked it up?"

Klein thought a bit. "I don't know. It's hard to remember. I put it in my jacket pocket, or in my coat pocket after we got our overcoats out of hock."

"Did you do anything with it once you got home?"

"No, as a matter of fact. I forgot all about it. All this matchbook bit just passed out of my head till Manny Rubin mentioned about his wife collecting bulls."

"You're not wearing the same jacket now, are you?"

"No. But I'm wearing the same coat."

"Would you look in the coat pocket and see if you have the matchbook there?"

Klein vanished into the private cloakroom used by the Black Widowers on the occasion of their meetings.

"What are you getting at, Henry?" asked Trumbull.

"Probably nothing," said Henry. "I'm playing a long chance, and we've already had one this evening."

"Which is that?"

"That Mr. Klein had lunch with a man who turns out to be someone you've been stalking, and that you find out about it the day after. Asking for two chances like that is a bit much, perhaps."

"Here it is," said Klein joyously, returning with a small object held high. "I've got it."

He tossed it on the table and everyone rose to look at it. It said "Cock and Bull" upon it in semi-archaic lettering, and there was the small picture of a bull's head, with a rooster perched on one horn. Gonzalo reached for it.

"If you please, Mr. Gonzalo," said Henry. "I don't think anyone ought to touch it yet. . . . Mr. Klein, this is the matchbook that was at your table, the one you used to light a cigarette and which Mr. Ottiwell then used to demonstrate some points about the place where the friction strip is located and so on?"

"Yes."

"And he put it down and you picked it up?"

"Yes."

"Did you happen to notice how many matches were present in the matchbook when you lit your cigarette?"

Klein looked surprised. "I don't know. I didn't pay any attention."

"But, in any case, you tore off one match to light your cigarette?"

"Oh, yes."

"So that even if it had been a full book of matches to begin with, there would be one missing now. Since this looks like a standard matchbook, with thirty matches, there can't be more than twenty-nine matches in it right now—and maybe less."

"I suppose so."

"And how many matches are there in the book now? Would you look and see?"

Klein paused and then opened the matchbook. He stared at it for quite a while, then said, "It hasn't been touched. It's got all thirty matches in it. Let me count them. . . . Yes, there are thirty."

"But you did pick it up from your table, and you did think it was the matchbook you had used? You didn't pick it up from another table altogether?"

"No, no, it was our matchbook. Or at least I was convinced it was."

"All right. If you gentlemen would care to look at it

now, please do so. If you'll notice, there is no mark on the friction strip, no sign of any match being lighted."

Trumbull said, "You mean that Ottiwell substituted this matchbook for the one that was on the table?"

"I thought such a thing was possible as soon as you said he was passing information, Mr. Trumbull. I agreed with you, Mr. Trumbull, that Mr. Ottiwell would make use of matchbooks. The psychology seemed sound to me. But I also agreed with Mr. Avalon that indirection might be used. It's just that Mr. Avalon did not quite see the possible subtlety of the indirection."

"Being too crooked myself to see clearly," sighed Avalon. "I know."

"By concentrating on his collection," said Henry, "and on his mailing and receiving matchbooks, he had you quite firmly pinned there, Mr. Trumbull. Yet it seemed to me that Mr. Ottiwell was not involved with matchbooks *only* in connection with his collection. Every time he ate in a decent restaurant, which might be often, he would be near a matchbook. Even if he were with others, it would be easy for him to substitute another matchbook for the one already on the table. Once he and the rest of the party left, a confederate could pick it up."

"Not this time," said Rubin sardonically.;

"No, not this time. When the party left, the table was empty of matchbooks. This leads to some bothersome thoughts. Have you been followed, Mr. Klein?"

Klein looked alarmed. *"No!* At least—at least—I don't know. I didn't notice anyone."

"Any pocket-picking attempts?"

"No! None that I know of."

"In that case, they may not be sure who took it—after all there were four others at the table besides yourself and Ottiwell; and a waiter might have cleared it, too. Or else they think that a lost matchbook will cause far less trouble than an attempt at retrieval might. Or else I'm all wrong from beginning to end."

Trumbull said, "Don't worry, Klein. I'll arrange to have an eye kept on you for a while."

He then went on. "I see the point you're making,

Henry. There are dozens of these matchbooks in any given restaurant at any given time, all of them identical. Ottiwell could easily have picked up one or two on a previous visit—or a dozen, if he wanted to—and then use them as substitutes. Who would notice? Who would care? And are you suggesting now that that one little substitute matchbook would carry the information?"

"It certainly would seem a strong possibility to me," said Henry.

"Go, little Book! from this my solitude/I cast thee on the waters—go thy way!" muttered Halsted. "That's Robert Southey!"

"But how would it work?" said Trumbull, ignoring Halsted's whispered verse. He turned the matchbook from side to side between his fingers. "It's one matchbook, just like all the rest. It says 'Cock and Bull' on it, plus an address and a phone number. Where would there be any information on this one as opposed to others?"

"We would have to look in the right place," said Henry.

"And where would that be?" said Trumbull.

"I go by what you said, sir," said Henry. "You said Mr. Ottiwell would be sure to use the matchbook in a way that would involve its unique qualities, and I agree. But what is unique about the message that matchbooks carry? In almost every case, it is just advertising matter, and you'll find such matter in almost any number of other places from cereal boxtops to the inside covers of magazines."

"Well, then?"

"Only one thing is truly unique about a matchbook—and that is the matches it contains. In the standard matchbook there are thirty matches that seem to be arranged in a moderately complicated pattern. If you study the bottom of the matches, though, you will see that there are two pieces of cardboard, from each of which there arise fifteen matches. If you count from left to right, first the back row—as you look at them from the direction of the opened flap—and then the front row, say, you can give each match a definite and unequivocal number from 1 to 30."

"Yes," said Trumbull, "but all the matches are identical with each other and with the matches in other matchbooks of the same kind. The matches in this particular matchbook are absolutely standard."

"But do the matches have to stay identical, sir? Suppose you took out one match—any one match. There would be thirty different ways of taking out one match. If you took out two matches, or three, there would be many more additional ways."

"No matches are missing."

"Just a manner of speaking. Tearing out matches would be far too crude a way of differentiating. Suppose certain matches had pinholes in them, or little scratches, or a tiny drop of fluorescent paint on the tips that would show up under ultraviolet light. With thirty matches, how many different patterns could you produce by marking any number, from none at all to all thirty?"

"I'll tell you that," interrupted Halsted. "Two to the thirtieth power, which comes to—oh, a little over one billion; that's *billion,* not million. And if you also marked or didn't mark the flap just behind the matches, you would double that to two billion."

"Well," said Henry, "if you could give a particular matchbook any number from zero to two billion, such numbers could encode considerable information, perhaps."

"As many as six words, easily," said Trumbull thoughtfully. "Damn!" he shouted, jumping to his feet. "Give me that thing. I'm leaving now."

He left for the cloakroom at a run and was back fumbling into his coat and shouting, "Get your coat, Klein, you're coming with me. I need your statement and you'll be safer."

Henry said, "I may be quite wrong, sir."

"Wrong, *hell!* You're right; I know you are. The whole thing fits a few items you don't know about. . . . Henry, would you consider getting involved in this sort of thing? I mean, professionally."

"Hey," shouted Rubin, "don't you go taking Henry away from us."

"No fear, Mr. Rubin," said Henry softly, "I find it much more exciting here."

Afterword

This story first appeared in a slightly shorter version, in the December 1972 issue of *Ellery Queen's Mystery Magazine,* under the title "The Matchbook Collector." Once again, I consider the magazine title pedestrian.

I'll leave it up to you. The phrase "Go, little Book!" is the beginning of a line from Chaucer and from a poem by Robert Southey, and that line from Southey was satirized very effectively by Lord Byron, so it has meaning in the history of English literature. On top of that, it perfectly expresses the nub of the story in which the little (match) books are sent outward on errands of information.

What do you say, then? Don't I owe it to all mankind to change "The Matchbook Collector" back into "Go, Little Book!"?

Sure I do.

By the way, when I first wrote the story I calculated out the value of 2^{30} (that is, 30 two's multiplied together) in my head out of sheer vainglory. Naturally, I got an answer that was off a little, and serves me right. A young lady named Mildred L. Stover wrote me a letter in which the value was carefully calculated out, multiplication by multiplication, and I corrected my mistake for the book. If you are interested, $2^{30} = 1,073,741,824$. Thank you, Miss Stover.

5

Early Sunday Morning

Geoffrey Avalon swirled his second drink as he sat down to the table. It had not yet diminished to the halfway mark and he would take one more sip before abandoning it. He looked unhappy.

He said, "This is the first time within my memory that the Black Widowers have met without a guest." His bushy eyebrows, still black (although his mustache and trim beard had become respectably gray with the years), seemed to twitch.

"Oh, well," said Roger Halsted, flicking his napkin with an audible slap before placing it over his knees. "As host this session, it's my decision. No appeal. Besides, I have my reasons." He placed the palm of his hand on his high forehead and made a motion as though to brush back hair that had disappeared from the forepart of his pate years before.

"Actually," said Emmanuel Rubin, "there's nothing in the bylaws that says we *must* have a guest. The only thing we *must* have present at the dinner is no women."

"The *members* can't be women," said Thomas Trumbull, glowering out of his perpetually tanned face. "Where does it say that a guest can't be a woman?"

"No," said Rubin sharply, his sparse beard quivering. "Any guest is a member *ex officio* for the meal and must abide by all the rules, including not being a woman."

"What does *ex officio* mean, anyway?" asked Mario Gonzalo. "I always wondered."

But Henry was already presenting the first course, which seemed to be a long roll of pasta, stuffed with spiced cheese, broiled, and sauce-covered.

At last Rubin, looking pained, said, "As near as I can make out this seems to be a roll of pasta, stuffed—"

But by that time, the conversation had grown general and Halsted seized a break to announce that he had his limerick for the third book of the *Iliad*.

Trumbull said, "Damn it to hell, Roger, are you going to inflict one of those on us at every meeting?"

"Yes," said Halsted thoughtfully. "I was planning just that. It keeps me working at it. Besides, you have to have some item of intellectual worth at the dinner. . . . Say, Henry, don't forget that if it's steak tonight, I want mine rare."

"Trout tonight, Mr. Halsted," said Henry, refilling the water glasses.

"Good," said Halsted. "Now here it is:

> *"Menelaus, though not very mighty,*
> *Was stronger than Paris, the flighty.*
> *Menelaus did well in*
> *The duel over Helen,*
> *But was foiled by divine Aphrodite."*

Gonzalo said, "But what does it mean?"

Avalon interposed, "Oh, well, in the third book, the Greeks and Trojans decide to settle the matter by means of a duel between Menelaus and Paris. The latter had eloped with the former's wife, Helen, and that was what caused the war. Menelaus won, but Aphrodite snatched Paris away just in time to save his life. . . . I'm glad you didn't use Venus in place of Aphrodite, Roger. There's too much of the use of Roman analogues."

Halsted, through a full mouth, said, "I wanted to avoid the temptation of obvious rhyming."

"Didn't you ever read the *Iliad*, Mario?" asked James Drake.

"Listen," said Gonzalo, "I'm an artist. I have to save my eyes."

It was with dessert on the table that Halsted said, "Okay, let me explain what I have in mind. The last four times we met, there's been some sort of crime that's come up every discussion, and in the course of that discussion, it's been solved."

"By Henry," interrupted Drake, stubbing out his cigarette.

"All right, by Henry. But what kind of crimes? Rotten crimes. The first time I wasn't here, but I gather the crime was a robbery, and not much of one either, from what I understand. The second time, it was worse. It was a case of cheating on an examination, for heaven's sake."

"That's not such a minor thing," muttered Drake.

"Well, it's not exactly a major thing. The third time— and I was here then—it was theft again, but a better one. And the fourth time it was a case of espionage of some sort."

"Believe me," said Trumbull, "that wasn't minor."

"Yes," said Halsted in his mild voice, "but there was no violence anywhere. Murder, gentlemen, murder!"

"What do you mean, murder?" asked Rubin.

"I mean that every time we bring a guest, something minor turns up because we take it as it comes. We don't deliberately invite guests who can offer us interesting crimes. In fact, they're not even supposed to offer us crimes at all. They're just guests."

"So?"

"So there are now six of us present, no guests, and there must be one of us who knows of some killing that's a mystery and—"

"Hell!" said Rubin in disgust. "You've been reading Agatha Christie. We'll each tell a puzzling mystery in turn and Miss Marple will solve it for us. . . . Or Henry will."

Halsted looked abashed. "You mean they do things like that—"

"Oh, God," said Rubin emotionally.

"Well, you're the writer," said Halsted. "I don't read murder mysteries."

"That's your loss," said Rubin, "and it shows what an idiot you are. You call yourself a mathematician. A proper mystery is as mathematical a puzzle as anything you can prepare and it has to be constructed out of much more intractable material."

"Now wait a while," said Trumbull. "As long as we're here, why don't we see if we can dig up a murder?"

"Can you present one?" said Halsted hopefully. "You're with the government, working on codes or whatever. You must have been involved with murder, and you don't have to name names. You know that nothing gets repeated outside these walls."

"I know that better than you," said Trumbull, "but I don't know about any murders. I can give you some interesting code items but that's not what you're after. . . . How about you, Roger? Since you bring this up, I suppose you have something up your sleeve. Some mathematical murder?"

"No," said Halsted thoughtfully, "I don't think I can recall being involved in a single murder."

"You don't think? You mean there's a doubt in your mind?" aked Avalon.

"I guess I'm certain. How about you, Jeff? You're a lawyer."

"Not the kind that gets murderers for clients," Avalon said, with an apparently regretful shake of his head. "Patent complications are my thing. You might ask Henry. He's more at home with crimes than we are, or he sounds it."

"I'm sorry, sir," said Henry softly as he poured the coffee with practiced skill. "In my case, it is merely theory. I have been fortunate enough never to be involved with violent death."

"You mean," said Halsted, "that with six of us here— seven, counting Henry—we can't scare up a single murder?"

Drake shrugged. "In my game, there's always a good chance of death. I haven't witnessed one in the chem lab personally, but there've been poisonings, explosions, even electrocutions. At worst, though, it's murder through negligence. I can't tell you anything about any of them."

Trumbull said, "How come you're so quiet, Manny? In

all your colorful career, you mean you've never had occasion to kill a man?"

"It would be a pleasure sometimes," said Rubin, "like now. But I don't really have to. I can handle them perfectly well at any size without having to lay a hand on them. Listen, I remember—"

But Mario Gonzalo, who had been sitting there with his lips clamped tightly together, suddenly said, "I've been involved in a murder."

"Oh? What kind?" asked Halsted.

"My sister," he said broodingly, "about three years ago. That was before I joined the Black Widowers."

"I'm sorry," said Halsted. "I guess you don't want to talk about it."

"I wouldn't mind talking about it," said Mario, shrugging, his large and prominent eyes looking them all in the face, one by one, "but there's nothing to talk about. No mystery. It's just another one of those things that make this city the fun place it is. They broke into the apartment, tried to loot it, and killed her."

"Who did?" asked Rubin.

"Who knows? Addicts! It happens all the time in that neighborhood. In the apartment house she and her husband lived in, there'd been four burglaries since New Year's and it was only the end of April when it happened."

"Were they all murders?"

"They don't have to be. The smart looter picks a time when the apartment is empty. Or if someone's there, they just scare them or tie them up. Marge was stupid enough to try to resist, to fight back. There were plenty of signs of a struggle." Gonzalo shook his head.

Halsted said, after a painful pause, "Did they ever get the ones who did it?"

Gonzalo's eyes lifted and stared into Halsted's without any attempt at masking the contempt they held. "Do you think they even looked? That sort of thing goes on all day long. Nobody can do anything. Nobody even cares. And if they got them, so what? Would it bring back Marge?"

"It might keep them from doing it to others."

"There'd be plenty of other miserable creeps to do it." Gonzalo drew a deep breath, then said, "Well, maybe I'd *better* talk about it and get it out of my system. It's all my fault, you see, because I wake up too early. If it weren't for that, maybe Marge would be alive and Alex wouldn't be the wreck he is now."

"Who's Alex?" asked Avalon.

"My brother-in-law. He was married to Marge, and I liked him. I think I liked him better than I ever did her, to be truthful. She never approved of me. She thought being an artist was just my way of goofing off. Of course, once I started making a decent living—no, she never really approved of me even then and most of the time she was, meaning no disrespect to the dead, one big pain. She liked Alex, though."

"He wasn't an artist?" Avalon was carrying the burden of the questioning and the others seemed willing to leave it to him.

"No. He wasn't much of anything when they married, just a drifter, but afterward he became exactly what she wanted. She was what he needed to get a little push into him. They needed each other. She had something to care for—"

"No children?"

"No. None. Unless you want to count one miscarriage. Poor Marge. Something biological, so she couldn't have kids. But it didn't matter. Alex was her kid, and he flourished. He got a job the month he was married, got promoted, did well. They were getting to the point where they were planning to move out of that damned death trap, and then it happened. Poor Alex. He was as much to blame as I was. More, in fact. Of all days, he had to leave the house on that one."

"He wasn't in the apartment, then?"

"Of course not. If he was, he might have scared them off."

"Or he might have gotten killed himself."

"In which case they would probably have run off and

left Marge alive. Believe me, I've listened to him list the possibilities. No matter how he slices it, she'd still be alive if he hadn't left that day, and it bothers him. And let me tell you, he's gone to pot since it happened. He's just a drifter again now. I give him money when I can and he gets odd jobs now and then. Poor Alex. He had that five years of marriage when he was really making it. He was a go-getter. Now it's all for nothing. Nothing to show for it."

Gonzalo shook his head. "What gets me is that the victim isn't the one who gets the worst of it. It's a senseless murder—hell, everything they got in the apartment amounted to no more than about ten, fifteen dollars in small bills—but at least Marge died quickly. The knife was right in the heart. But Alex suffers every day of his life now, and my mother took it hard. And it bothers me, too."

"Listen," said Halsted, "if you don't want to talk about it—"

"It's all right. . . . I think of it nights sometimes. If I didn't wake up early that day—"

"That's the second time you said that," said Trumbull. "What's your waking up early got to do with it?"

"Because people who know me count on it. Look, I always wake up at eight A.M. sharp. It doesn't vary by as much as five minutes one way or the other. I don't even bother keeping the clock by my bed; it stays in the kitchen. It's got something to do with rhythms in the body."

"The biological clock," muttered Drake. "I wish it worked that way with me. I *hate* getting up in the morning."

"It works with me all the time," said Gonzalo, and even under the circumstances, there was a hint of complacence in his voice as he said so. "Even if I go to sleep late—three in the morning, four—I always wake up at exactly eight. I go back to sleep later in the day if I'm knocked out, but at eight I wake up. Even on Sunday. You'd think I'd have the right to sleep late on Sunday, but even then, damn it, I wake up."

"You mean it happened on a Sunday?" asked Rubin.

Gonzalo nodded. "That's right. I should have been asleep. I should have been the kind of person people would know better than to wake early Sunday morning—but they don't hesitate. They know I'll be awake, even on Sunday."

"Nuts," said Drake, apparently still brooding over his difficulties in the morning. "You're an artist and make your own hours. Why do you have to get up in the morning?"

"Well, I work best then. Besides, I'm time-conscious, too. I don't have to live by the clock, but I like to know what time it is at all times. That clock I have. It's trained, you know. After it happened, after Marge was killed, I wasn't home for three days and it just happened to stop either eight P.M. Sunday or eight A.M. Monday. I don't know. Anyway, when I came back there it was with the hands pointing to eight as though rubbing it in that that was wake-up time."

Gonzalo brooded for a while and no one spoke. Henry passed around the small brandy glasses with no expression on his face, unless you counted the merest tightening of his lips.

Gonzalo finally said, "It's a funny thing but I had a rotten night, that night before, and there was no reason for it. That time of year, end of April, cherry-blossom time, is my favorite. I'm not exactly a landscape artist, but that's the one time I do like to get into the park and make some sketches. And the weather was good. I remember it was a nice mild Saturday, the first really beautiful weekend of the year, and my work was doing pretty well, too.

"I had no reason to feel bad that day, but I got more and more restless. I remember I turned off my little television set just before the eleven-o'clock news. It was as though I felt that I didn't want to hear the news. It was as though I felt there would be bad news. I *remember* that. I didn't make it up afterward, and I'm not a mystic. But I had a premonition. I just did."

Rubin said, "More likely you had a touch of indigestion."

"All right," said Gonzalo, moving his hands as though to take in and welcome the suggestion. "Call it indigestion. All I know is that it was before eleven P.M. and I went into the kitchen and wound the clock—I always wind it at night—and said to myself, 'I can't go to bed *this* early,' but I did.

"Maybe it *was* too early, because I couldn't sleep. I kept tossing and worrying—I don't remember about what. What I should have done was get up, do some work, read a book, watch some late movie—but I just didn't. I just made up my mind to stay in bed."

"Why?" asked Avalon.

"Don't know. It seemed important at the time. God, how I remember that night, because I kept thinking, maybe I'll sleep late because I'm not sleeping now and I knew I wouldn't. I must have dropped off at about four A.M., but at eight I was up and crawled out of bed to get myself breakfast.

"It was another sunny day. Pleasant and cool, but you knew it was going to have all the warmth of spring with none of the heat of summer. Another nice day! You know it hurts me, now and then, that I didn't like Marge better than I did. I mean, we got along all right, but we weren't close. I swear I visited them more to be with Alex than to be with her. And then I got a call."

Halsted said, "You mean a telephone call?"

"Yes. Eight o'clock of a Sunday morning. Who would make a call at that time to anyone unless they knew the jerk always got up at eight. If I had been asleep and had been awakened, and growled into the mouthpiece, the whole thing would have been different."

"Who was it?" asked Drake.

"Alex. He asked if he woke me. He knew he didn't, but he felt guilty calling that early, I suppose. He asked what time it was. I looked at the clock and said, 'It's eight-oh-nine A.M. Of course I'm awake.' I was sort of proud of it, you see.

"And then he asked if he could come over, because he

had had an argument with Marge and had stamped out of
the house and didn't want to go back till she had cooled
down. . . . I tell you, I'm glad I never married.

"Anyway, if I'd only said no. If I'd only told him I'd
had a bad night and I needed my sleep and I didn't want
company, he'd have gone back to his apartment. He had
no place else to go. And then it all wouldn't have happened. But no, big-hearted Mario was so proud of being
an early riser that he said, 'Come on over and I'll fix you
coffee and eggs,' because I knew Marge wasn't one for
early Sunday breakfasts, and I knew Alex hadn't eaten.

"So he was over in ten minutes and by eight-thirty I
had the scrambled eggs and bacon in front of him, and
Marge was alone in the apartment, waiting for murderers."

Trumbull said, "Did your brother-in-law tell his wife
where he was going?"

Gonzalo said, "I don't think so. I assumed he didn't. I
figure what happened was he stamped out in a fit of rage
without even knowing where he was going himself. Then
he thought of me. Even if he knew he was going to visit
me, he might not have told her. He would figure: Let her
worry."

"All right," said Trumbull, "and then when the junkies
came to the door and maybe tried the lock, she figured it
was Alex coming back and she opened the door to them.
I'll bet the lock wasn't broken."

"No, it wasn't," said Gonzalo.

"Isn't Sunday morning a queer time for junkies to
make the rounds?" asked Drake.

"Listen," said Rubin, "they'll do it any time. The crav-
ing for drugs knows no season."

"What was the fight about?" asked Avalon suddenly. "I
mean, between Alex and Marge?"

"Oh, I don't know. A little thing. Alex had done something at work that must have looked bad and that was one
thing that Marge couldn't stand. I don't even know what
it was, but whatever it was, it must have been a blow at
her pride in him and she was sore.

"The trouble was that Alex never learned to just let her

run down. When we were kids, I always did that. I would say, 'Yes, Marge; yes, Marge,' and then she'd run down. But Alex would always try to defend himself and then things would just get worse. That time, most of the night was filled with argument. . . . Of course, he says now that if he only hadn't made a federal case out of it, he wouldn't have left, and then none of it would have happened."

"The moving finger writes,' " said Avalon. "Brooding on these ifs does no good."

"Sure, but how do you stop, Jeff? Anyway, they had a bad night and I had a bad night. It was as though there were some kind of telepathic communication."

"Oh, bull," said Rubin.

"We were twins," said Gonzalo defensively.

"Only fraternal twins," said Rubin, "unless you're a girl underneath all those clothes."

"So what?"

"So it's only identical twins that are supposed to have this telepathic sympathy, but that's bull, too."

"Anyway," said Gonzalo, "Alex was with me and I ate and he didn't eat much, and he cried on my shoulder about how hard Marge was on him sometimes, and I sympathized and said, 'Listen, why do you pay so much attention to her? She's a good kid if you'll only not take her seriously.' You know all the consoling things people say. I figured in a couple of hours he'd be talked out and he'd go home and make it up and I'd go out to the park or maybe back to bed. Only in a couple of hours the telephone rang again, and it was the police."

"How'd they know where to find Alex?" asked Halsted.

"They didn't. They called *me*. I'm her brother. Alex and I went over and identified her. For a while there, he looked like a dead man. It wasn't just that she was dead. After all, he'd had a fight with her and the neighbors must have heard. Now she was dead, and they always suspect the husband. Of course, they questioned him and he admitted the fight and leaving the apartment and coming to my place—the whole thing."

"It must have sounded phony as hell," said Rubin.

"I corroborated the fact that he was at my place. I said he'd arrived at my place at eight-twenty, maybe eight twenty-five, and had been there since. And the murder had taken place at nine."

"You mean there were witnesses?" asked Drake.

"Hell, no. But there'd been noise. The people underneath heard. The people across the hall heard. Furniture being overturned; a scream. Of course, no one saw anyone; no one saw anything. They sat behind their locked doors. But they heard the noise and it was around nine o'clock. They all agreed to that.

"That settled it as far as the police were concerned. In that neighborhood, if it isn't the spouse, it's some petty thief, probably an addict. Alex and I went out and he got drunk and I stayed with him a couple of days because he was in no condition to be left alone and that's all there is to the story."

Trumbull said, "Do you ever see Alex these days?"

"Once in a while. I lend him a few bucks now and then. Not that I expect to get paid back. He quit his job the week after Marge was killed. I don't think he ever went back to work. He was just a broken man—because he blamed himself, you know. Why did he have to argue with her? Why did he have to leave the house? Why did he have to come over to my place? Anyway, there it is. It's a murder but no mystery."

There was silence for a time, and then Halsted said, "Do you mind, Mario, if we speculate about it, just—just—"

"Just for fun?" said Mario. "Sure, go ahead, have fun. If you have questions, I'll answer as best I can but as far as the murder is concerned, there's nothing to say."

"You see," said Halsted awkwardly, "no one *saw* anybody. It's only an assumption that some nameless addicts came in and killed her. Someone might have killed her with a better reason, knowing that it would be blamed on addicts and he'd be safe. Or she, maybe."

"Who's the someone?" said Mario skeptically.

"Didn't she have any enemies? Did she have money that somebody wanted?" said Halsted.

"Money? What there was was in the bank. It all went to Alex, of course. It was his to begin with; everything was joint."

"How about jealousy?" said Avalon. "Maybe she was having an affair. Or he was. Maybe that's what the argument was about."

"And he killed her?" said Gonzalo. "The fact is he was in my apartment at the time she was killed."

"Not necessarily he. Suppose it was her boy friend, or his girl friend. The boy friend, because she was threatening to break off the affair. The girl friend, because she wanted to marry your brother-in-law."

Mario shook his head. "Marge was no femme fatale. I was always surprised she made it with Alex. For that matter, maybe she didn't."

"Did Alex complain about that?" asked Trumbull with sudden interest.

"No, but then he's no great lover, either. Listen, he's been a widower for three years now and I'm willing to swear he has no girl of any kind. No boy, either, before you start talking about that."

Rubin said, "Hold it, you still don't know what the argument was really about. You said it was something that happened at work. Did he actually tell you what it was and you've just forgotten; or did he never tell you?"

"He didn't go into detail, and I didn't ask. It wasn't my business."

"All right," said Rubin, "how about this? It was an argument about something big at work. Maybe Alex had stolen fifty thousand dollars and Marge was sore about it, and that was the argument. Or Marge had made him steal it and he was getting cold feet about it and that was the argument. And maybe the fifty thousand was in the house and someone knew about it and that someone killed her and took it and Alex doesn't dare mention it."

"What someone?" demanded Gonzalo. "What theft? Alex wasn't that kind of guy."

"Famous last words," intoned Drake.

"Well, he wasn't. And if he had done it, the firm he worked for wouldn't have kept quiet. No chance."

Trumbull said, "How about the kind of in-fighting that goes on in apartment houses? You know, feuds between tenants. Was there someone who hated her and finally let her have it?"

"Hell, if there were anything that serious, I'd know about it. Marge never kept things like that quiet."

Drake said, "Could it be suicide? After all, her husband had just walked out on her. Maybe he said he was never coming back and she was in despair. In a fit of irrational depression, she killed herself."

"It was a knife from the kitchen," said Gonzalo. "There's that. But Marge isn't the suicidal type. She might kill someone else, but not herself. Besides, why would there be that struggle and the scream if she had killed herself?"

Drake said, "In the first place, things might have been knocked about during the argument with her husband. In the second place, she might have faked a murder to get her husband into trouble. Vengeance is mine, saith the aggrieved wife."

"Oh, come on," said Gonzalo contemptuously. "Marge wouldn't do something like that in a million years."

"You know," said Drake, "you don't really know all that much about another person—even if she's a twin."

"Well, you won't get me to believe it."

Trumbull said, "I don't know why we're wasting our time. Why don't we ask the expert? . . . Henry?"

Henry, whose face mirrored only polite interest, said, "Yes, Mr. Trumbull?"

"How about telling us all about it? Who killed Mr. Gonzalo's sister?"

Henry's eyebrows lifted slightly. "I do not represent myself to be an expert, Mr. Trumbull, but I must say that all the suggestions made by the gentlemen at the table, including yours, are unlikely in the extreme. I myself think that the police are perfectly correct and that if, in this case, the husband did not do it, then housebreakers did. And these days, one must assume that those housebreakers were drug addicts desperate for money or for something they can convert into money."

"You disappoint me, Henry," said Trumbull.

Henry smiled gently.

"Well, then," said Halsted, "I guess we'd better adjourn after we settle who hosts next time, and I suppose we'd better go back to having guests. This scheme of mine didn't work out so well."

"Sorry I couldn't make it better, folks," said Gonzalo.

"I didn't mean it that way, Mario," said Halsted hastily.

"I know. Well, let's forget it."

They were leaving, with Mario Gonzalo bringing up the rear. A light tap at his shoulder caused Gonzalo to turn.

Henry said, "Mr. Gonzalo, could I see you privately, without the others knowing? It's quite important."

Gonzalo stared a moment and said, "Okay, I'll go out, say my goodbyes, take a taxi, and have it bring me back." He was back in ten minutes.

"Is this something about my sister, Henry?"

"I'm afraid so, sir. I thought I had better talk to you, privately."

"All right. Let's go back into the chamber. It's empty now."

"Better not, sir. Anything said in that room can't be repeated outside and I do not wish to talk in confidence. I don't mind finding myself hushed up about average run-of-the-mill misdeeds, but murder is another thing altogether. There's a corner here that we can use."

They went together to the indicated place. It was late and the restaurant was virtually empty.

Henry said, in a low voice, "I listened to the account and I would like your permission to repeat some of it just to make sure I have it right."

"Sure, go ahead."

"As I understand it, on a Saturday toward the end of April, you felt uneasy and went to bed before the eleven-o'clock news."

"Yes, just before eleven o'clock."

"And you didn't hear the news."

"Not even the opening headlines."

"And that night, even though you didn't sleep, you

didn't get out of bed. You didn't go to the bathroom or the kitchen."

"No, I didn't."

"And then you woke up at exactly the same time you always do."

"That's right."

"Well, now, Mr. Gonzalo, that is what disturbs me. A person who wakes up every morning at exactly the same time, thanks to some sort of biological clock inside him, wakes up at the wrong time twice a year."

"What?"

"Twice a year, sir, in this state, ordinary clocks are shifted, once when Daylight Saving Time starts, and once when it ends, but biological time doesn't change suddenly. Mr. Gonzalo, on the last Sunday in April, Daylight Saving Time starts. At one A.M. Sunday morning the clocks are shifted to two A.M. If you had listened to the eleven-o'clock news you would have been reminded to do that. But you wound you clock before eleven P.M. and you said nothing about adjusting it. Then you went to bed and never touched it during the night. When you woke at eight A.M., the clock should have said *nine* A.M. Am I right?"

"Good Lord," said Gonzalo.

"You left after the police called and you didn't come back for days. When you came back the clock was stopped, of course. You had no way of knowing that it was an hour slow when it had stopped. You set it to the correct time and never knew the difference."

"I never thought of that, but you're perfectly right."

"The police should have thought of that, but it's so easy these days to dismiss run-of-the-mill crimes of violence as the work of addicts. You gave your brother-in-law his alibi and they followed the line of least resistance."

"You mean he—"

"It's possible, sir. They fought, and he killed her at nine A.M. as the statements of the neighbors indicated. I doubt that it was premeditated. Then, in desperation, he thought of you—and rather clever of him it was. He called you and asked you what time it was. You said eight-oh-nine and he knew you hadn't altered the clock and rushed over to your place. If you had said nine-oh-nine, he would have tried to get out of town."

"But, Henry, why should he have done it?"

"It's hard to tell with married couples, sir. Your sister may have had too high standards. You said she disapproved of your way of life, for instance, and probably made that very plain, plain enough to cause you not to like her very well. Now she must have disapproved of her husband's way of life, as it was before she had married him. He was a drifter, you said. She made of him a respectable, hard-working employee and he may not have liked it. After he finally exploded and killed her, he became a drifter again. You think this is so out of despair; he may have nothing more than the feeling of relief."

"Well . . . What do we do?"

"I don't know, sir. It would be a hard thing to prove. Could you really remember, after three years, that you didn't adjust the clock? A cross-examining attorney would tear you apart. On the other hand, your brother-in-law might break down if faced with it. You'll have to consider whether you wish to go to the police, sir."

"I?" said Gonzalo hesitantly.

"It was your sister, sir," said Henry softly.

Afterword

This story first appeared in the March 1973 issue of *Ellery Queen's Mystery Magazine,* under the title "The Biological Clock."

In this case it seems to me that the magazine title stresses something I would rather the reader slurred over, since it is the key to the puzzle. If he concentrates too hard on that because of the title, he will outguess me. Therefore, it's back to "Early Sunday Morning," which refers to the matter also, so that it's fair, but is sufficiently neutral to give *me* a fair chance, too.

6

The Obvious Factor

Thomas Trumbull looked about the table and said, with some satisfaction, "Well, at least you won't get yourself pen-and-inked into oblivion, Voss. Our resident artist isn't here. . . . *Henry!*"

Henry was at Trumbull's elbow before the echo of the bellow had died, with no sign of perturbation on his bright-eyed and unlined face. Trumbull took the scotch and soda the waiter had on his tray and said, "Has Mario called, Henry?"

"No, sir," said Henry calmly.

Geoffrey Avalon had reduced his second drink to the halfway point and swirled it absently. "After last month's tale about his murdered sister, it could be that he didn't—"

He did not complete the sentence, but put down his glass carefully at the seat he intended to take. The monthly banquet of the Black Widowers was about to begin.

Trumbull, who was host, took the armchair at the head of the table and said, "Have you got them all straight, Voss? At my left is James Drake. He's a chemist and knows more about pulp fiction than about chemistry, and that probably isn't much. Then Geoffrey Avalon, a lawyer who never sees the inside of a courtroom; Emmanuel Rubin, who writes in between talking, which is practically never; and Roger Halsted. . . . Roger, you're not inflicting another limerick on us this session, are you?"

"A limerick?" said Trumbull's guest, speaking for the first time. It was a pleasant voice, light and yet rich, with all consonants carefully pronounced. He had a white beard, evenly cut from temple to temple, and white hair,

96

too. His youthful face shone pinkly within its fence of white. "A poet, then?"

"A poet?" snorted Trumbull. "Not even a mathematician, which is what he claims to be. He insists on writing a limerick for every book of the *Iliad*."

"And *Odyssey*," said Halsted, in his soft, hurried voice. "But, yes, I have my limerick."

"Good! It's out of order," said Trumbull. "You are not to read it. Host's privilege."

"Oh, for heaven's sake," said Avalon, the flat lines of his well-preserved face set in disappointment. "Let him recite the poor thing. It takes thirty seconds and I find it fun."

Trumbull pretended not to hear. "You've all got it straight about my guest now? He's Dr. Voss Eldridge. He's a Ph.D. So is Drake, Voss. We're all doctors, though, by virtue of membership in the Black Widowers." He then raised his glass, gave the monthly invocation to Old King Cole, and the meal was officially begun.

Halsted, who had been whispering to Drake, passed a paper to him. Drake rose and declaimed:

> *"Next a Lycian attempted a ruse*
> *With an arrow—permitted by Zeus.*
> > *Who will trust Trojan candor, as*
> > *This sly deed of Pandarus*
> > *Puts an end to the scarce-proclaimed truce?"*

"Damn it," said Trumbull. "I ruled against reading it."

"Against *my* reading it," said Halsted. "Drake read it."

"It's disappointing not to have Mario here," said Avalon. "He would ask what it means."

"Go ahead, Jeff," said Rubin. "I'll pretend I don't understand it and you explain."

But Avalon maintained a dignified silence while Henry presented the appetizer and Rubin fixed it with his usual suspicious stare.

"I hate stuff," he said, "that's so chopped up and drowned in goop that you can't see what the ingredients are."

Henry said, "I think you'll find it quite wholesome."

"Try it; you'll like it," said Avalon.

Rubin tried it, but his face showed no signs of liking it. It was noted later, however, that he had finished it.

Dr. Eldridge said, "Is there a necessity of explaining these limericks, Dr. Avalon? Are there tricks to them?"

"No, not at all, and don't bother with the doctorate. That's only for formal occasions, though it's good of you to humor the club idiosyncrasy. It's just that Mario has never read the *Iliad;* few have, these days."

"Pandarus, as I recall, was a go-between and gives us the word 'pander.' That, I take it, was the sly deed mentioned in the limerick."

"Oh, no, no," said Avalon, unsuccessfully hiding his delight. "You're thinking now of the medieval Troilus tale, which Shakespeare drew on for his *Troilus and Cressida.* Pandarus was the go-between there. In the *Iliad* he was merely a Lycian archer who shot at Menelaus during a truce. That was the sly deed. He is killed in the next book by the Greek warrior Diomedes."

"Ah," said Eldridge, smiling faintly, "it's easy to be fooled, isn't it?"

"If you want to be," said Rubin, but he smiled as the London broil arrived. There was no mistaking the nature of the components there. He buttered a roll and ate it as though to give himself time to contemplate the beauty of the meat.

"As a matter of fact," said Halsted, "we've solved quite a few puzzles in recent meetings. We did well."

"We did lousy," said Trumbull. "Henry is the one who did well."

"I *include* Henry when I say 'we,' " said Halsted, his fair face flushing.

"Henry?" asked Eldridge.

"Our esteemed waiter," said Trumbull, "and honorary member of the Black Widowers."

Henry, who was filling the water glasses, said, "You honor me, sir."

"Honor, hell. I wouldn't come to any meeting if you weren't taking care of the table, Henry."

"Its good of you to say so, sir."

Eldridge remained thoughtfully quiet thereafter, as he followed the tide of conversation that, as was usual, grew steadily in intensity. Drake was making some obscure distinction between Secret Agent X and Operator 5, and Rubin, for some reason known only to himself, was disputing the point.

Drake, whose slightly hoarse voice never rose, said, "Operator 5 may have used disguises. I won't deny that. It was Secret Agent X, however, who was 'the man of a thousand faces.' I can send you a Xerox of a contents page of a magazine from my library to prove it." He made a note to himself in his memo book.

Rubin, scenting defeat, shifted ground at once. "There's no such thing as a disguise, anyway. There are a million things no one can disguise, idiosyncrasies of stance, walk, voice; a million habits you can't change because you don't even know you have them. A disguise works only because no one *looks*."

"People fool themselves, in other words," said Eldridge, breaking in.

"Absolutely," said Rubin. "People *want* to be fooled."

The ice-cream parfait was brought in, and not long after that, Trumbull struck his water glass with his spoon.

"Inquisition time," he said. "As Grand Inquisitor I pass, since I'm the host. Manny, will you do the honors?"

Rubin said, at once, "Dr. Eldridge, how do you justify the fact of your existence?"

"By the fact that I labor to distinguish truth from folly."

"Do you consider that you succeed in doing so?"

"Not as often as I wish, perhaps. And yet as often as most. To distinguish truth from folly is a common desire; we all try our hands at it. My interpretation of Pandarus' deed in Halsted's limerick was folly and Avalon corrected me. The common notion of disguise you claimed to be folly and you corrected it. When I find folly, I try to correct it, if I can. It's not always easy."

"What is your form of folly correction, Eldridge? How would you describe your profession?"

"I am," said Eldridge, "Associate Professor of Abnormal Psychology."

"Where do you . . . ?" began Rubin.

Avalon interrupted, his deep voice dominating, "Sorry, Manny, but I smell an evasion. You asked Dr. Eldridge's profession and he gave you a title . . . What do you do Dr. Eldridge, to occupy your time most significantly?"

"I investigate parapsychological phenomena," said Eldridge.

"Oh, God," muttered Drake, and stubbed out his cigarette.

Eldridge said, "You disapprove of that, sir?" There was no sign of annoyance on his face. He turned to Henry and said, "No, thank you, Henry, I've had enough coffee," with perfect calmness.

Henry passed on to Rubin, who was holding his cup in the air as a signal of its emptiness.

"It's not a question of approval or disapproval," said Drake. "I think you're wasting your time."

"In what way?"

"You investigate telepathy, precognition, things like that?"

"Yes. And ghosts and spiritual phenomena, too."

"All right. Have you ever come across something you couldn't explain?"

"Explain in what way? I could explain a ghost by saying, 'Yes, that's a ghost.' I take it that's not what you mean."

Rubin broke in. "I hate to be on Drake's side right now, but he means to ask, as you well know, whether you have ever come across any phenomenon you could not explain by the accepted and prosaic laws of science."

"I have come across many such phenomena."

"That you could not explain?" asked Halsted.

"That I could not explain. There's not a month that passes but that something crosses my desk that I cannot explain," said Eldridge, nodding his head gently.

There was a short silence of palpable disapproval and then Avalon said, "Does that mean that you are a believer in these psychic phenomena?"

"If you mean: Do I think that events take place that violate the laws of physics? No! Do I think, however, that I know all there is to know about the laws of physics? Also, no. Do I think anyone knows all there is to know about the laws of physics? No, a third time."

"That's evasion," said Drake. "Do you have any evidence that telepathy exists, for instance, and that the laws of physics, as presently accepted, will have to be modified accordingly?"

"I am not ready to commit myself that far. I well know that in even the most circumstantial stories, there are honest mistakes, exaggerations, misinterpretations, outright hoaxes. And yet, even allowing for all that, I come across incidents I cannot quite bring myself to dismiss."

Eldridge shook his head and continued, "It's not easy, this job of mine. There are some incidents for which no conceivable run-of-the-mill explanation seems possible; where the evidence for something quite apart from the known rules by which the universe seems to run appears irrefutable. It would seem I *must* accept—and yet I hesitate. Can I labor under a hoax so cleverly manipulated, or an error so cleverly hidden, that I take for the gold of fact what is only the brass of nonsense? I can be fooled, as Rubin would point out."

Trumbull said, "Manny would say that you *want* to be fooled."

"Maybe I do. We all want dramatic things to be true. We want to be able to wish on a star, to have strange powers, to be irresistible to women—and would inwardly conspire to believe such things no matter how much we might lay claim to complete rationality."

"Not me," said Rubin flatly. "I've never kidded myself in my life."

"No?" Eldridge looked at him thoughtfully. "I take it then that you will refuse to believe in the actual existence of parapsychological phenomena under all circumstances?"

"I wouldn't say that," said Rubin, "but I'd need damned good evidence—better evidence than I've ever seen advanced."

"And how about the rest of you gentlemen?"

Drake said, "We're all rationalists. At least I don't know about Mario Gonzalo, but he's not here this session."

"You, too, Tom?"

Trumbull's lined face broke into a grim smile. "You've never convinced me with any of your tales before this, Voss. I don't think you can convince me now."

"I never told you tales that convinced *me*, Tom. . . . But I have one now; something I've never told you and that no one really knows about outside my department. I can tell it to you all and if you can come up with an explanation that would require no change in the fundamental scientific view of the universe, I would be greatly relieved."

"A ghost story?" said Halsted.

"No, not a ghost story," said Eldridge. "It is merely a story that defies the principle of cause and effect, the very foundation stone on which all science is built. To put it another way, it defies the concept of the irreversible forward flow of time."

"Actually," said Rubin, at once, "it's quite possible, on the sub-atomic level, to consider time as flowing either—"

"Shut up, Manny," said Trumbull, "and let Voss talk."

Quietly, Henry had placed the brandy before each of the diners. Eldridge lifted his small glass absently and sniffed at it, then nodded to Henry, who returned a small, urbane smile.

"It's an odd thing," said Eldridge, "but so many of those who claim to have strange powers, or have it claimed for them, are young women of no particular education, no particular presence, no particular intelligence. It is as though the existence of a special talent has consumed what would otherwise be spread out among the more usual facets of the personality. Maybe it's just more noticeable in women.

"At any rate, I am speaking of someone I'll just call Mary for now. You understand I'm not using her real name. The woman is still under investigation and it would be fatal, from my point of view, to get any kind of publicity hounds on the track. You understand?"

Trumbull frowned severely. "Come on, Voss, you know I told you that nothing said here is ever repeated outside the confines of these walls. You needn't feel constrained."

"Accidents happen," said Eldridge equably. "At any rate, I'll return to Mary. Mary never completed grade school and has earned what money she could earn by serving behind a counter at the five-and-ten. She is not attractive and no one will sweep her away from the counter, which may be good, for she is useful there and serves well. You might not think so, since she cannot add correctly and is given to incapacitating headaches, during which she will sit in a back room and upset the other employees by muttering gibberish to herself in a baleful sort of way. Nevertheless, the store wouldn't dream of letting her go."

"Why not?" asked Rubin, clearly steeling himself to skepticism at every point.

"Because she spots shoplifters, who, as you know, can these days bleed a store to death through a thousand small cuts. It isn't that Mary is in any way shrewd or keen-eyed or unrelenting in pursuit. She just knows a shoplifter when he or she enters the store, even if she has never seen the person before, and even if she doesn't actually see the person come in.

"She followed them herself at first for brief intervals; then grew hysterical and began her muttering. The manager eventually tied the two things together—Mary's characteristic behavior and the shoplifting. He started to watch for one, then the other, and it didn't take long for him to find out that she never missed.

"Losses quickly dropped to virtually nothing in that particular five-and-ten despite the fact that the store is in a bad neighborhood. The manager, of course, received the credit. Probably, he deliberately kept the truth from being known lest anyone try to steal Mary from him.

"But then I think he grew afraid of it. Mary fingered a shoplifter who wasn't a shoplifter but who later was mixed up in a shooting incident. The manager had read about some of the work my department does, and he came to us. Eventually, he brought Mary to us.

"We got her to come to the college regularly. We paid her, of course. Not much, but then she didn't ask for much. She was an unpleasant not-bright girl of about twenty, who was reluctant to talk and describe what went on in her mind. I suppose she had spent a childhood having her queer notions beaten out of her and she had learned to be cautious, you see."

Drake said, "You're telling us she had a gift for precognition?"

Eldridge said, "Since precognition is just Latin for seeing-things-before-they-happen, and since she sees things before they happen, how else can I describe it? She sees unpleasant things only, things that upset or frighten her, which, I imagine, makes her life a hell. It is the quality of becoming upset or frightened that breaks down the time barrier."

Halsted said, "Let's set our boundary conditions. What does she sense? How far ahead in time does she see things? How far away in space?"

"We could never get her to do much for us," said Eldridge. "Her talent wasn't on tap at will and with us she could never relax. From what the manager told us and from what we could pick up, it seemed she could never detect anything more than a few minutes ahead in time. Half an hour to an hour at the most."

Rubin snorted.

"A few minutes," said Eldridge mildly, "is as good as a century. The principle stands. Cause and effect is violated and the flow of time is reversed.

"And in space, there seemed no limits. As she described it, when I could get her to say anything at all, and as I interpreted her rather clumsy and incoherent words, the background of her mind is a constant flickering of frightening shapes. Every once in a while, this is lit up, as though by a momentary lightning flash, and she sees, or becomes aware. She sees most clearly what is close by or what she is most concerned about—the shoplifting, for instance. Occasionally, though, she sees what must be taking place farther away. The greater the disaster, the farther she can sense things. I suspect she could detect a nuclear bomb getting ready to explode anywhere in the world."

Rubin said, "I imagine she speaks incoherently and you fill in the rest. History is full of ecstatic prophets whose mumbles are interpreted into wisdom."

"I agree," said Eldridge, "and I pay no attention—or at least not much—to anything that isn't clear. I don't even attach much importance to her feats with shoplifters. She might be sensitive enough to detect some characteristic way in which shoplifters look and stand, some aura, some *smell*—the sort of thing you talked about, Rubin, as matters no one can disguise. But then—"

"Then?" prompted Halsted.

"Just a minute," said Eldridge. "Uh—Henry, could I have a refill in the coffeecup after all?"

"Certainly," said Henry.

Eldridge watched the coffee level rise. "What's *your* attitude on psychic phenomena, Henry?"

Henry said, "I have no general attitude, sir. I accept whatever it seems to me I must accept."

"Good!" said Eldridge. "I'll rely on you and not on these prejudiced and preconcepted rationalists here."

"Go on, then," said Drake. "You paused at the dramatic moment to throw us off."

"Never," said Eldridge. "I was saying that I did not take Mary seriously, until one day she suddenly began to squirm and pant and mumble under her breath. She does that now and then, but this time she muttered 'Eldridge. Eldridge.' And the word grew shriller and shriller.

"I assumed she was calling me, but she wasn't. When I responded, she ignored me. Over and over again, it was 'Eldridge! Eldridge!' Then she began to scream, 'Fire! Oh, Lord! It's burning! Help! Eldridge! Eldridge!' Over and over again, with all kinds of variations. She kept it up for half an hour.

"We tried to make sense out of it. We spoke quietly, of

course, because we didn't want to intrude more than we had to, but we kept saying, 'Where? Where?' Incoherently enough, and in scraps, she told us enough to make us guess it was San Francisco, which, I need not tell you, is nearly three thousand miles away. There's only one Golden Gate Bridge after all, and in one spasm, she gasped out, 'Golden Gate,' over and over. Afterward it turned out she had never heard of the Golden Gate Bridge and was quite shaky as to San Francisco.

"When we put it all together, we decided that there was an old apartment house somewhere in San Francisco, possibly within eyeshot of the Bridge, that had gone up in fire. A total of twenty-three people were in it at the time it burst into fire, and of these, five did not escape. The five deaths included that of a child."

Halsted said, "And then you checked and found there *was* a fire in San Francisco and that five people had died, including a child."

"That's right," said Eldridge. "But here's what got me. One of the five deaths was that of a woman, Sophronia Latimer. She had gotten out safely and then discovered that her eight-year-old boy had not come out with her. She ran wildly back into the house, screaming for the boy, and never came out again. The boy's name was Eldridge, so you can see what she was shouting in the minutes before her death.

"Eldridge is a very uncommon first name, as I need not tell you, and my feeling is that Mary captured that particular event, for all that it was so far away, entirely because she had been sensitized to the name, by way of myself, and because it was surrounded by such agony."

Rubin said, "You want an explanation, is that it?"

"Of, course," said Eldridge. "How did this ignorant girl see a fire in full detail, get all the facts correct—and believe me, we checked it out— at three thousand miles."

Rubin said, "What makes the three-thousand-mile distance so impressive? These days it means nothing; it's one sixtieth of a second at the speed of light. I suggest that she heard the tale of the fire on radio or on television—more likely the latter—and passed it on to you.

That's why she chose that story; because of the name Eldridge. She figured it would have the greatest possible effect on you."

"Why?" asked Eldridge. "Why should she put through such a hoax?"

"Why?" Rubin's voice faded out momentarily, as though with astonishment, then came back in a shout. "Good God, you've been working with these people for years and don't realize how much they *want* to hoax you. Don't you suppose there's a feeling of power that comes with perpetrating a good hoax; and money, too, don't forget."

Eldridge thought about it, then shook his head. "She doesn't have the brains to put something like this across. It takes brains to be a faker—a good one, anyway."

Trumbull broke in. "Well, now, Voss. There's no reason to suppose she's in it on her own. A confederate is possible. She supplies the hysteria, he supplies the brains."

"Who might the confederate be?" asked Eldridge softly.

Trumbull shrugged. "I don't know."

Avalon cleared his throat and said, "I go along with Tom here, and my guess is that the confederate is the manager of the five-and-ten. He had noted her ability to guess at shoplifters, and thought he could put this to use in something more splashy. I'll bet that's it. He heard about the fire on television, caught the name Eldridge, and coached her."

"How long would it take to coach her?" asked Eldridge. "I keep telling you that she's not very bright."

"The coaching wouldn't be difficult," said Rubin quickly. "You say she was incoherent. He would just tell her a few key words: Eldridge, fire, Golden Gate, and so on. She then keeps repeating them in random arrangements and you intelligent parapsychologists fill it in."

Eldridge nodded, then said, "That's interesting, except that there was no time at all to coach the girl. That's what precognition is all about. We know exactly what time she had her fit and we know exactly what time the fire broke out in San Francisco. It so happens the fire broke out at just about the minute that Mary's fit died down. It was as though once the fire was actual, it was no longer a matter of precognition, and Mary lost contact. So you see, there could be no coaching. The news didn't hit the network TV news programs till that evening. That's when *we* found out and began our investigation in depth."

"But wait," said Halsted. "What about the time difference? There's a three-hour time difference between New York and San Francisco, and a confederate in San Francisco—"

"A confederate in San Francisco?" said Eldridge, opening his eyes wide, and staring. "Are you imagining a continental conspiracy? Besides, believe me, I know about the time difference also. When I say that the fire started just as Mary finished, I mean allowing for the time difference. Mary's fit started at just about one-fifteen P.M. Eastern Standard Time, and the fire in San Francisco started at just about ten forty-five A.M. Pacific Standard Time."

Drake said, "I have a suggestion."

"Go on," said Eldridge.

"This is an uneducated and unintelligent girl—you keep saying that over and over—and she's throwing a fit, an epileptic fit, for all I know."

"No," said Eldridge firmly.

"All right, a prophetic fit, if you wish. She's muttering and mumbling and screaming and doing everything in the world but speaking clearly. She makes sound which *you* interpret, and which you make fit together. If it had occurred to you to hear her say something like 'atom bomb,' then the word you interpreted as 'Eldridge' would have become 'Oak Ridge,' for instance."

"And Golden Gate?"

"You might have heard that as 'couldn't get' and fitted it in somehow."

"Not bad," said Eldridge. "Except that we know that it is hard to understand some of these ecstatics and we are bright enough to make use of modern technology. We routinely tape-record our sessions and we tape-recorded this one. We've listened to it over and over and there is no question but that she said 'Eldridge' and not 'Oak Ridge,' 'Golden Gate' and not 'couldn't get.' We've had different people listen and there is no disagreement on any of this. Besides, from what we heard, we worked out all the details of the fire before we got the facts. We had to make no modifications afterward. It all fit exactly."

There was a long silence at the table.

Finally Eldridge said, "Well, there it is. Mary foresaw the fire three thousand miles away by a full half-hour and got all the facts correct."

Drake said uneasily, "Do *you* accept it? Do *you* think it was precognition?"

"I'm trying not to," said Eldridge. "But for what reason can I disbelieve it? I don't want to fool myself into believing it, but what choice have I? At what point am I fooling myself? It it wasn't precognition, what was it? I had hoped that perhaps one of you gentlemen could tell me."

Again a silence.

Eldridge went on. "I'm left in a position where I must refer to Sherlock Holmes's great precept: 'When the impossible has been eliminated, then whatever remains, however improbable, is the truth.' In this case, if fakery of any kind is impossible, the precognition must be the truth. Don't you all agree?"

The silence was thicker than before, until Trumbull cried out, "Damn it all, Henry is grinning. No one's asked *him* yet to explain this. Well, Henry?"

Henry coughed. "I should not have smiled, gentlemen, but I couldn't help it when Professor Eldridge used that quotation. It seems the final bit of evidence that you gentlemen *want* to believe."

"The hell we do," said Rubin, frowning.

"Surely, then, a quotation from President Thomas Jefferson would have sprung to mind."

"What quotation?" asked Halsted.

"I imagine Mr. Rubin knows," said Henry.

"I probably do, Henry, but at the moment I can't think

of an appropriate one. Is it in the Declaration of Independence?"

"No, sir," began Henry, when Trumbull interrupted with a snarl.

"Let's not play Twenty Questions, Manny. Go on, Henry, what are you getting at?"

"Well, sir, to say that when the impossible has been eliminated, whatever remains, however improbable, is the truth, is to make the assumption, usually unjustified, that everything that is to be considered has indeed been considered. Let us suppose we have considered ten factors. Nine are clearly impossible. Is the tenth, however improbable, therefore true? What if there were an eleventh factor, and a twelfth, and a thirteenth . . ."

Avalon said severely, "You mean there's a factor we haven't considered?"

"I'm afraid so, sir," said Henry, nodding.

Avalon shook his head. "I can't think what it can be."

"And yet it is an obvious factor, sir; the *most* obvious one."

"What is it, then?" demanded Halsted, clearly annoyed. "Get to the point!"

"To begin with," said Henry, "it is clear that to explain the ability of the young lady to foretell, as described, the details of a fire three thousand miles away except by precognition is impossible. But suppose precognition is also to be considered impossible. In that case—"

Rubin got to his feet, straggly beard bristling, eyes magnified through thick-lensed glasses, staring. "Of course! The fire was *set*. The woman could have been coached for weeks. The accomplice goes to San Francicso and they coordinate. She predicts something she *knows* is going to happen. He causes something he *knows* she will predict."

Henry said, "Are you suggesting, sir, that a confederate would deliberately plan to kill five victims, including an eight-year-old boy?"

"Don't start trusting in the virtue of mankind, Henry," said Rubin. "You're the one who is sensitive to wrongdoing."

"The minor wrongdoings, sir, the kind most people

overlook. I find it difficult to believe that anyone, in order to establish a fancied case of precognition, would deliberately arrange a horrible multi-murder. Besides, to arrange a fire in which eighteen of twenty-three people escape and five specific people die requires a bit of precognition in itself."

Rubin turned stubborn. "I can see ways in which five people can be trapped; like forcing a card in conjuring—"

"Gentlemen!" said Eldridge peremptorily, and all turned to look at him. "I have not told you the cause of the fire."

He went on, after looking about the table to make sure he had the attention of all, "It was a stroke of lightning. I don't see how a stroke of lightning could be arranged at a specified time." He spread out his hands helplessly. "I tell you. I've been struggling with this for weeks. I don't want to accept precognition, but . . . I suppose this spoils your theory, Henry?"

"On the contrary, Professor Eldridge, it confirms it and makes it certain. Ever since you began to tell us this tale of Mary and the fire, your every word has made it more and more certain that fakery is impossible and that precognition has taken place. If, however, precognition is impossible, then it follows of necessity, Professor, that you have been lying."

Not a Black Widower but exclaimed at that, with Avalon's shocked "Henry!" loudest of all.

But Eldridge was leaning back in his chair, chuckling. "Of course I was lying. From beginning to end. I wanted to see if all you so-called rationalists would be so eager to accept parapsychological phenomena that you would overlook the obvious rather than spoil your own thrill. When did you catch me out, Henry?"

"It was a possibility from the start, sir, which grew stronger each time you eliminated a solution by inventing more information. I was certain when you mentioned the lightning. That was dramatic enough to have been brought in at the beginning. To be mentioned only at the very end made it clear that you created it on the spot to block the final hope."

"But why was it a possibility from the start, Henry?" demanded Eldridge. "Do I *look* like a liar? Can you detect liars the way I had Mary detect shoplifters?"

"Because this is *always* a possibility and something to be kept in mind and watched for. That is where the remark by President Jefferson comes in."

"What was that?"

"In 1807, Professor Benjamin Silliman of Yale reported seeing the fall of a meteorite at a time when the existence of meteorites was not accepted by scientists. Thomas Jefferson, a rationalist of enormous talent and intelligence, on hearing the report, said, 'I would sooner believe that a Yankee professor would lie than that a stone would fall from heaven.' "

"Yes," said Avalon at once, "but Jefferson was wrong. Silliman did *not* lie and stones *did* fall from heaven."

"Quite so, Mr. Avalon," said Henry, unruffled. "That is why the quotation is remembered. But considering the great number of times that impossibilities have been reported, and the small number of times they have been proven possible after all, I felt the odds were with me."

Afterword

This story first appeared in the May 1973 issue of *Ellery Queen's Mystery Magazine,* under the title I gave it.

I hope that no reader thinks the solution in this tale "isn't fair." In real life, a great many reports of unconventional phenomena are the results of deviations from the truth, either deliberate or unconscious. And I am sick and tired of mysteries that end up with some indication that perhaps, after all, something supernatural really did happen.

As far as I am concerned, if, when everything impossible has been eliminated and what remains is supernatural, then someone is lying. If that be treason, make the most of it.

7

The Pointing Finger

It was a rather quiet Black Widowers banquet until Rubin and Trumbull had their nose-to-nose confrontation.

Mario Gonzalo had been first to arrive, subdued and with the shadow of trouble upon him.

Henry was still setting up the table when Gonzalo arrived. He stopped and asked, "How are you, sir?" in quiet and unobtrusive concern.

Gonzalo shrugged. "All right, I guess. Sorry I missed the last meeting, but I finally decided to go to the police and I wasn't up to much for a while. I don't know if they can do anything, but it's up to them now. I almost wish you hadn't told me."

"Perhaps I ought not to have done so."

Gonzalo shrugged. "Listen, Henry," he said. "I called each of the guys and told him the story."

"Was that necessary, sir?"

"I had to. I'd feel constrained if I didn't. Besides, I didn't want them to think you had failed."

"Not an important consideration, sir."

The others came one by one, and each greeted Gonzalo with a hearty welcome that ostentatiously ignored a murdered sister, and each then subsided into a kind of uneasy quiet.

Avalon, who was hosting the occasion, seemed, as always, to add the dignity of that office to his natural solemnity. He sipped at his first drink and introduced his guest, a young man with a pleasant face, thinning black hair, and an amazingly thick mustache which seemed to be waiting only for the necessary change in fashion to be waxed at the end.

"This is Simon Levy," said Avalon. "A science writer and a splendid fellow."

Emmanuel Rubin promptly said, "Didn't you write a book on the laser, *Light in Step?*"

"Yes," said Levy with the energetic delight of an author greeting unexpected recognition. "Have you read it?"

Rubin, who was carrying, as he always did, the self-conscious soul of a six-footer in his five-foot-four body, looked solemnly at the other through his thick glasses and said, "I did, and found it quite good."

Levy's smile weakened, as though he considered a judgment of "quite good" no good at all.

Avalon said, "Roger Halsted won't be with us today. He's out of town on something or other. Sends his regrets and says to say hello to Mario if he shows up."

Trumbull said with his mouth down-curved in a sneer, "We're spared a limerick."

"I missed last month's," said Gonzalo. "Was it any good?"

"You wouldn't have understood it, Mario," said Avalon gravely.

"That good, eh?"

And then things quieted down to a near whisper until somehow the Act of Union came up. Afterward, neither Rubin nor Trumbull could remember exactly how.

Trumbull said, in what was considerably more than an ordinary speaking voice, "The Act of Union forming the United Kingdom of England, Wales, and Scotland was made law at the Treaty of Utrecht in 1713."

"No, it wasn't," said Rubin, his straw-colored and straggly beard wagging indignantly. "The Act was passed in 1707."

"Are you trying to tell me, you dumb jackass, that the Treaty of Utrecht was signed in 1707?"

"No, I'm not," shouted Rubin, his surprisingly loud voice reaching a bellow. "The Treaty of Utrecht was signed in 1713. You guessed that part right, though God only knows how."

"If the Treaty was signed in 1713, then that settles the Act of Union."

"No, it doesn't, because the Treaty had nothing to do with the Act of Union, which was 1707."

"Damn you, five dollars says you don't know the Act of Union from a union suit."

"Here's my five dollars. Where's yours? Or can you spare a week's pay at that two-bit job you've got?"

They were standing up now, leaning toward each other over James Drake, who philosophically added a fresh dollop of sour cream and chives to the last of his baked potato, and finished it.

Drake said, "No use shouting back and forth, my fellow jackasses. Look it up."

"Henry!" roared Trumbull.

There was the smallest of delays and then Henry was at hand with the third edition of the *Columbia Encyclopedia.*

"Host's privilege," said Avalon. "I'll check, as an impartial observer."

He turned the pages of the fat volume, muttering, "Union, union, union, ah, Act of." He then said, almost at once, "1707. Manny wins. Pay up, Tom."

"What?" cried Trumbull, outraged. "Let's see that."

Rubin quietly picked up the two five-dollar bills which had been lying on the table and said in a ruminating voice, "A good reference book, the *Columbia Encyclopedia.* Best one-volume all-round reference in the world and more useful than the *Britannica,* even if it does waste an entry on Isaac Asimov."

"On whom?" asked Gonzalo.

"Asimov. Friend of mine. Science fiction writer and pathologically conceited. He carries a copy of the *Encyclopedia* to parties and says, 'Talking of concrete, the *Columbia Encyclopedia* has an excellent article on it only 249 pages after their article on me. Let me show you.' Then he shows them the article on himself."

Gonzalo laughed. "Sounds a lot like you, Manny."

"Tell him that and he'll kill you—if I don't first."

Simon Levy turned to Avalon and said, "Are there arguments like that all the time here, Jeff?"

"Many arguments," said Avalon, "but they generally

don't get to the wager and reference book stage. When it does happen, Henry's prepared. We have not only the *Columbia Encyclopedia,* but copies of the Bible, both the King James and the New English; Webster's unabridged —second edition, of course; *Webster's Biographical Dictionary; Webster's Geographical Dictionary; The Guinness Book of Records; Brewer's Dictionary of Phrase and Fable;* and *The Complete Works of Shakespeare.* It's the Black Widowers' library and Henry is the custodian. It usually settles all arguments."

"I'm sorry I asked," said Levy.

"Why?"

"You mentioned Shakespeare and I react to that, right now, with nausea."

"To Shakespeare?" Avalon gazed down at his guest with lofty disapproval.

"You bet. I've been living with him for two months, reading him backward and forward till one more 'Why, marry' or 'fretful porpentine' and I'll throw up."

"Really? Well, wait. . . . Henry, is dessert coming up?"

"Directly, sir. *Coupe aux marrons.*"

"Good! . . . Simon, wait till dessert's finished and we'll carry on."

Ten minutes later, Avalon placed spoon to water glass and tinkled the assemblage to silence. "Host's privilege," he said. "It is time for the usual inquisition, but our honored guest has let it slip that for two months past he has been studying Shakespeare with great concentration, and I think this ought to be investigated. Tom, will you do the honors?"

Trumbull said indignantly, "Shakespeare? Who the hell wants to talk about Shakespeare?" His disposition had not been improved by the loss of five dollars and by the look of unearthly virtue upon Rubin's face.

"Host's privilege," said Avalon firmly.

"Humph. All right. Mr. Levy, as a science writer, what is your connection with Shakespeare?"

"None, as a science writer." He spoke with a distinct Brooklyn accent. "It's just that I'm after three thousand dollars."

"In Shakespeare?"

"Somewhere in Shakespeare. Can't say I've had any luck, though."

"You speak in riddles, Levy. What do you mean three thousand dollars somewhere in Shakespeare that you can't find?"

"Oh, well, it's a complicated story."

"Well, *tell* it. That's what we're here for. It's a long-standing rule that nothing that is said or done in this room is ever repeated outside under any circumstances, so speak freely. If you get boring, we'll stop you. Don't worry about that."

Levy spread out his arms. "All right, but let me finish my tea."

"Go ahead, Henry will bring you another pot, since you aren't civilized enough to drink coffee. . . . Henry!"

"Yes, sir," murmured Henry.

"Don't start till he comes back," said Trumbull. "We don't want him to miss any of this."

"The waiter?"

"He's one of us. Best man here."

Henry arrived with a new pot of tea and Levy said, "It's a question of a legacy, sort of. It's not one of those things where the family homestead is at stake, or millions in jewels, or anything like that. It's just three thousand dollars which I don't really need, but which would be nice to have."

"A legacy from whom?" asked Drake.

"From my wife's grandfather. He died two months ago at the age of seventy-six. He'd been living with us for five years. A little troublesome, but he was a nice old guy and, being on my wife's side of the family, she took care of most of it. He was sort of grateful to us for taking him in. There were no other descendants and it was either us or a hotel for old people."

"Get to the legacy," said Trumbull, showing some signs of impatience.

"Grandpa wasn't rich but he had a few thousand. When he first came to us, he told us that he had bought three thousand dollars' worth of negotiable bonds and would give them to us when he died."

"Why when he died?" asked Rubin.

"I suppose the old guy worried about our getting tired of him. He held out the three thousand to us as a reward for good behavior. If he was still with us when he was dying, he would give the bonds to us, and if we kicked him out, he wouldn't. I guess that was what was in his mind."

Levy went on, "He hid them in various places. Old guys can be funny. He'd change the hiding place now and then whenever he began to fear we might find them. Of course, we usually did find them before long, but we'd never let on and we'd never touch them. Except once! He put them in the clothes hamper and we had to give them back to him and ask him to put them elsewhere, or sooner or later they would get into the washing machine.

"That was about the time he had a small stroke—no connection, I'm sure—and after that he was a little harder to handle. He grew morose and didn't talk much. He had difficulties in using his right leg and it gave him a feeling of mortality. After that, he must have hidden the bonds more efficiently, for we lost track of them, though we didn't attach much importance to that. We assumed he would tell us when he was ready.

"Then two months ago, little Julia, that's my younger daughter, came running to us to tell us that Grandpa was lying on the couch and looking funny. We ran to the living room, and it was obvious that he had had another stroke. We called the doctor, but it was clear that his right side was gone entirely. He couldn't speak. He could move his lips and make sounds, but they came to no words.

"He kept moving his left arm and trying to speak and I said, 'Grandpa, are you trying to tell me something?' He could just about tremor his head into a small nod. 'About the bonds?' Again a small nod. 'You want us to have them?' Again a nod and his hand began to move as though he were trying to point.

"I said, 'Where are they?' His left hand trembled and

continued to point. I couldn't help but say, 'What are you pointing at, Grandpa?' but he couldn't tell me. His finger just kept pointing in an anxious, quivering way, and his face seemed in agony as he tried to talk and failed. I was sorry for him. He wanted to give the bonds to us, to reward us, and he was dying without being able to.

"My wife, Caroline, was crying and saying, 'Leave him alone, Simon,' but I *couldn't* leave him alone. I couldn't let him die in despair. I said, 'We'll have to move the couch toward whatever it is he's pointing to.' Caroline didn't want to, but the old man was nodding his head.

"Caroline got at one end of the couch and I at the other and we moved it, little by little, trying not to jar him. He was no light-weight, either. His finger kept pointing, always pointing. He turned his head in the direction in which we were moving him, making moaning sounds as though to indicate whether we were moving him in the right direction or not. I would say, 'More to the right, Grandpa?' 'More to the left?' And sometimes he would nod.

"Finally, we got him up against the line of bookcases, and slowly his head turned. I wanted to turn it for him, but I was afraid to harm him. He managed to get it round and stared at the books for a long time. Then his finger moved along the line of books till it pointed toward one particular book. It was a copy of *The Complete Works of Shakespeare,* the Kittredge edition.

"I said, 'Shakespeare, Grandpa?' He didn't answer, he didn't nod, but his face relaxed and he stopped trying to speak. I suppose he didn't hear me. Something like a half-smile pulled at the left side of his mouth and he died. The doctor came, the body was taken away, we made arrangements for the funeral. It wasn't till after the funeral that we went back to the Shakespeare. We figured it would wait for us and it didn't seem right to grab for it before we took care of the old man.

"I assumed there would be something in the Shakespeare volume to tell us where the bonds were, and that's when the first shock came. We turned through every page, one by one, and there was nothing there. Not a scrap of paper. Not a word."

Gonzalo said, "What about the binding? You know, in between the stuff that glues the pages and the backstrip?"

"Nothing there."

"Maybe someone took it?"

"How? The only ones who knew were myself and Caroline. It isn't as though there were any robbery. Eventually, we thought there was a clue somewhere in the book, in the written material, in the plays themselves, you know. That was Caroline's idea. In the last two months, I've read every word of Shakespeare's plays; every word of his sonnets and miscellaneous poems—twice over. I've gotten nowhere."

"The hell with Shakespeare," said Trumbull querulously. "Forget the clue. He had to leave them somewhere in the house."

"Why do you suppose that?" said Levy. "He might have put it in a bank vault for all we know. He got around even after his first stroke. After we found the bonds in the clothes hamper, he might have thought the house wasn't safe."

"All right, but he still might have put them in the house somewhere. Why not just search?"

"We did. Or at least Caroline did. That was how we divided the labor. She searched the house, which is a big, rambling one—one reason we could take in Grandpa— and I searched Shakespeare, and we both came out with nothing."

Avalon untwisted a thoughtful frown and said, "See here, there's no reason we can't be logical about this. I assume, Simon, that your grandfather was born in Europe."

"Yes. He came to America as a teen-ager, just as World War I was starting. He got out just in time."

"He didn't have much of a formal education, I suppose."

"None at all," said Levy. "He went to work in a tailor shop, eventually got his own establishment, and stayed a tailor till he retired. No education at all, except for the usual religious education Jews gave each other in Tsarist Russia."

"Well, then," said Avalon, "how do you expect him to indicate clues in Shakespeare's plays? He wouldn't know anything about them."

Levy frowned and leaned back in his chair. He hadn't touched the small brandy glass Henry had put in front of him some time before. Now he picked it up, twirled the stem gently in his fingers, and put it down again.

"You're quite wrong, Jeff," he said, a little distantly. "He may have been uneducated but he was quite intelligent and quite well-read. He knew the Bible by heart, and he'd read *War and Peace* as a teen-ager. He read Shakespeare, too. Listen, we once went to see a production of *Hamlet* in the park and he got more out of it than I did."

Rubin suddenly broke in energetically, "I have no intention of ever seeing *Hamlet* again till they get a Hamlet who looks as Hamlet is supposed to look. Fat!"

"Fat!" said Trumbull indignantly.

"Yes, fat. The Queen says of Hamlet in the last scene, 'He's fat, and scant of breath.' If Shakespeare says Hamlet is fat—"

"That's his mother talking, not Shakespeare. It's the typical motherly oversolicitousness of a not-bright woman—"

Avalon banged the table. "Not now, gentlemen!"

He turned to Levy. "In what language did your grandfather read the Bible?"

"In Hebrew, of course," Levy said coldly.

"And *War and Peace?*"

"In Russian. But Shakespeare, if you don't mind, he read in English."

"Which is not his native tongue. I imagine he spoke with an accent."

Levy's coolness had descended into the frigid. "What are you getting at, Jeff?"

Avalon harumphed. "I'm not being anti-Semitic. I'm just pointing out the obvious fact that if your wife's grandfather was not at home with the language, there was

a limit to how subtly he could use Shakespeare as a reference. He's not likely to use the phrase 'and there the antick sits' from *Richard II* because, however well-read he
is, he isn't likely to know what an antick is."

"What is it?" asked Gonzalo.

"Never mind," said Avalon impatiently. "If your
grandfather used Shakespeare, it would have to be some
perfectly obvious reference."

"What was your father's favorite play?" asked Trumbull.

"He liked *Hamlet* of course. I know he didn't like the
comedies," said Levy, "because he felt the humor undig-
nified, and the histories meant nothing to him. Wait, he
liked *Othello*."

"All right," said Avalon. "We ought to concentrate on
Hamlet and *Othello*."

"I read them," said Levy. "You don't think I left them
out, do you?"

"And it would have to be some well-known passage,"
Avalon went on, paying no attention. "No one would
think that just pointing to Shakespeare would be a useful
hint if it were some obscure line that were intended."

"The only reason he just pointed," said Levy, "was
that he couldn't talk. It *might* have been something very
obscure which he would have explained if he could have
talked."

"If he could have talked," said Drake reasonably, "he
wouldn't have had to explain anything. He would just
have told you where the bonds were."

"Exactly," said Avalon. "A good point, Jim. You said,
Simon, that after the old man pointed to Shakespeare, his
face relaxed and he stopped trying to speak. He felt that
he had given you all you needed to know."

"Well, he didn't," said Levy morosely.

"Let's reason it out, then," said Avalon.

"Do we have to?" said Drake. "Why not ask Henry
now? . . . Henry, which verse in Shakespeare would suit
our purpose?"

Henry, who was noiselessly taking up the dessert
dishes, said, "I have an average knowledge of the plays of

Shakespeare, sir, but I must admit that no appropriate verse occurs to me."

Drake looked disappointed, but Avalon said, "Come on, Jim. Henry has done very well on past occasions but there's no need to feel that we are helpless without him. I flatter myself I know Shakespeare pretty well."

"I'm no novice, either," said Rubin.

"Then between the two of us, let's solve this. Suppose we consider *Hamlet* first. If it's *Hamlet,* then it has to be one of the soliloquies, because they're the best-known portions of the play."

"In fact," said Rubin, "the line 'To be or not to be, that is the question' is the best-known line of Shakespeare. It epitomizes him as the 'Quartet' from *Rigoletto* typifies opera."

"I agree," said Avalon, "and that soliloquy talks of dying, and the old man was dying. 'To die: to sleep; No more; and by a sleep to say we end the heart-ache and the thousand natural shocks that flesh is——' "

"Yes, but what good does that do?" said Levy impatiently. "Where does it get us?"

Avalon, who always recited Shakespeare in what he insisted was Shakespearean pronunciation (which sounded remarkably like an Irish brogue), said, "Well, I'm not sure."

Gonzalo said suddenly, "Is it in *Hamlet* where Shakespeare says, 'The play's the thing'?"

"Yes," said Avalon. " 'The play's the thing wherein I'll catch the conscience of the king.' "

"Well," said Gonzalo, "if the old man was pointing out a book of plays, maybe that's the line. Do you have a picture of a king, or a carving, or a deck of cards, maybe."

Levy shrugged. "That doesn't bring anything to mind."

"What about *Othello?*" asked Rubin. "Listen. The best-known part of the play is Iago's speech on reputation, 'Good name in man and woman, dear my lord . . .' "

"So?" said Avalon.

"And the most famous line in it, and one which the old man was sure to know because it's the one everyone knows, even Mario, is 'Who steals my purse steals trash; 'tis something, nothing; 'twas mine, 'tis his . . .' and so on."

"So?" said Avalon again.

"So it sounds as though it applies to the legacy. ' 'Twas mine, 'tis his,' and it also sounds as though the legacy were gone. 'Who steals my purse steals trash.' "

"What do you mean, 'gone'?" said Levy.

"After you found the bonds in the clothes hamper, you lost track of them, you said. Maybe the old man took them off somewhere to be safe and doesn't remember where. Or maybe he mislaid them or gave them away or lost them to some confidence scheme. Whatever it was, he could no longer explain it to you without speech. So to die in peace, he pointed to the works of Shakespeare. You would remember the best-known line of his favorite play, which tells you that his purse is only trash—and that is why you have found nothing."

"I don't believe that," said Levy. "I asked him if he wanted us to have the bonds and he nodded."

"All he could do was nod, and he *did* want you to have them, but that was impossible. . . . Do you agree with me, Henry?"

Henry, who had completed his tasks and was quietly listening, said, "I'm afraid I don't, Mr. Rubin."

"I don't, either," said Levy.

But Gonzalo was snapping his fingers. "Wait, wait. Doesn't Shakespeare say anything about bonds?"

"Not in his time," said Drake, smiling.

"I'm sure of it," said Gonzalo. "Something about bonds being nominated."

Avalon said, "Ah! You mean 'Is it so nominated in the bond?' The bond is a legal contract, and the question was whether something was a requirement of the contract."

Drake said, "Wait a bit. Didn't that bond involve a sum of three thousand ducats?"

"By Heaven, so it did," said Avalon.

Gonzalo's grin split his head from ear to ear. "I think I've got something there: bonds involving three thousand units of money. That's the play to look into."

Henry interrupted softly. "I scarcely think so, gentlemen. The play in question is *The Merchant of Venice* and the person asking whether something was nominated in the bond was the Jew, Shylock, intent on a cruel revenge. Surely the old man would not enjoy this play."

Levy said, "That's right. Shylock was a dirty word to him—and not so clean to me, either."

Rubin said, "What about the passage that goes: 'Hath not a Jew eyes? hath not a Jew hands, organs, dimensions, senses, affections, passions . . .'?"

"It wouldn't appeal to my grandfather," said Levy. "It pleads the obvious and cries out for an equality my grandfather would not, in his heart, be willing to grant, since I'm sure he felt superior in that he was a member of God's uniquely chosen."

Gonzalo looked disappointed. "It seems we're not getting anywhere."

Levy said, "No, I don't think we are. I went through the entire book. I read all the speeches carefully; all the passages you mentioned. None of them meant anything to me."

Avalon said, "Granted they don't, but you may be missing something subtle—"

"Come on, Jeff, you're the one who said it couldn't be subtle. My grandfather was thinking of something tailored for the mind of myself and my wife. It was something we would get, and probably get at once; and we didn't."

Drake said, "Maybe you're right. Maybe some in-joke is involved."

"I've just said that."

"Then why don't you try it backward? Can you think of something, some gag, some phrase? . . . Is there some expression he used every time?"

"Yes. When he disapproved of someone he would say, 'Eighteen black years on him.'"

"What kind of an expression is that?" asked Trumbull.

"In Yiddish it's common enough," said Levy. "Another one was 'It will help him like a dead man cups.'"

"What does that mean?" asked Gonzalo.

"It refers to cupping. You place a lighted piece of

paper in a small round glass cup and then put the open edge against the skin. The paper goes out but leaves a partial vacuum in the cup and circulation is sucked into the superficial layers. Naturally, cupping can't improve the circulation of a corpse."

"All right," said Drake, "is there anything about eighteen black years, or about cupping dead men, that reminds you of something in Shakespeare?"

There was a painful silence and finally Avalon said, "I can't think of anything."

"And even if you did," said Levy, "what good would it do? What would it mean? Listen, I've been at this for two months. You're not going to solve it for me in two hours."

Drake turned to Henry again and said, "Why are you just standing there, Henry? Can't you help us?"

"I'm sorry, Dr. Drake, but I now believe that the whole question of Shakespeare is a false lead."

"No," said Levy. "You can't say that. The old man pointed to *The Collected Works* without any question. His fingertip was within an inch of it. It couldn't have been any other book."

Drake said suddenly, "Say, Levy, you're not diddling us, are you? You're not telling us a pack of lies to make jackasses out of us?"

"What?" said Levy in amazement.

"Nothing, nothing," said Avalon hastily. "He's just thinking of another occasion. Shut up, Jim."

"Listen," said Levy. "I'm telling you exactly what happened. He was pointing exactly at Shakespeare."

There was a short silence and then Henry sighed and said, "In mystery stories—"

Rubin broke in with a "Hear! Hear!"

"In mystery stories," Henry repeated, "the dying hint is a common device, but I have never been able to take it seriously. A dying man, anxious to give last-minute information, is always pictured as presenting the most complex hints. His dying brain, with two minutes' grace, works out a pattern that would puzzle a healthy brain with hours to think. In this particular case, we have an old man dying of a paralyzing stroke who is supposed to have quickly invented a clue that a group of intelligent men have failed to work out; and with one of them having worked at it for two months. I can only conclude there is no such clue."

"Then why should he have pointed to Shakespeare, Henry?" asked Levy. "Was it all just the vague delusions of a dying man?"

"If your story is correct," said Henry, "then I think he was indeed trying to do something. He cannot, however, have been inventing a clue. He was doing the only thing his dying mind could manage. He was pointing to the bonds."

"I beg your pardon," said Levy huffily. "I was there. He was pointing to Shakespeare."

Henry shook his head. He said, "Mr. Levy, would you point to Fifth Avenue?"

Levy thought a while, obviously orienting himself, and then pointed.

"Are you pointing to Fifth Avenue?" asked Henry.

"Well, the restaurant's entrance is on Fifth Avenue, so I'm pointing to it."

"It seems to me, sir," said Henry, "that you are pointing to a picture of the Arch of Titus on the western wall of this room."

"Well, I am, but Fifth Avenue is beyond it."

"Exactly, sir. So I only know that you are pointing to Fifth Avenue because you tell me so. You might be pointing to the picture or to some point in the air before the picture, or to the Hudson River, or to Chicago, or to the Planet Jupiter. If you point, and nothing more, giving no hint, verbal or otherwise, as to what you're pointing at, you are only indicating a direction and nothing more."

Levy rubbed his chin. "You mean my grandfather was only indicating a direction?"

"It must be so. He didn't *say* he was pointing to Shakespeare. He merely pointed."

"All right, then, what was he pointing at? The—the—" He closed his eyes and fingered his mustache gently, as he oriented the room in his house. "The Verrazano Bridge?"

"Probably not, sir," said Henry. "He was pointing in the direction of *The Collected Works*. His finger was an inch from it, you said, so it is doubtful that he could be pointing at anything in front of it. What was behind the book, Mr. Levy?"

"The bookcase. The wood of the bookcase. And when you took the book out, there was nothing behind it. There was nothing pushed up against the wood, if that's what you have in mind. We would have seen it at once if anything at all had been there."

"And behind the bookcase, sir?"

"The wall."

"And between the bookcase and the wall, sir?"

Now Levy fell silent. He thought a while, and no one interrupted those thoughts. He said, "Is there a phone I can use, Henry?"

"I'll bring you one, sir."

The phone was placed in front of Levy and plugged in. Levy dialed a number.

"Hello, Julia? What are you doing up so late? . . . Never mind the TV and get to bed. But first call Mamma, dear. . . . Hello, Caroline, it's Simon. . . . Yes, I'm having a good time, but listen, Caroline, listen. You know the bookcase with the Shakespeare in it? . . . Yes, *that* Shakespeare. Of course. Move it away from the wall. . . . The bookcase. . . . Look, you can take the books out of it, can't you? Take them all out, if you have to, and dump them on the floor. . . . No, no, just move the end of the bookcase near the door a few inches; just enough to look behind and tell me if you see anything. . . . Look about where the Shakespeare book would be. . . . I'll wait, yes."

They were all frozen in attitudes. Levy was distinctly pale. Some five minutes passed. Then, "Caroline? . . . Okay, take it easy. Did you move . . . ? Okay, okay, I'll be home soon."

He hung up and said, "If that doesn't beat everything. The old guy had them taped to the back of the bookcase. He must have moved that thing sometime when we were out. It's a wonder he didn't have a stroke then and there."

"You did it again, Henry," said Gonzalo.

Levy said, "Agent's fee is three hundred dollars, Henry."

Henry said, "I am well paid by the club, and the banquets are my pleasure, sir. There is no need for more."

Levy reddened slightly and changed the subject. "But how did you get the trick of it? When the rest of us—"

"It was not difficult," said Henry. "The rest of you happened to track down all the wrong paths, and I simply suggested what was left."

Afterword

This story first appeared in the July 1973 issue of *Ellery Queen's Mystery Magazine,* under the title I gave it.

In the magazine the story has a slightly different beginning because it was thought that one story in the series shouldn't refer to events in earlier stories. After all, the reasoning is, many of the magazine readers don't get all the issues and might not have read the one with the earlier story. Or if they did, and if that had been half a year ago or so, they wouldn't remember.

That's perfectly right, but here in the book I restore the original beginning. In fact, it occurs to me that if I had written the series for the book version to begin with, I would have interlocked them quite a bit. For instance, I wouldn't have let the matter of Halsted's limerick version of the *Iliad* and the *Odyssey* drop. As it was though, I felt that to come across them out of order, or missing some and reading others, would spoil the effect.

Oh, well.

8

Miss What?

There was a certain frostiness about the monthly meeting of the Black Widowers and it clearly centered on the guest brought by Mario Gonzalo. He was a large man. His cheeks were plump and smooth, his hair was almost nonexistent, and he wore a vest, something no one had seen at the Black Widowers in living memory.

His name was Aloysius Gordon and the trouble began when he calmly introduced himself by name and occupation, announcing himself quite casually as being connected with the 17th Precinct. It was like lowering a window shade against the sun, for the spark went out of the dinner at once.

Gordon had no way of comparing the quiet now prevailing with the hubbub characteristic of the usual Black Widowers dinner. He had no way of knowing how unusual it was that Emmanuel Rubin was almost supernaturally reserved and had not contradicted anyone once; that Thomas Trumbull's voice, even when it was used, was subdued; that Geoffrey Avalon actually finished his second drink; that twice James Drake had stubbed out a cigarette before it was down to the quick; and that Roger Halsted, having unfolded the piece of paper on which he had written the limerick based on the fifth book of the *Iliad,* merely looked at it mildly, wrinkled his high, pink forehead, and put it away.

In fact, Gordon seemed interested only in Henry. He followed the waiter with his eyes, and there was an unmistakable light of curiosity in them. Henry, ordinarily perfect in his job, upset a glass of water, to the horror of all. His cheekbones seemed to show in his unlined face.

Trumbull rose rather ostentatiously and moved in the direction of the men's room. The gesture he made was unobtrusive but none the less urgent for that, and a minute later Gonzalo left the table, too.

In the men's room, Trumbull said in a harsh whisper, "Why the hell did you bring that fellow?"

"He's an interesting guy," said Gonzalo defensively, "and it's host's privilege. I can bring anyone I want."

"He's a policeman."

"He's a plainclothesman."

"What's the difference? Do you know him, or is he here professionally?"

Gonzalo raised his hands in a kind of helpless anger. His dark eyes bulged as they usually did in moments of passion. "I know him personally. I met him—it's none of your business how I met him, Tom—I *know* him. He's an interesting guy and I want him here."

"Yes? What did you tell him about Henry?"

"What do you mean, what did I tell?"

"Oh, come on, you dumb jerk. Don't play games. Haven't you seen the guy watching Henry's every move? Why should he watch a waiter?"

"I told him Henry's a whiz at solving puzzles."

"In how much detail?"

"No detail at all," said Gonzalo with heat. "Don't you suppose I know that nothing that goes on in the banquet room is mentioned outside? I just said Henry was a whiz at solving puzzles."

"And he was interested, I suppose."

"Well, he said he would like to be at one of our meetings and I—"

Trumbull said, "You realize this could be very embarrassing for Henry. Did you consult him?"

Gonzalo played with one of the brass buttons of his blazer. "If I see that Henry's embarrassed, I'll use host's privilege and cut the proceedings."

"What if this Gordon guy doesn't play along?"

Gonzalo looked miserable and shrugged. They returned to the table.

When Henry was pouring out the coffee and it came time for the game of placing the guest on the griddle, there was still no increase in verve. Gonzalo offered the role of inquisitor to Trumbull, as was traditional, and Trumbull looked unhappy about it.

The traditional first question came out. "Mr. Gordon, how do you justify your existence?"

"At the moment," said Gordon, in a rather rich baritone, "by adding to the pleasure of this occasion, I hope."

"In what way?" asked Avalon glumly.

"It is my understanding, gentlemen," said Gordon, "that guests are expected to pose a problem which the members of the club then attempt to solve."

Trumbull shot a furious glance at Gonzalo and said, "No, no, that's all wrong. Some guests have presented problems, but that was more or less a side issue. All that's expected of them is interesting conversation."

"Besides," said Drake in his dry voice, "it's Henry who does the solving. The rest of us just bat things around foolishly."

"For God's sake, Jim," began Trumbull, but Gordon's voice overrode his.

"That's exactly what I've been given to understand," he said. "Now I am here in a strictly social capacity and not as a member of the Police Department at all. Just the same, I can't help having a professional interest in the matter. In fact, I'm damned curious about Henry, and I've come to test him. . . . If I may, that is," he added in response to the cold silence that had fallen over everyone else.

Avalon was frowning, and on his face, with its neat mustache, its closely cut and neatly kept chin beard, and its absolutely luxurious eyebrows, a frown was a portentous phenomenon.

He said, "Mr. Gordon, this is a private club, the meetings of which serve no purpose but social camaraderie. Henry is our waiter and we value him and we do not wish him to be disturbed in this room. If your presence here is purely social and not professional, as you say, I think it would be best if we leave Henry to himself."

Henry had just completed the coffee ritual and he interrupted with the faintest trace of agitation in his voice. He said, "Thank you, Mr. Avalon. I appreciate your concern. However, it may improve the situation if I explain something to Mr. Gordon."

He turned to the guest and went on earnestly, "Mr. Gordon, on some half-dozen occasions I have been able to make some obvious point or other in connection with some problem that arose at the dinners. The puzzles were, in themselves, trivial, and not at all the sort that would interest a policeman. I know quite well that in solving the kind of cases that interest policemen, what is most important are records, informants, rather tedious procedural work, the cooperation of many different men and agencies. All of this is quite beyond my abilities.

"In fact, I could not even do what I have done were it not for the other members of the club. The Black Widowers are ingenious men who can find complicated answers to any problem. When they are all done then, assuming none of the complicated answers are correct, I can sometimes wiggle past the complications to the simple truth. That is all I do, and I assure you that it is not worth your while to test me."

Gordon nodded his head. "In other words, Henry, if there's a gangland killing and we have to track down half a dozen hoods and investigate their alibis, or try to find some bystanders not too afraid to tell us what they saw, you couldn't help us."

"Not at all, sir."

"But if I have an odd piece of paper that carries some words that might make sense and might not, and that may require a little thought past the complications to the simple truth, you could help."

"Probably not, sir."

"But would you look at the paper and give me your thoughts on the matter?"

"Is that the test, sir?"

"I suppose we can call it that," said Gordon.

"Well, then," said Henry, with a slow shake of his head. "Mr. Gonzalo is the host. If he's willing to have you introduce it, then, by the rules of the club, you may."

Gonzalo looked uncomfortable. Then he said defiantly, "Go on, Lieutenant, show it to him."

"Hold on," said Trumbull, pointing his blunt finger at Gonzalo. "Have you seen it, Mario?"

"Yes."

"Can you make sense out of it?"

"No," said Gonzalo, "but it's the kind of thing Henry might be able to handle."

Rubin said, "I don't think we ought to put Henry on the spot like that."

But Henry said, "It's host's privilege, sir. I'm willing to look at it."

Gordon brought a piece of paper, folded into quarters, out of his upper right vest pocket. He held it over his shoulder and Henry took it. Henry looked at it for a moment, then handed it back.

"I'm sorry, sir," he said, "but I cannot see anything in it except what it says."

Drake held out his hand. "How about passing it around? Is that all right, Mr. Gordon?"

"I'm willing to pass it around," said Gordon. He gave it to Halsted, who sat at his right. Halsted read it and passed it on. There was absolute silence till it had made its circle and returned to Gordon. Gordon glanced at it briefly and put it back in his pocket.

The message, in full, written in a scrawled hand, went:

> *Woe unto you, Jezebels.*
> *Death unto you, Rahab.*

"It sounds Biblical," said Gonzalo. "Doesn't it?" He looked automatically at Rubin, who was the Biblical authority of the group.

"It sounds Biblical," said Rubin, "and it may have

been written by a Bible nut, but that is not a quotation from the Bible. You can take my word on that."

"No one's likely to question your word on the Bible, Manny," said Avalon agreeably.

Gordon said, "That note was delivered to a girl at the entrance to a restaurant within which the Miss Earth contestants were holding a press conference."

"Who delivered it?" asked Trumbull.

"A drifter. He had been given a dollar to hand the note to the girl and he couldn't describe the person who had given it to him, except that it was a man. There is no reason to suppose the drifter was more than an intermediary. We checked him out."

Halsted said, "Any fingerprints?"

Gordon said, "Any number of superimposed smudges. Nothing useful."

Avalon looked austere and said, "I suppose that the Jezebels mentioned in the note referred to the young ladies of the Miss Earth contest."

"That seems a natural thought," said Gordon. "The question is: Which one?"

"All of them, I should say," said Avalon. "The note used the plural, and the kind of person who uses the term in this context would not make fine distinctions. Anyone who presents her beauty to the public gaze for judgment would be a Jezebel. All of them would be Jezebels."

"But what about the second phrase?" asked Gordon.

Rubin said, with just a trace of self-importance, "I'll explain that. Suppose the writer is a Bible nut; I mean the kind who reads the Bible every day and hears God whispering in his ear, directing him to destroy immorality. Such a guy would automatically write in Biblical style. It so happens that the chief poetic device in Biblical times was the repetition of the same sentence in a slightly different way, such as . . ." He thought for a while, then said, "For instance, *How goodly are thy tents, O Jacob, and thy tabernacles, O Israel.* Another one is *Hear my words, O ye wise men; and give ear unto me, ye that have knowledge.*"

Rubin's straggly beard grew stragglier as his lips parted

in a broad smile and his eyes glinted through his thick spectacles as he said, "That second one is from the Book of Job."

"Parallelism," muttered Avalon.

Gordon said, "You mean he's just saying the same thing twice?"

"That's right," said Rubin. "First he predicts woe and then he predicts the ultimate woe, death. First he calls them Jezebels, then he calls them Rahabs."

"Not quite," said Gordon. " 'Jezebel' is in the plural. 'Rahab' isn't. The fellow who wrote that speaks of 'Jezebels,' plural, when he yells 'Woe'; but only 'Rahab,' singular, when he predicts 'Death.' "

"Can I see that paper again?" said Rubin. It was passed to him and he studied it. Then he said, "The way this fellow writes, I don't know whether we can expect exact spelling. He may have meant to put in the 's.' "

"He *may* have," said Gordon, "but we can't rely on that. His spelling and punctuation are correct and, scrawl or not, the other 's' is clear and sharp."

"It seems to me," said Avalon, "it would be safer to assume the singular is what is meant, unless we have good reason to the contrary."

Drake tried to blow a smoke ring (an attempt at which no one had ever seen him succeed) and said, "Do you take this thing seriously, Mr. Gordon?"

"My private inclinations," said Gordon, "are not in question. The note has a certain psychotic quality about it and I feel pretty safe in saying that if the writer is not playing a stupid practical joke, then he's crazy. And crazy people have to be taken seriously. Suppose the writer is someone who considers himself a spokesman for the wrath of God. Naturally, he announces it; he sends for the word of God because that's what the Biblical prophets did."

"And he announces it in poetic terms," began Halsted.

"Because that's what the Biblical prophets did, too," said Gordon, nodding. "A man like that may just possibly decide to be the arm of God as well as His voice. We can't take a chance. You understand that the Miss Earth contest offers a more ticklish situation than the Miss America contest does."

"Because there are foreign contestants, I suppose," said Rubin.

"That's right. There are about sixty contestants altogether, and exactly one—Miss United States—is homegrown. We'd just as soon nothing happened to any of them, even a minor incident. I don't say that it would plunge the world into a crisis if anything happened, but the State Department would be very unhappy. So a note like this means that the police have to supply protection for all sixty girls and these days we don't have all that manpower to waste."

"If you don't mind," said Trumbull frowning, "what the hell do you expect us to do about it?"

Gordon said, "It's just possible he may not be planning to kill all the girls. He may have only one in mind, so that is why he uses the singular when he talks of death. Perhaps Henry might give us some ideas as to how to narrow it down. We'd rather concentrate on ten girls than on sixty. We'd rather concentrate on one girl only, in fact."

"From that note?" said Trumbull, with perfectly obvious disgust. "You want Henry to pick out one Miss Earth contestant from that note?"

He turned to look at Henry, and Henry said, "I have *no* idea, Mr. Trumbull."

Gordon put the note away again. "I thought you might tell me who Rahab is. Why should he call one particular girl Rahab and threaten to kill her?"

Gonzalo said suddenly, "Why should we suppose that Rahab applies to the girl he's after? Maybe it's his signature. Maybe it's a pseudonym he's using because Rahab was some important prophet or executioner in the Bible."

Rubin let out his breath in a snort. "Oh, boy! Mario, how can even an artist know so little? 'Rahab' is part of the line. If it were the signature, he would put it on the bottom. If he's the kind of guy who wants to call down the wrath of God in public, he would sign it proudly and unmistakably if he signed it at all. And if he did, he would never take the pseudonym of Rahab, not if he knew anything at all about the Bible. Rahab was . . . No, I tell you what. Henry, get us the King James from the reference shelf. We might as well make sure we get the words exactly right."

"You mean you don't know the Bible by heart?" said Trumbull.

"I miss a word now and then, Tom," said Rubin loftily.

He took the Bible from Henry. "Thanks, Henry. Now the only person named Rahab in the Bible was a harlot."

"She was?" said Gonzalo incredulously.

"That's right. Here it is—first verse of the second chapter of the Book of Joshua. *And Joshua the son of Nun sent out of Shittim two men to spy secretly, saying, Go view the land, even Jericho. And they went, and came into an harlot's house, named Rahab, and lodged there.*"

"And that's part of the parellelism," said Avalon thoughtfully. "Is that what you think?"

"Of course. And that's why I think 'Jezebel' and 'Rahab' both apply to all the girls and should both be plural. Both Jezebel and Rahab are Biblical representatives of immoral women, and I take it that our note writer, whoever he may be, conceives all the Miss Earth candidates to be just that."

"Are they?" asked Gonzalo. "I mean, immoral."

Gordon smiled slightly. "I won't guarantee their private lives, but I don't think they set any records in immorality. They're young women, carefully selected to represent their countries. I doubt that anything really notorious would slip by the judges."

Avalon said, "When a Fundamentalist who's a little past the bend speaks of immorality, or when he starts calling someone a Jezebel, there is no need, in my opinion, for the existence of real immorality. It's probably purely subjective. Any woman who rouses feelings of sexual excitement within him will seem to him to be immoral; and the one who does so most will seem to him to be most immoral."

"You mean," said Gordon, swiveling his eyes toward

Avalon, "that he's after the most beautiful one and aims to kill her?"

Avalon shrugged. "What's beauty? He may be after the one *he* thinks is most beautiful, but what are his standards? It might not even be beauty in the most literal sense. It might be that one of them reminds him of his dead mother, his childhood sweetheart, or some teacher he once had. How can we tell?"

"All right," said Gordon. "You may be quite correct in all you say, but it doesn't matter. Tell me who he's after; tell me who Rahab is; and we can worry about motives afterward."

Avalon shook his head. "I don't know that we can dismiss motive quite that easily, but, in any case, we won't get anywhere if we head down the wrong path. Despite what Manny says, I don't think there's any parallelism between Jezebel and Rahab."

"There certainly is," said Rubin, his jaw lifting at once.

"Where is it? To begin with, Jezebel wasn't a harlot. She was the Queen of Israel and there is no hint in the Bible that she was in any way sexually immoral. It's just that she was an idolator and opposed the Yahvists; that is, those who worshipped Yahveh—or Jehovah, to use the more common but less accurate name."

Rubin said, "I'll explain it to you, if you want. Jezebel was the daughter of the King of Tyre, who was also a priest of Astarte. She was probably a priestess herself. As for Rahab, she was probably not a common harlot, but a priestess who participated in fertility rites. To the Israelites that was being a harlot."

Halsted said, "Not everybody has gone into the Bible the way you have, Manny. The Bible calls Jezebel a queen and Rahab a harlot, and the average reader wouldn't go past that."

"But that's not the point I'm trying to make," said Avalon. "Jezebel, whatever her status, came to a bad end. She died in a palace coup and was eaten by dogs. Rahab, however, came to a good end. She was saved alive after

the fall of Jericho, because she had kept the spies hidden
and safe. One can assume she was converted to the worship of the God of Israel and was no longer a harlot or a
pagan priestess. In fact . . . Manny, let me have the
Bible."

Avalon took it and turned its pages rapidly. "It's just at
the opening of the Book of Matthew. Here it is: *And
Salmon begat Booz of Rachab; and Booz begat Obed of
Ruth; and Obed begat Jesse; and Jesse begat David the
king.* There, that's the fifth and sixth verse of the first
chapter of the Gospel of St. Matthew. According to that,
Rahab married a prominent Israelite and was the great-
great-grandmother of David and therefore a distant an-
cestress of Jesus himself. Having helped the Israelites take
Jericho, having married an Israelite, and being the ances-
tress of David and Jesus, Rahab couldn't possibly be used
as a symbol of immorality by any Fundamentalist."

The Bible passed from hand to hand, and Halsted said,
"The name isn't spelled the same. It's 'Rachab' in Matthew."

Avalon said, "The New Testament is translated into
English from the Greek; the Old Testament from the Hebrew. The transliterations aren't consistent. 'Booz' in the
passage I just read is 'Boaz' in the Old Testament Book
of Ruth."

"Besides," said Rubin, "in this case 'Rachab' is more
nearly the correct spelling. The Hebrew letter that occurs
in the middle of the name is correctly pronounced like the
guttural German 'ch.'"

"So if we are going to associate Rahab with one of the
Miss Earth contestants," said Avalon, "we had better forget about the parallelism with Jezebel and look for something else."

"But what?" asked Drake.

"Don't worry." Avalon lifted an admonitory finger. "I
have something in mind. Manny, isn't 'Rahab' used in the
Bible as the poetic equivalent of Egypt?"

Rubin said excitedly, "Yes, you're right. It's not the
same word in Hebrew. There the middle letter *is* an 'h.'
Still, it's the same word in English. Usually it's translated

into 'pride' or 'might' or something like that, but it's left untranslated in at least one place. . . . Somewhere in the Psalms, I think."

He turned the pages and muttered, "I wish we had a Bible dictionary. That's something the club ought to buy and add to the reference shelf." Then, with his voice rising to a shout, he said, "Here it is, by God! Fourth verse of the 87th Psalm: *I will make mention of Rahab and Babylon to them that know me: behold Philistia, and Tyre, with Ethiopia.*"

"How do you know that 'Rahab' means Egypt there?" asked Gonzalo.

"Because throughout Old Testament history the rival great powers were those in the Tigris-Euphrates Valley and on the Nile. Babylon clearly typifies the former, so Rahab must typify the latter. There's no dispute there. Biblical scholars agree that 'Rahab' stands for Egypt there."

"In that case," said Avalon, "I don't think we have to fall back on Henry. I suspect that it's Miss Egypt that our mysterious friend is after. And that makes sense, too. There are a couple of million Jewish people in this city and considering the present situation between Israel and Egypt, one of them, with a little derangement, might feel called upon to threaten Miss Egypt."

Gordon said, "An interesting thought. There's only one trouble."

"What's that, sir?"

"There isn't any Miss Egypt. You see, the Miss Earth contest isn't as cut-and-dried as the Miss America contest. In the Miss America you have one contestant from each of the fifty states because foreign policy doesn't enter into it. In the Miss Earth contest, nations hostile to the United States, or those which look down on beauty contests as decadent, don't enter. This year, no Arab state is represented. On the other hand, some nations are represented by more than one entry, each with a different name. Some years ago, I understand, there were two German beauties. The top winner went as Miss Germany and the second went as Miss Bavaria."

Avalon looked distinctly annoyed. "If there's no Miss Egypt, then I don't know what 'Rahab' can mean."

"What does it mean in the Bible?" asked Gonzalo. "Why do they give that name to Egypt? There has to be some reason."

Rubin said, "Oh, well. Egypt was a river kingdom and Rahab was associated with the waters. In fact, it was a mythological remnant of a pre-Israelite creation myth. The land was viewed by the Sumerians as having been created from the sea. They visualized the sea as an enormous monster called Tiamat that had to be split in two so that the land emerged from between the halves. In Babylonian mythology, it was Marduk who killed Tiamat.

"The priestly writers of the first book of Genesis cleaned up the Babylonian myths and removed the polytheism, but they left traces. In the beginning, before the first day of creation, according to Chapter 1, Verse 2 of Genesis, *And the earth was without form and void; and darkness was upon the face of the deep. And the Spirit of God moved upon the face of the waters.* Well, the Hebrew word translated as 'the deep' is 'tehom' and some commentators think that is a version of Tiamat and that this verse is all that is left of the cosmic struggle."

"That's pretty farfetched," said Drake.

"I don't know. There are occasional verses in the Bible which seem to refer to the earlier and less sophisticated creation myth. There's one toward the end of Isaiah, if I can find it. . . . I used to know where all these references are."

He turned pages back and forth feverishly, ignoring the small glass of brandy Henry had placed before him. Gordon sipped at his own brandy and watched calmly. He made no attempt to stop Rubin or to attempt to bring the discussion back to the point.

It was Trumbull who said, "Is this getting us anywhere?"

But Rubin waved excitedly. "I've got it. I've got it. Listen to this: Isaiah, Chapter 51, Verse 9: *Awake, awake, put on strength, O arm of the Lord; awake, as in the ancient days, in the generations of old. Art thou not it that hath cut Rahab and wounded the dragon?* You see, 'cut Rahab' and 'wounded the dragon' is another example of parallelism. Rahab and the dragon are alternate expressions that symbolize the raging ocean that has to be defeated and split before dry land can be formed. Some commentators maintain this refers to Egypt and the division of the Red Sea, but in my opinion it is certainly a version of the fight with Tiamat."

There was perspiration on Rubin's forehead and he kept waving his left hand for silence, even while his right hand continued to turn pages. "There are references to it in the Psalms, too. I can find them if you'll give me a minute. Ah! Psalm 89, Verses 9 and 10: *Thou rulest the raging of the sea: when the waves thereof arise, thou stillest them. Thou hast broken Rahab in pieces, as one that is slain.* And then another one, Psalm 74, Verses 13 and 14: *Thou didst divide the sea by thy strength: thou brakest the heads of the dragons in the waters. Thou brakest the heads of leviathan in pieces.* Leviathan was another name for the primeval ocean."

Trumbull shouted, "God damn it, Manny. You're not a revivalist preacher any more. Where's this all getting us?"

Rubin looked up indignantly and closed the Bible. "If you'll let me talk, Tom," he said, with exaggerated dignity, "and curb your impulse to bellow, I'll tell you."

He looked about impressively. "I now suspect that to the fellow who wrote this note, Rahab meant the raging power of the sea. Now what is the raging power of the sea today? Who controls the sea? The United States does. With our aircraft carriers, our nuclear submarines, our Polaris missiles, we have the power of Rahab. I think maybe he's after Miss United States."

"Is that so?" said Halsted. "The United States has been the predominant sea power only since World War II. It hasn't had time to enter legend. It's Great Britain that's the ruler of the sea in song and story. 'Britannia rules the waves.' I vote for Miss Great Britain."

Gordon interposed. "There's no Miss Great Britain. There's a Miss England, though."

"All right. I vote for Miss England."

Drake said, "There's no way of getting into this nut's head. Maybe he was just using the name to indicate his method of operation. Rubin said 'brakest the head' and 'broken in pieces' when he read those verses. Maybe the writer meant he was going to use a blunt instrument."

Rubin shook his head. "In one of the verses it was 'cut Rahab.'"

Gonzalo said, "If Rahab is an arch opponent of God, the writer might be thinking of the Nazis. Jeff said the writer might be Jewish and after Miss Egypt; why not after Miss Germany?"

Trumbull said, "Why does the writer have to be Jewish? Most Fundamentalists are Protestants and they've had some neat terms in their time for the Pope. He was the 'Whore of Babylon' to some of them and Rahab was a harlot. I don't suppose there's a Miss Vatican City, but how about Miss Italy?"

Henry said, "I beg your pardon, gentlemen."

Gordon looked up. "Ah, you have a suggestion, Henry?"

"Yes, I have, sir. Whether it's useful or not, I don't know. . . . You said, Mr. Gordon, that the rules are rather flexible in the Miss Earth contest as far as the nations represented are concerned. Some nations have no representatives, some have two or more under different names. You mentioned a Miss Germany and a Miss Bavaria, for instance."

"That's right," said Gordon.

"And you said there was no Miss Great Britain, but that there was a Miss England."

"Right again," said Gordon.

"Does the Miss England imply the presence of a Miss Scotland as well?"

"It does, as a matter of fact." Gordon's eyes narrowed. "And a Miss Ireland and Miss Northern Ireland as well."

Gonzalo brought both hands before him down on the table. "I'll bet I know what Henry is driving at. If the writer of the note is Irish, he may be after Miss Northern

Ireland. He would consider her as representing a political division that's a puppet of England, and England rules the waves and is Rahab."

Henry shook his head. "It's not as complicated as that, I think. I have always thought that all things being equal, the simplest explanation is best."

"Occam's razor," muttered Avalon.

"I must admit," said Henry, "I never heard of Rahab before, but Mr. Rubin's explanation was quite enlightening. If Rahab is a monster representing the sea, and if the monster is also called leviathan, and if leviathan is sometimes used as a name for an actual sea monster, and the largest that lives, why might not the writer be referring to Miss Wales?"

"Ah," said Gordon.

Henry turned to him. "Was that the answer, Mr. Gordon?"

Gordon said gravely, "It's a possibility."

"No, Mr. Gordon," said Henry. "You know better than that. You came here to test me. How can you test me with a puzzle to which you don't know the answer?"

Gordon broke into a laugh. "You win again, Henry," he said. "Everything I told you is true enough, but it happened last year. The person in question was caught. He had a knife in his hand, but he wasn't really dangerous. He surrendered quietly and he's in a mental hospital now. He was quite incoherent. We could never be sure what his motive was except that he was sure his victim was particularly wicked.

"The trouble was," Gordon went on, "we had to stake out a lot of men and we never did find out what Rahab meant. . . . But when we caught him he was making his way into the dressing room of Miss Wales. We should have had you last year, Henry. You're a remarkable detective."

"The Black Widowers are. They explore the problem; I only pick up what's left," said Henry.

Afterword

This story first appeared in the September 1973 issue of *Ellery Queen's Mystery Magazine,* under the title "A Warning to Miss Earth," which I simply don't like. Back to "Miss What?"

I don't always remember the exact genesis of a particular story, but I remember this one. Mrs. Anita Summer, who works with the Leonard Lyons column on the *New York Post,* and who is a science fiction reader, invited me to come with her to a cocktail party being given for the contestants for the Miss Universe award.

Well, of course, I was delighted to go and I wandered from contestant to contestant in a happy daze. Anita, pleased at my artless delight, said, "Are you going to write a story about this, Isaac?"

And I said, "All right." And I did. So this story, "Miss What?", is dedicated to Anita Summer.

9

The Lullaby of Broadway

For the first time in the history of the Black Widowers, the monthly banquet was being given in a private apartment. Emmanuel Rubin had insisted and his straggly straw-colored beard had waggled strenuously as he argued it out in parliamentary fashion.

He was going to be the next host, he said, and the host was an absolute monarch within the wording of the bylaws and nowhere in the bylaws was the place of meeting specifically fixed.

"According to tradition," began Geoffrey Avalon with the kind of solemnity that befitted his profession as patent lawyer, "we have always met right here."

"If tradition is the master," said Rubin, "why the bylaws?"

And in the end he had had his way, carrying it finally when he pointed out that he was a gourmet cook and Mario Gonzalo had grinned and said, "Let's go and smell him burn the hamburgers."

"I do not serve hamburgers," said Rubin hotly, but by that time everyone had conceded the point.

So Avalon and James Drake, who had both come in from across the Hudson on the same train, stood in the lobby of Rubin's West Side apartment house and waited for the doorman to pay attention to them. It was quite clear that they could not get in without the doorman's permission by anything short of violence.

Avalon muttered, "It's the fortress mentality. It's all over New York. You can't go anywhere without having to pass the gimlet eye and being frisked for weapons."

"I don't blame them," said Drake in his soft, hoarse voice. He lit a cigarette. "It's better than being mugged in the elevator."

"I suppose so," said Avalon gloomily.

The doorman turned to them. He was short, round-faced, and bald-headed, with a gray fringe of hair that was repeated in his mustache, which was as short and bristly as Drake's but which occupied a more generous space of upper lip. He did not look in the least formidable but his gray uniform lent him the cachet of authority and, presumably, that was enough to quell the intruder.

"Yes?" he said.

Avalon cleared his throat, and spoke in his most impressively rich baritone in order to conceal the shyness that no one could believe anyone as tall, straight, and impressive as he could have. "We are Dr. Drake and Mr. Avalon calling on Mr. Emmanuel Rubin in 14-AA."

"Drake and Avalon," repeated the doorman. "One minute." He moved to the bank of apartment bells and spoke into the intercom. The squawking sound of Rubin's voice came clearly. "Send them up. Send them up."

The doorman held the door open for them, but Avalon hesitated on the threshold. "Do you have many incidents here, by the way?"

The doorman nodded importantly. "Sometimes, sir. No matter what you do, things happen! Apartment on the twentieth floor was robbed last year. There was a lady got hurt in the laundry room not too long ago. Things like that happen."

A voice said gently, "May I join you, gentlemen?"

Drake and Avalon both turned to look at the newcomer. There was a perceptible moment in which neither recognized him. And then Drake chuckled briefly, and said, "Henry, when you're not waiting on us at the restaurant, you're beautiful."

Avalon said, considerably more explosively, "Henry! What are you doing . . . ?" He choked it off and looked uncomfortable.

"Mr. Rubin invited me, sir. He said that as long as the dinner was not to be held in the restaurant and I could not have the privilege of waiting on you, then I would be his guest. I believe that was his purpose in insisting the dinner be held here. One would not think it, but Mr. Rubin is a sentimental gentleman."

"Splendid," said Avalon with great enthusiasm, as though to make up for his previous surprise. "Doorman, this gentleman is with us."

Henry hung back. "Would you like to inquire of Mr. Rubin, sir?"

The doorman, having held the door patiently through this, said, "No, that's all right. You go right ahead."

Henry nodded, and all three advanced through the large blue lobby to the bank of elevators.

Drake said, "Henry, I haven't seen an outfit like yours in years. They'll mob you in New York if you go around dressed like that."

Henry looked down upon himself briefly. His suit was a charcoal brown and cut so conservatively that Drake was clearly wondering where the establishment could be found that would have such garments for sale. The shoes were a sober black, the shirt a gleaming white, and the tie, a narrow and somber gray held with a neat tie clip.

Crowning it all was the dark-brown derby which Henry now doffed, holding it lightly by the brim.

"I haven't seen a derby in a long time," said Avalon.

"Or a hat at all," said Drake.

"It is the freedom of the times," said Henry. "We each do our thing now, and this is mine."

Avalon said, "The trouble is that some people consider the thing to do to be molesting women in laundries."

"Yes," said Henry, "I heard what the doorman said. At least we can hope there will be no trouble today."

One of the elevators arrived at the lobby and a lady with a dog got off. Avalon looked inside, right and left, then entered. They rose to the fourteenth floor without trouble.

They were all gathered, or almost all. Rubin was wearing his wife's apron (it had a large "Jane" crocheted on it) and he was looking harried. The sideboard had a full collection of bottles and Avalon had appointed himself an impromptu bartender, after fending off Henry.

"Sit down, Henry," said Rubin in a loud voice. "You're the guest."

Henry looked uncomfortable.

Halsted said, with his very slight stutter, "You've got a nice apartment, Manny."

"It's all right—let me get past you for a minute—but it's small. Of course, we don't have children, so we don't need it much larger, and being in Manhattan has its conveniences for a writer."

"Yes," said Avalon. "I listened to some of the conveniences downstairs. The doorman said women have trouble in the laundry."

"Oh, hell," said Rubin contemptuously. "Some of the dames here *want* trouble. Ever since the Chinese delegation to the United Nations took over a motel a few blocks down, some of the dowagers here see the yellow menace everywhere."

"And robberies, too," said Drake.

Rubin looked chagrined as though any slur against Manhattan were a personal attack. "It could happen anywhere. And Jane was careless."

Henry, the only one sitting at the table, and with an as yet untouched drink before him, looked surprised—an expression which somehow did not put a single wrinkle into his unlined face. He said, "Pardon me, Mr. Rubin. Do you mean *your* apartment was entered?"

"Well, yes, the apartment lock can be opened with a strip of celluloid, I think. That's why everyone puts in fancy locks in addition."

"But when was this?" asked Henry.

"About two weeks ago. I'm telling you, it was Jane's fault. She went down the hall to see someone about recipes or something and didn't double-lock the door. That's just asking for it. The hoodlums have an instinct for it, a special ESP. She came back just as the bum was leaving and there was a hell of a fuss."

"Did she get hurt?" asked Gonzalo, his ordinarily prominent eyes bulging slightly.

"Not really. She was shook up, that's all. She yelled like anything—about the best thing she could have done. The guy ran. If I'd been there, I'd have taken after him and caught him, too. I'd have—"

"It's better not to try," said Avalon austerely, stirring his drink by moving the ice with his forefinger. "The end result of a chase could be a knife in the ribs. *Your* ribs."

"Listen," said Rubin, "I've faced guys with knives in my time. They're easy to han— Hold it, something's burning." He dashed into the kitchen.

There was a knock at the door.

"Use the peephole," said Avalon.

Halsted did, and said, "It's Tom." He opened the door to let Thomas Trumbull in.

Avalon said, "How come you weren't announced?"

Trumbull shrugged. "They know me here. I've visited Manny before."

"Besides," said Drake, "an important government operative like you is above suspicion."

Trumbull snorted and his lined face twisted into a scowl, but he didn't rise to the bait. That he was a code expert all the Black Widowers knew. What he did with it, none of the Black Widowers knew, though all had the same suspicion.

Trumbull said, "Any of you counted the bulls yet?"

Gonzalo laughed. "It does seem a herd."

The bookcases that lined the wall were littered with bulls in wood and ceramic and in all sizes and colors. There were several on the end tables, others on the television set.

"There are more in the bathroom," said Drake, emerging.

"I'll bet you," said Trumbull, "that if we each count all the bulls in the place, we'll each come out with a different answer and every one of them will be wrong."

"I'll bet *you*," said Halsted, "that Manny doesn't know how many there are himself."

"Hey, Manny," shouted Gonzalo, "how many bulls have you got?"

"Counting me?" called back Rubin, amid the clatter of

pottery. He put his head out of the kitchen door. "One thing about eating here is you know damn well you don't get any liver in the appetizer. You're getting an eggplant dish with all kinds of ingredients in it and don't ask the details because it's my recipe. I invented it. . . . And, Mario, that bull will chip if you drop it and Jane knows them all by heart and she'll inspect each one when she comes back."

Avalon said, "Did you hear about the robbery here, Tom?"

Trumbull nodded. "He didn't get much, I understand."

Rubin hustled out, carrying dishes. "*Don't* help, Henry. Say, Jeff, put down the drink a minute and help me put out the cutlery. . . . It's roast turkey, so all of you get ready to tell me if you want light meat or dark and don't change your mind once you've made it up. And you're all getting stuffing whether you want it or not because that's what makes or—"

Avalon put out the last of the knives with a flourish and said, "What did they get, Rubin?"

"You mean the guy who broke in? Nothing. Jane must have come back just as he started. He messed up some of the items in the medicine chest; looking for drugs, I suppose. I think he picked up some loose change, and my recording equipment was knocked about. He may have been trying to carry off my portable stereo to hock it, but he just had a chance to move it a bit. . . . Who wants music, by the way?"

"No one," shouted Trumbull indignantly. "You start making your damned noise, and *I'll* steal the stereo and kick every one of your tapes into the incinerator."

Gonzalo said, "You know, Manny, I hate to say it, but the stuffing is even better than the eggplant was."

Rubin grunted. "If I had a bigger kitchen—"

The wail of a siren sounded from outside. Drake jerked a thumb over his shoulder toward the open window. "The lullaby of Broadway."

Rubin waved his hand negligently. "You get used to it. If it isn't a fire engine, it's an ambulance; if it isn't an ambulance, it's a police car; if it isn't . . . The traffic doesn't bother me."

For a moment he seemed lost in thought. Then a look of the deepest malignancy crossed his small face. "It's the *neighbors* who bother me. Do you know how many pianos there are on this floor alone? And how many record players?"

"You have one," said Trumbull.

"I don't play it at two A.M. at top volume," said Rubin. "It wouldn't be so bad if this were an old apartment house with walls as thick as the length of your arm. The trouble is, this place is only eight years old and they make the walls out of coated aluminum foil. Hell, the walls *carry* sound. Put your ear to the wall and you can hear noise from any apartment on any floor, three up and three down.

"And it's not as though you can really hear the music and enjoy it," he went on. "You just hear that damned bass, thump, thump, thump, at a subsonic level that turns your bones to water."

Halsted said, "I know. In my place, we've got a couple who have fights and my wife and I listen, but we can never hear the words, just the tone of voice. Infuriating. Sometimes it's an interesting tone of voice, though."

"How many families do you have here in this apartment house?" asked Avalon.

Rubin spent a few moments computing with moving lips. "About six hundred fifty," he said.

"Well, if you insist on living in a beehive," said Avalon, "you have to take the consequences." His neat and graying beard seemed to bristle with high morality.

"That's a real fat hunk of comfort," said Rubin. "Henry, you're going to have another helping of turkey."

"No, really, Mr. Rubin," said Henry, with a kind of helpless despair. "I just can't—" And he stopped with a sigh, since his plate was heaped high.

He said, "You seem very put out, Mr. Rubin; and somehow I feel there is more to it than someone's piano playing."

Rubin nodded and, for a moment, his lips actually trembled, as though in passion. "You bet it is, Henry. It's that Goddamn carpenter. You might be able to hear him now."

He tilted his head in an attitude of listening and, automatically, all conversation stopped and all listened. Except for the steady whine of traffic outside, there was nothing.

Rubin said, "Well, we're lucky. He isn't doing it now; hasn't for a while, in fact. Listen, everyone, dessert was a kind of disaster and I had to improvise. If anyone doesn't want to eat it, I've got cake from the bakery, which I wouldn't ordinarily recommend, you understand——"

"Let me help this course," said Gonzalo.

"Okay. Anyone but Henry."

"That," said Trumbull, "is a kind of reverse snobbery. Henry, this guy Rubin is putting you in your place. If he weren't so damned conscious that you're a waiter, he'd let you help wait on us."

Henry looked at his plate, still piled high, and said, "My frustration is not so much at being unable to help wait on table, as at being unable to understand."

"Unable to understand what?" asked Rubin, coming in with desserts on a tray. They looked very much like chocolate mousse.

"Are you having a carpenter working in this apartment house?" asked Henry.

"What carpenter? . . . Oh, you mean what I said. No, I don't know what the hell he is. I just call him a carpenter. He's forever banging. Three in the afternoon. Five in the morning. He's forever banging. And always when I'm writing and want it particularly quiet. . . . How's the Bavarian cream?"

"Is that what this is?" asked Drake, staring at it suspiciously.

"That's what it started *out* to be," said Rubin, "but the gelatin wouldn't set properly and I had to improvise."

"Tastes great to me, Manny," said Gonzalo.

"Little too sweet," said Avalon, "but I'm not much of a dessert man."

"It *is* a little too sweet," said Rubin magnanimously. "Coffee coming up in a minute; and not instant, either."

"Banging what, Mr. Rubin?" asked Henry.

Rubin had bustled away, and it wasn't till five minutes afterward, with the coffee poured, that Henry could ask again, "Banging what, Mr. Rubin?"

"What?" asked Rubin.

Henry pushed his chair back from the table. His mild face seemed to set into a harder outline. "Mr. Rubin," he said, "you are the host; and I am the guest of the club at this dinner. I would like to ask a privilege which, as host, you can grant."

"Well, ask," said Rubin.

"As guest, it is traditional that I be quizzed. Frankly, I do not wish to be, since, unlike other guests, I will be at next month's banquet and at the one after that, in my ordinary capacity as waiter, of course, and I prefer—" Henry hesitated.

"You prefer your privacy, Henry?" asked Avalon.

"Perhaps I would not quite put it—" began Henry, and then, interrupting himself, he said, "Yes, I *would* quite put it that way. I want my privacy. But I want something more. I want to quiz Mr. Rubin."

"What for?" asked Rubin, his eyes widening behind the magnifying effect of his thick-lensed spectacles.

"Something I have heard this night puzzles me and I cannot get you to answer my questions."

"Henry, you're drunk. I've been answering every question."

"Nevertheless, may I quiz you formally, sir?"

"Go ahead."

"Thank you," said Henry. "I want to know about the annoyance you have been having."

"You mean the carpenter, and his lullaby of Broadway?"

"*My* line," said Drake quietly, but Rubin ignored him.

"Yes. How long has it been going on?"

"How long?" said Rubin passionately. "For months."

"Very loud?" asked Henry.

Rubin thought a while. "No, not loud, I suppose. But you can hear it. It comes at odd moments. You can never predict it."

"And who's doing it?"

Rubin brought his fist down on the table suddenly, so that his coffeecup clattered. "You know, *that's* it. It isn't the noise so much, irritating though it might be. I could *stand* it if I understood it; if I knew who it was; if I knew what he was doing; if I could go to someone and ask him not to do it for a while when I'm having particular trouble with a plot line. It's like being persecuted by a poltergeist."

Trumbull held up his hand. "Wait a while. Let's not have any of this poltergeist horse manure. Manny, you're not going to try to bring in the supernatural, here. Let's get one thing straight first—"

Halsted said, "It's Henry that's doing the quizzing, Tom."

"I'm aware of that," said Trumbull, nodding his head frigidly. "Henry, may I ask a question?"

"If," said Henry, "you are about to ask why Mr. Rubin, hearing a noise, can't tell where it's coming from, it is what I am about to ask."

"Go ahead," said Trumbull. "I'll help myself to more coffee."

Henry said, "Would you answer the question, Mr. Rubin?"

Rubin said, "I suppose it is hard for you all to understand. Let's see now, two of you live across the Hudson, one of you lives down in one of the older sections of Brooklyn, and one of you is in Greenwich Village. Tom lives in a reconverted brownstone. I'm not sure where Henry lives but I'm sure it's not a modern beehive, as Avalon calls it. None of you live in one of these modern apartment complexes with twenty-five stories or more, and twenty-five apartments on a floor, and nice sound-carrying concrete for a skeleton.

"If someone had a good loud record player on, I might be able to tell if it's from upstairs or from downstairs, though I wouldn't bet on it. If I wanted to, I could go from door to door all along this floor, then door to door all along the floor beneath, and again all along the floor above, and I guess I would be able to tell what apartment it is by plastering my ear against the right door.

"If it's just a soft hammering, though, it's impossible to tell. You can listen at a door and it wouldn't help. Sound doesn't carry so much through the air and the door. It goes through the walls. Listen, I've gone from door to door when I got mad enough. I don't know how many times I've crept through the corridors."

Gonzalo laughed. "If you get caught doing that, that doorman downstairs will be getting reports about vicious-looking hoodlums sneaking around."

"That doesn't worry me," said Rubin. "The doorman knows me." A look of coy modesty suddenly dripped over Rubin's face. "He's a fan of mine."

"I knew you had one somewhere," said Trumbull, but Henry pushed at the turkey on his plate and seemed more distressed than ever.

"Suppose your fan isn't on duty," said Gonzalo argumentatively. "You've got to have doormen around the clock and your fan has to sleep."

"They all know me," said Rubin. "And this one, the guy at the door now, Charlie Wiszonski, takes the four-to-twelve evening shift weekdays, which is the heavy shift. He's senior man. . . . Look, let me clear the table."

Henry said, "Could you have someone else do that, Mr. Rubin? I want to continue questioning you and I want to get back to the carpenter. If sound carries through the walls and you hear him, don't many other people hear him, too?"

"I suppose so."

"But if he disturbs so many—"

"That's another irritating thing," said Rubin. "He

doesn't. . . . Thanks, Roger, just pile all the dishes in the sink. I'll take care of them afterward. . . . This carpenter doesn't seem to bother anyone. During the day husbands are away and so are lots of the wives and the apartment house isn't rich in children. The wives that are home are doing housework. In the evening, everyone has the television set on. What does anyone care for an occasional banging? *I* care because I'm home night and day and I'm a *writer*. I care because I'm a creative person who has to do some *thinking* and needs a little *quiet*."

"Have you asked others about it?" said Henry.

"Oh, occasionally, yes." He tapped his spoon restlessly against the cup. "I suppose your next question is to ask what they said."

"I should guess," said Henry, "from the look of frustration about you, that no one admitted ever hearing it."

"Well, you're wrong. One or two would say something about hearing it once or twice. The trouble is, no one *cared*. Even if they heard it, they didn't care. New Yorkers get so deadened to noise, you could blow them up and they wouldn't care."

"What do you suppose he's doing to make that noise, whoever he is?" asked Avalon.

Rubin said, "I say he's a carpenter. Maybe not professionally, but he works at it. I could swear he has a workshop up there. I can still swear it. Nothing else will explain it."

"What do you mean, you can *still* swear it?" asked Henry.

"I consulted Charlie about it."

"The doorman?"

"What's the good of the doorman?" asked Gonzalo. Why didn't you go to the superintendent? Or the owner?"

"What good are they?" said Rubin impatiently. "All I know about the owner is the fact that he lets the air conditioning blow out every heat wave because he prefers to patch it with the finest grade of chewing gum. And to get the superintendent you have to pull in Washington. Besides, Charlie's a good guy and we get along. Hell, when

Jane had the run-in with the hoodlum, and me not there, Charlie was the one she called."

"Didn't she call the police?" asked Avalon.

"Sure she did. But first Charlie!"

Henry looked terribly unhappy. He said, "So you consulted the doorman about the banging. What did he say?"

"He said there were no complaints. It was the first he had heard of it. He said he would investigate. He did and he swore up and down that there were no carpenter's workshops anywhere in the building. He said he had men go into each apartment to check air conditioners—and that's one sure way of getting in anywhere."

"So then the doorman dropped the matter?"

Rubin nodded. "I suppose so. And that bugged me, too. It bothered me. I could see that Charlie didn't believe me. He didn't think there was any banging. I was the only one to mention it, he said."

"Doesn't Mrs. Rubin hear it?"

"Of course she does. But I have to call it to her attention. It doesn't bother her, either."

Gonzalo said, "Maybe it's some gal practicing with castanets, or some percussion instrument."

"Come on. I can tell something rhythmic from just random banging."

"It could be a kid," said Drake, "or some pet. I lived in an apartment in Baltimore once and I had banging directly overhead, like someone dropping something a few hundred times a day. And that's what it was. They had a dog that kept picking up some toy bone and dropping it. I got them to put down a cheap rug."

"It's no kid and it's no pet," said Rubin stubbornly. "I wish you wouldn't all assume I don't know what I'm hearing. Listen, I worked in a lumberyard once. I'm a pretty fair carpenter myself. I know the sound of a hammer on wood."

"Maybe someone's doing some home repairs," said Halsted.

"For months? It's more than that."

Henry said, "Is that where the situation stands now?

Did you make any other effort to find the source after the doorman failed you?"

Rubin frowned. "I tried but it wasn't easy. Everyone has an unlisted number around here. It's part of the fortress mentality Avalon talks about. And I only know a couple of people to talk to. I tried knocking on the most likely doors and introducing myself and asking and all I got were hard stares."

"I'd give up," said Drake.

"Not I," said Rubin, tapping himself on the chest. "The main trouble was that everyone thought I was some kind of nut. Even Charlie, I think. There's a kind of general suspicion about writers on the part of ordinary people."

"Which may be justified," said Gonzalo.

"Shut up," said Rubin. "So I thought I would present some concrete evidence."

"Such as?" asked Henry.

"Well, by God, I recorded the damned banging. I spent two or three days keeping my senses alert for it and then, whenever it started, I tripped the switch and recorded it. It played hell with my writing but I ended up with about forty-five minutes of banging—not loud, but you could hear it. And it was an interesting thing to do because if you listened to it you could tell just from the banging that the bum is a rotten carpenter. The blows weren't even and strong. He had no control over that hammer, and that kind of irregularity wears you out. Once you get the proper rhythm, you can hammer all day without getting tired. I did that many a time—"

Henry interrupted. "And did you play the recording for the doorman?"

"No. A month ago I went to a higher court."

Gonzalo said, "Then you did see the super?"

"No. There's such a thing as a tenants' organization."

There was a general smile of approval at the table which left only Henry untouched. "Didn't think of that," said Avalon.

Rubin grinned. "People wouldn't in a case like this. That's because the only purpose of the organization is to get after the landlord. It's as though no one ever heard of a tenant annoying another tenant and yet I'd say that nine-tenths of the annoyances in an apartment house are caused by tenant-tenant interactions. I said that. I—"

Henry interrupted again. "Are you a regular member of the organization, Mr. Rubin?"

"I'm a member, sure. Every tenant is a member automatically."

"I mean do you attend meetings regularly?"

"As a matter of fact, this was only the second meeting I'd attended."

"Do the regular attendees know you?"

"Some of them do. Besides, what difference does that make? I announced myself. Rubin, I said, 14-double-A, and I made my speech. I had my tape recording with me and I held it up and waved it. I said that was the proof some damn fool was a public nuisance; that I had it labeled with dates and times and would have it notarized if necessary and see my lawyer. I said that if the landlord had made that noise, everyone in the audience would be howling for united action against the nuisance. Why not react the same to one of the tenants?"

"It must have been a most eloquent address," growled Trumbull. "A pity I wasn't there to hear you. What did they say?"

Rubin scowled. "They wanted to know who was the tenant who made the noise and I couldn't tell them. So they let it drop. Nobody heard the noise; anyway, nobody was interested."

"When did the meeting take place?" asked Henry.

"Nearly a month ago. And they haven't forgotten about it, either. It *was* an eloquent address, Tom. I fried them. I did it deliberately. The word was going to spread, and it did. Charlie the doorman said he heard half the tenants talking about it—which was what I wanted. I wanted that carpenter to hear it. I wanted him to know I was after him."

"Surely you don't intend violence, Mr. Rubin," said Henry.

"I don't need violence. I just wanted him to know. It's

been pretty quiet the last few weeks, and I'll bet it stays quiet."

"When's the next meeting?" asked Henry.

"Next week. . . . I may be there."

Henry shook his head. He said, "I wish you wouldn't, Mr. Rubin. I think it might be better if you dropped the whole thing."

"I'm not scared of whoever it is."

"I'm sure you're not, Mr. Rubin, but I find the situation peculiar on several counts—"

"In what way?" asked Rubin hastily.

"I—I— It seems melodramatic, I admit but— Mr. Avalon, you and Dr. Drake arrived downstairs in the lobby just ahead of me. You spoke to the doorman."

"Yes, that's right," said Avalon.

"Perhaps I came too late. I may have missed something. It seems to me, Mr. Avalon, that you asked the doorman if there had been any incidents of a distressing nature in the apartment house and he said there had been a robbery in a twentieth-floor apartment the last year and that a woman had been hurt in some fashion in the laundry room."

Avalon looked thoughtful and nodded.

Henry said, "Yet he knew that we were heading for Mr. Rubin's apartment. How is it that he didn't mention that this apartment had been broken into only two weeks before?"

There was a thoughtful pause. Gonzalo said, "Maybe he didn't like to gossip."

"He told us about other incidents. There might have been a harmless explanation, but when I heard of the break-in, I grew perturbed. Everything I've heard since has increased my feeling of uneasiness. He was a fan of Mr. Rubin. Mrs. Rubin had turned to him at the time. Yet he never spoke of it."

"What do you make of it, Henry?" asked Avalon.

"Is he involved, somehow?"

"Come *on*, Henry," said Rubin at once. "Are you trying to say Charlie is part of a holdup ring?"

"No, but if there is something peculiar going on in this

apartment house, it might be very useful to slip the door-man a ten-dollar bill now and then. He might not know what it's for. What is wanted may seem quite harmless to him—but then when your apartment is invaded, it may be that he suddenly understands more than he did before. He feels involved and he won't talk of it any more. For his own sake."

"Okay," said Rubin. "But what would be so peculiar going on here? The carpenter and his banging?"

Henry said, "Why should someone haunt the floor waiting for you and Mrs. Rubin to leave the apartment untenanted and single-locked? And why, when Mr. Avalon mentioned the matter of the woman in the laundry early in the evening, Mr. Rubin, did you promptly dismiss the matter with some reference to the Chinese delegation to the United Nations. Is there a connection?"

Rubin said, "Only that Jane told me some of the tenants were worried about the Chinese getting in here."

"Somehow I feel that is too weak a reason to account for your *non sequitur*. Did Mrs. Rubin say that the man she had surprised in the apartment was an Oriental?"

"Oh, you can't go by that," said Rubin, drawing his shoulders into an earnest shrug. "What can anyone really notice—"

Avalon said, "Now wait a while, Manny. No one's asking you if the burglar was *really* Chinese. All Henry is asking is whether Jane *said* he was."

She said she *thought* he was; she had the *impression* he was. . . . Come on, Henry. Are you proposing espionage?"

Henry said stolidly, "Combine all this with the matter of the irregular banging—I believe Mr. Rubin mentioned the irregularity specifically as the sign of a poor carpenter. Might the irregularity be the product of a clever spy? It seems to me that the weak point of any system of espionage is the transfer of information. In this case, there would be no contact between sender and receiver, no intermediate checkpoint, nothing to tap or intercept. It would be the most natural and harmless sound in the world that no one would hear except for the person listening—and, as luck would have it, a writer trying to concentrate on his writing and distracted by even small sounds. Even then it would be considered merely some-one hammering—a carpenter."

Trumbull said, "Come on, Henry. That's silly."

Henry said, "But then what about a break-in where virtually nothing was taken?"

"Nuts," said Rubin. "Jane came back too soon. If she had stayed away five minutes more, the stereo would have been gone."

Trumbull said, "Look here, Henry. You've done some remarkable things in the past and I wouldn't totally dismiss *anything* you say. Just the same, this is very thin."

"Perhaps I can present evidence."

"What kind?"

"It would involve the recordings Mr. Rubin made of the banging. Could you get them, Mr. Rubin?"

Rubin said, "Easiest thing in the world." He stepped through an archway.

Trumbull said, "Henry, if you think I'm going to listen to some stupid hammering and tell you if it's in code, you're crazy."

"Mr. Trumbull," said Henry, "what connections you have with the government, I don't know, but it is my guess that in a few moments you will want to get in touch with the proper people and my suggestion is that you begin by having the doorman thoroughly questioned, and that—"

Rubin came back, frowning and red-faced. "Funny. I can't find them. I thought I knew exactly where they were supposed to be. They're not there. So much for your evidence, Henry. I'll have to . . . Did I leave them somewhere?"

"It's the absence that's the evidence, Mr. Rubin," said Henry, "and I think we know now what the burglar was after, and why there's been no hammering since."

Trumbull said hastily, "I'd better make—" Then he paused as the doorbell sounded.

For a moment all were frozen, then Rubin muttered,

"Don't tell me Jane is getting home early." He rose heavily, moved to the door, and peered out the peephole.

He stared a moment, then said, "What the hell!" and flung the door open. The doorman was standing there, red-faced and clearly uneasy.

The doorman said, "It took time to get someone to stand in for me. . . . Listen," he said, his eyes darting uneasily from person to person. "I don't want trouble, but—"

"Close the door, Manny!" cried Trumbull.

Rubin pulled the doorman inside and closed the door. "What is it, Charlie?"

"It's been getting to me. And now someone asked me about troubles here. . . . You did, sir," he said to Avalon. "Then more people came and I think I know what it must be about. I guess some of you are investigating the break-in and I didn't know what was going on but I guess I was out of line and I want to explain. This fellow—"

"Name and apartment number," said Trumbull.

"King! He's in 15-U," said Charlie.

"Okay, come into the kitchen with me. Manny, I'm going to make that phone call on the phone in here." He closed the kitchen door.

Rubin looked up, as though listening. Then he said, "Hammering messages? Who'd believe it?"

"Exactly why it worked, Mr. Rubin," said Henry softly, "and might have continued to work had there not been in the same apartment house a writer of your—if I may say so—marked eccentricity."

Afterword

This story, and the two that follow, did not appear in *Ellery Queen's Mystery Magazine,* but, as I explained in the Introduction, were written especially for the book.

This one is an example of how writing enriches one's life. The business about hearing mysterious banging from one's apartment is taken from actual fact. Someone in my apartment house bangs away at all hours. I've never taken the strong action Manny Rubin took, but have contented myself with shaking my head and gritting my teeth.

I was getting more and more irritated at it and might have worked myself into an ulcer when it occurred to me that I might use it as the central point of a short story. So I did. This one.

Now when I hear the banging (it isn't really so often or so bad) I just shrug cheerfully and remember that it supplied me with a story. Then I don't mind it at all.

10
Yankee Doodle Went to Town

It was general knowledge among the Black Widowers that Geoffrey Avalon had served as an officer in World War II and had reached the rank of major. He had never seen active service, as far as any of them knew, however, and he never talked about wartime experiences. His stiff bearing, however, seemed suited to the interior of a uniform, so that it never surprised anyone to know that he had once been Major Avalon.

When he walked into the banquet room with an army officer as his guest, it seemed, therefore, entirely natural. And when he said, "This is my old army friend Colonel Samuel Davenheim," everyone greeted him cordially without so much as a raised eyebrow. Any army buddy of Avalon's was an army buddy of theirs.

Even Mario Gonzalo, who had served an uneventful hitch in the army in the late fifties, and who was known to have acerbic views concerning officers, was pleasant enough. He propped himself on one of the sideboards and began sketching. Avalon looked over Gonzalo's shoulder briefly, as though to make sure the artist member of the Black Widowers would not, somehow, draw the Colonel's head upward into a crown of ass's ears.

It would have been most inappropriate for Gonzalo to have done so, for there was every indication of clear intelligence about Davenheim. His face, round and a little plump, was emphasized by outmoded hair, short above and absent below. His mouth curved easily into a friendly smile, his voice was clear, his words crisp.

He said, "I've had you all described to me, for Jeff, as

you probably all know, is a methodical man. I ought to be able to identify you all. For instance, you're Emmanuel Rubin since you're short, have thick glasses, a sparse beard—"

"Straggly beard," said Rubin, unoffended, "is what Jeff usually calls it because his own is dense, but I've never found that density of facial hair implies—"

"And are talkative," said Davenheim firmly, overriding the other with the calm authority of a colonel. "And you're a writer. . . . You're Mario Gonzalo, the artist, and I don't even need your description since you're drawing. . . . Roger Halsted, mathematician, partly bald. The only member without a full head of hair, so that's easy. . . . James Drake, or, rather, Dr. James Drake—"

"We're all doctors by virtue of being Black Widowers," said Drake from behind a curl of cigarette smoke.

"You're right, and Jeff explained that carefully. You're Doctor Doctor Drake because you smell of tobacco smoke at ten feet."

"Well, Jeff should know," said Drake philosophically.

"And Thomas Trumbull," said Davenheim, "because you're scowling, and by elimination. . . . Have I got everyone?"

"Only the members," said Halsted. "You've left out Henry, who's all-important."

Davenheim looked about, puzzled. "Henry?"

"The waiter," said Avalon, flushing and staring at his drink. "I'm sorry, Henry, but I didn't know what to tell Colonel Davenheim about you. To say you're the waiter is ridiculously insufficient and to say more would endanger Black Widower confidentiality."

"I understand," said Henry agreeably, "but I think it would be well to serve the Colonel. What is your pleasure, sir?"

For a moment the Colonel looked blank. "Oh, you mean drinks? No, that's all right. I don't drink."

"Some ginger ale, perhaps?"

"All right." Davenheim was plainly grasping at straws. "That will be fine."

Trumbull smiled. "The life of a non-drinker is a difficult one."

"Something wet must be pressed on one," said Davenheim wryly. "I've never managed to adjust."

Gonzalo said, "Have a cherry put in your ginger ale. Or better yet, put water in a cocktail glass and add an olive. Then drink and replace the water periodically. Everyone will admire you as a man who can hold his liquor. Though, frankly, I've never seen an officer who could—"

"I think we'll be eating any minute," said Avalon hastily, looking at his watch.

Henry said, "Won't you be seated, gentlemen?" and placed one of the bread baskets directly in front of Gonzalo as though to suggest he use his mouth for that purpose.

Gonzalo took a roll, broke it, buttered one half, bit into it, and said in muffled tones, "—keep from getting sloppy drunk on one martini," but no one listened.

Rubin, finding himself between Avalon and Davenheim, said, "What kind of soldier was Jeff, Colonel?"

"Damned good one," said Davenheim gravely, "but he didn't get much of a chance to shine. We were both in the legal end of matters, which meant desk work. The difference is that he had the sense to get out once the war was over. I didn't."

"You mean you're still involved with military law?"

"That's right."

"Well, I look forward to the day when military law is as obsolete as feudal law."

"I do, too," said Davenheim calmly. "But it isn't as yet."

"No," said Rubin, "and if you—"

Trumbull interrupted. "Damn it, Manny, can't you wait for grilling time?"

"Yes," said Avalon, coughing semi-stentorially, "we might as well let Sam eat before putting him through his paces."

"If," said Rubin, "military law applied the same considerations to those—"

"Later!" roared Trumbull.

Rubin looked through his thick-lensed glasses indignantly, but subsided.

Halsted said, in what was clearly intended to be a change of topic, "I'm not happy with my limerick for the fifth book of the *Iliad*."

"The what?" said Davenheim, puzzled.

"Pay no attention," said Trumbull. "Roger keeps threatening to put together five lines of crap for every book of the *Iliad*."

"And the *Odyssey*," said Halsted. "The trouble with the fifth book is that it deals chiefly with the feats of the Greek hero Diomedes, and I feel I ought to have him part of the rhyme scheme. I've been at it, off and on, for months."

"Is that why you've spared us limericks the last couple of sessions?" asked Trumbull.

"I've had one and I've been ready to read it, but I'm not quite satisfied with it."

"Then you've joined the great majority," said Trumbull.

"The thing is," said Halsted quietly, "that both 'Diomedes' and its legitimate variant 'Diomed' cannot be rhymed seriously. 'Diomedes' rhymes with 'Wheaties' and 'Diomed' rhymes with 'shy-a-bed' and what good are those?"

"Call him Tydeides," said Avalon. "Homer frequently used the patronymic."

"What's a patronymic?" asked Gonzalo.

"A father-name, which is the literal translation of the word," said Halsted. "Diomedes' father was Tydeus. Don't you think I've thought of that? It rhymes with 'didies' or, if you want to go Cockney, with 'lydies.' "

"How about 'ascites'?" said Drake.

"Wit seeks its own level," said Halsted. "How about this? All I need do is distort the stress and give 'Diomed' accents on first and last syllables."

"Cheating," said Rubin.

"A little," admitted Halsted, "but here it is:

"In courage and skill well ahead,
Into battle went brave Diomed.
Even gods were his quarries,
And the war-loving Ares
He struck down and left nearly for dead."

Avalon shook his head. "Ares was only wounded. He had enough strength left to rise, roaring, to Olympus."

"I must admit I'm not satisfied," said Halsted.

"Unanimous!!" said Trumbull.

"Veal parmesan!" said Rubin enthusiastically, for, with his usual agility, Henry was already placing the dishes before each.

Colonel Davenheim said, after he had devoted considerable time to the veal, "You do yourselves well here, Jeff."

"Oh, we do our poor best," said Avalon. "The restaurant charges in proportion, but it's only once a month."

Davenheim plied his fork enthusiastically and said, "Dr. Halsted, you're a mathematician—"

"I teach mathematics to reluctant youngsters, which isn't quite the same thing."

"But why, then, limericks on the epic poems?"

"Precisely because it is not mathematics, Colonel. It's a mistake to think that because a man has a profession that can be named, all his interests must bear that name."

"No offense," said the Colonel.

Avalon stared at a neatly cleaned plate and pushed thoughtfully at his untouched last half-glass of liquor. He said, "As a matter of fact, Sam knows what it is to have an intellectual hobby. He is an excellent phoneticist."

"Oh, well," said Davenheim, with heavy modesty, "in an amateur way."

Rubin said, "Does that mean you can tell jokes in accent?"

"In any accent you wish—within reason," said Davenheim. "But I can't tell jokes even in natural speech."

"That's all right," said Rubin, "I'd rather hear a bad joke in an authentic accent than a good one with a poor one."

Gonzalo said, "Then how do you account for the fact that you laugh only at your own jokes when they fail in both respects?"

Davenheim spoke quickly to cut off Rubin's rejoinder. He said, "You've got me off the subject." He leaned to one side to allow Henry to place the rum cake before him. "I mean, Dr. Halsted—very well, Roger—that perhaps you switch to the classics to get your mind off some knotty mathematics problem. Then, while your conscious mind is permutating rhymes, your unconscious mind is—"

"The funny thing about that," said Rubin, seizing his own chance to cut in, "is that it works. I've never been so stymied by a plot that I couldn't get it worked out by going to a movie. I don't mean a *good* movie that really absorbs me. I mean a bad one that occupies my conscious mind just sufficiently to allow my unconscious free reign. A spy-action film is best."

Gonzalo said, "I can't follow the plot of those things even when I'm paying attention."

"And yet they're aimed at the twelve-year-old mind," said Rubin, striking back at last.

Henry poured the coffee, as Davenheim said, "I agree with what Manny says. I happen to think that a day spent on phonetics is sometimes the best way of contributing to a problem at work. But isn't there another aspect to this? It's easy to see that by keeping the conscious mind occupied, we leave the unconscious free to do as it wishes underground. But will it stay underground? Might it not obtrude aboveground? Might it not make itself seen or heard, if not to the person himself—the person who is thinking—then to others?"

"Exactly what do you mean, Colonel?" asked Trumbull.

"Look," said Davenheim, "if we're on first-name terms, let it be first names all round. Call me Sam. What I mean is this. Suppose Manny is working on a plot involving an undetectable poison—"

"Never!" said Rubin strenuously. "Tarantulas are out, too, and mystic Hindus, and the supernatural. That's all nineteenth-century romanticism. I'm not sure that even the locked-room mystery hasn't become a matter of——"

"Just for *example*," said Davenheim, who had momentary trouble breasting the tide. "You do other things to let your unconscious work and as far as you yourself are concerned you can swear that you have completely forgotten the mystery, that you're not thinking about it, that it's completely wiped out. Then, when you're hailing a cab, you call, 'Toxic! Toxic!' "

Trumbull said thoughtfully, "That's farfetched and I don't accept it, but I'm beginning to get a notion. Jeff, did you bring Sam here because he has a problem on his mind?"

Avalon cleared his throat. "Not really. I invited him last month for many reasons—the most important of which was that I thought you would all like him. But he stayed over at my house last night and—— may I tell them, Sam?"

Davenheim shrugged. "This place is as quiet as the grave, you say."

"Absolutely," said Avalon. "Sam knows my wife almost as long as he knows me, but twice he called her Farber instead of Florence."

Davenheim smiled dimly. "My unconscious forcing its way through. I could have sworn I had put it out of my mind."

"You weren't aware of it," said Avalon. He turned to the others. "I didn't notice it. Florence did. The second time she said, 'What are you calling me?' and he said, 'What?' She said, 'You keep calling me Farber.' And he looked absolutely thunderstruck."

"Just the same," said Davenheim, "it's not my unconscious that's bothering me. It's *his*."

"Farber's?" asked Drake, tamping out his cigarette with his stained fingers.

"The other one's," said Davenheim.

Trumbull said, "It's about time for the brandy anyway, Jeff. Do you want to grill our esteemed guest, or ought someone else do so?"

"I don't know that he needs to be grilled," said Avalon.

"Perhaps he'll simply tell us what's occupying his unconscious when his conscious mind is being diverted."

"I don't know that I want to do that," said Davenheim grimly. "It's rather a delicate matter."

"You have my word," said Trumbull, "that everything said here is in strictest confidence. I'm sure Jeff has told you that already. And that includes our esteemed Henry. And, of course, you needn't go into full detail."

"I can't hide behind false names, though, can I?"

"Not if Farber is one of the true ones," said Gonzalo, grinning.

"Well, what the devil," sighed Davenheim. "Actually, it's not much of a story as stories go, and it may be nothing; nothing at all. I may be so *damned* wrong. But if I'm not wrong it's going to be embarrassing for the army, and expensive for the country. I could almost hope I was wrong, but I've committed myself so far that if I am wrong it may permanently—hamper my career. Yet I'm not so far away from retirement."

For a moment he seemed lost in thought, then he said fiercely, "No, I *want* to be right. However embarrassing, it's got to be stopped."

"Is it treason you're after?" asked Drake.

"No, not in the narrow sense of the word. I almost wish it were. There can be a colossal dignity about treason. A traitor is sometimes only the other side of the patriot coin. One man's traitor is another man's martyr. I'm not talking about the penny-ante handyman for hire. I'm talking about the man who thinks he is serving a higher cause than his country and wouldn't accept a penny for the risks he undergoes. We understand that quite well when it is the enemy's traitors we are dealing with. The men, for instance, whom Hitler considered—"

"It's not treason, then?" said Trumbull, a bit impatiently.

"No. Just corruption! Stinking, fetid corruption. A gang of men—soldiers, I'm sorry to say, officers, conceivably high officers—intent on bleeding Uncle Sam a bit."

"Why isn't that treason?" snapped Rubin. "It weakens us and spreads decay in the army. Soldiers who think so

little of their country as to steal from it are scarcely going
to think so much of it as to die for it."

"If it comes to that," said Avalon, "people put their
emotions and actions in separate compartments. It's quite
possible to steal from Uncle Sam today and die for him
tomorrow and be perfectly sincere about it both times.
Many a man who routinely cheats the national treasury
out of half his proper income tax considers himself a loyal
American patriot."

Rubin said, "Leave the income tax out of it. Considering what consumes most of federal spending, you can
make a good case for maintaining that the true patriot is
he who goes to jail rather than pay his taxes."

Davenheim said, "It's one thing not to pay your taxes
out of principle, to admit it, and go to jail for it. It's another thing to duck your share of the fair load for no
other reason than to see others carry their own burden
and yours to boot. Both actions are equally illegal, but I
have some respect for the former. In the case I'm talking
about the only motivation is simple greed. It is quite possible that millions of dollars of the taxpayers' money are
involved."

"Possible? Is that all?" asked Trumbull, his forehead
wrinkling into a washboard.

"That's all. So far. I can't prove it and it's a difficult
thing to track down without a damned good scent. If I
push too hard and can't back my suspicions all the way,
I'll be torn in half. Some big names might be involved—
and might not."

"What's Farber got to do with it?" asked Gonzalo..

"So far we have two men, a sergeant and a private. The
sergeant is Farber; Robert J. Farber. The other is Orin
Klotz. We've got nothing on them really."

"Nothing at all?" asked Avalon.

"Not really. As a result of the action of Farber and
Klotz, thousands of dollars of army equipment have
evaporated but we cannot show that their actions were illegal. They were covered in every case."

"You mean because higher-ups were involved?" Gonzalo smiled slowly. "Officers? With *brains?*"

"Unlikely as it seems," said Davenheim dryly. "That may be so. But I have no proof."

"Can't you question the two men you have?" said Gonzalo.

"I have," said Davenheim. "And with Farber I can get nothing. He is that most dangerous of men, the honest tool. I believe he was too stupid to know the significance of what he did, and that if he did know, he wouldn't have done it."

"Confront him with the truth," said Avalon.

"What is the truth?" asked Davenheim. "And I'm not ready to put my guesses on the table. If I tell what I know now, it will be dishonorable discharge for the two, at best, and the rest of the ring will pull in its horns for a breathing space and then start in again. No, I'd like to cover my hand until such time as I can get a lead, some lead I can be sufficiently sure of to run the risk I'm going to have to run."

"You mean a lead to someone higher up?" asked Rubin.

"Exactly."

"What about the other fellow?" asked Gonzalo.

Davenheim nodded. "He's the one. He knows. He's the brains of that pair. But I can't break his story. I've been over and over it with him and he's covered."

Halsted said, "If it's only a guess that there's something more to this than those two guys, why do you take it so seriously? Aren't the chances actually very good that you're wrong?"

"To other people it would seem so," said Davenheim. "And there's no way in which I could explain why I know I'm *not* wrong except by pleading experience. After all, Roger, an experienced mathematician can be quite certain that a particular conjecture is true and yet be unable to prove it by the strict rules of mathematical demonstration. Right?"

"I'm not sure that that's a good analogy," said Halsted.

"It seems a good one to me. I've talked to men who were guilty beyond a doubt and to men who were innocent beyond a doubt and the attitude of each under accusation is different and I can *sense* that difference. The trouble is that that sense I have is not admissible as evidence. Farber I can dismiss, but Klotz is just a shade too wary, just a shade too unconfused. He plays *games* with me and enjoys it, too, and that's one thing I can't possibly miss."

"If you insist that you can sense such things," said Halsted, dissatisfied, "there's no arguing about it, is there? You put it outside the rational."

"There's just no mistake in it," said Davenheim, unheeding, as though he were now caught up in the fury of his thoughts to the point where what Halsted said was just an outer sound that didn't impinge. "Klotz smiles just a little bit whenever I'm after him hotly. It's as though I'm a bull and he's a matador, and when I'm beginning to lunge at close quarters, he stands there rigidly with his cape flirting negligently to one side, daring me to gore him. And when I try, he's not there and the cape flips over my head."

"I'm afraid he's got you, Sam," said Avalon, shaking his head. "If you feel as though he's playing you for a fool, you've reached the point where you can't trust your judgment. Let someone else take over."

Davenheim shook his head. "No, if it's what I think it is, and I *know* it's what I think it is, I want to be the one to smash it."

"Look," said Trumbull. "I have a little experience in such things. Do you suppose Klotz can break the case wide open for you? He's only a private, and I suspect that even if there *is* some sort of conspiracy, he knows very little about it."

"All right. I'll accept that," said Davenheim. "I don't expect Klotz to hand me the moon. Yet he's got to know one other man, one man higher up. He's got to know some one fact, some one fact closer to the center than he himself is. It's that one man and that one fact I'm after. It's all I ask. And the thing that breaks me in two is that he's giving it away and I still don't get it."

"What do you mean, giving it away?" asked Trumbull.

"That's where the unconscious comes in. When he and I are sparring, he's entirely occupied with me, entirely engaged in stopping me, heading me off, stymying me, putting me behind the eight ball. It's a game he plays well, damn him. The last thing he's going to do is to give me the information I want, but it's in him just the same and when he's busy thinking of everything else but, that information bubbles out of him. Every time I'm close upon him and backing and maneuvering him into a corner—butting my horns against his damned cape just this far from his groin—he *sings*."

"He *what?*" exploded Gonzalo, and there was a general stir among the Black Widowers. Only Henry showed no trace of emotion as he refilled several of the coffeecups.

"He sings," said Davenheim. "Well, not quite—he hums. And it's always the same tune."

"What tune is that? Anything you know?"

"Of course I know it. Everyone knows it. It's 'Yankee Doodle.' "

Avalon said heavily, "Even President Grant, who had no ear for music, knew that one. He said he knew only two tunes. One was 'Yankee Doodle' and the other wasn't."

"And it's 'Yankee Doodle' that's giving the whole thing away?" asked Drake, with that look in his weary chemist's eyes that came when he began to suspect the rationality of another person.

"Somehow. He's masking the truth as cleverly as he can, but it emerges from his unconscious, just a bit; just the tip of the iceberg. And 'Yankee Doodle' is that tip. I don't get it. There's just not enough for me to grab hold of. But it's there! I'm sure of that."

"You mean there's a solution to your problem somewhere in 'Yankee Doodle'?" said Rubin.

"Yes!" said Davenheim emphatically. "I'm positive of that. The thing is he's not aware he's humming it. At one point I said, 'What's that?' and he was blank. I said, 'What are you humming?' and he just stared at me in what I could swear was honest amazement."

"As when you called Florence Farber," said Avalon.

Halsted shook his head. "I don't see where you can attach much importance to that. We all experience times when tunes run through our minds and we can't get rid of them for a while. I'm sure we're bound to hum them under our breath at times."

Davenheim said, "At *random* times, perhaps. But Klotz hums *only* 'Yaknee Doodle' and *only* at the specific times when I'm pressing him. When things get tense in connection with my probing for the truth about the corruption conspiracy I am sure exists, that tune surfaces. It *must* have meaning."

"Yankee Doodle," said Rubin thoughtfully, half to himself. For a moment he looked at Henry, who was standing near the sideboard, a small vertical crease between his eyebrows. Henry caught Rubin's eye but did not respond.

There was a ruminating silence for a few moments and all the Black Widowers seemed to be, to one degree or another, unhappy. Finally, Trumbull said, "You may be all wrong, Sam. What you may be needing here is psychiatry. This guy Klotz may hum 'Yankee Doodle' at *all* moments of tension. All it may mean is that he heard his grandfather sing it when he was six years old or that his mother sang him to sleep with it."

Davenheim lifted his upper lip in mild derision. "Can you believe I didn't think of that? I had a dozen of his close friends in. Nobody had ever heard him hum anything!"

"They might be lying," said Gonzalo. "I wouldn't tell an officer anything if I could avoid it."

"They might never have noticed," said Avalon. "Few people are good observers."

"Maybe they lied, maybe they didn't know," said Davenheim, "but, taken at face value, their testimony, all of it, would make me think that the humming of 'Yankee Doodle' is specifically associated with my investigation and nothing else."

"Maybe it's just associated with army life. It's a march associated with the Revolutionary War," said Drake.

"Then why only with me, not with anyone else in the army?"

Rubin said, "Okay, let's pretend 'Yankee Doodle'

means something in this connection. What can we lose? So let's consider how it goes. . . . For God's sake, Jeff, don't sing it."

Avalon, who had opened his mouth with the clear intention of singing, closed it with a snap. His ability to hold a true note rivaled that of an oyster and in his saner moments he knew it. He said, with a trace of hauteur, "I will recite the words!"

"Good," said Rubin, "but no singing."

Avalon, looking stern, struck an attitude and began declaiming in his most resonant baritone:

> *"Yankee Doodle went to town*
> *A-riding on a pony.*
> *Stuck a feather in his cap*
> *And called it macaroni.*
> *Yankee Doodle, keep it up,*
> *Yankee Doodle dandy.*
> *Mind the music and the step*
> *And with the girls be handy."*

Gonzalo said, "It's just a nonsense lyric."

"Nonsense, hell," said Rubin indignantly, and his straggly beard quivered. "It makes perfect sense. It's a satire on the country boy written by a city slicker. 'Doodle' is any primitive country instrument—a bagpipe, for instance—so a Yankee Doodle is a backwoods New Englander who's no more sophisticated than a bagpipe. He comes to town on his pony intent on cutting a fine figure, so he wears what he thinks are city clothes. He wears a feather in his hat and thinks he's a real dude. And in the late eighteenth century, that's what a 'macaroni' was, a city hepcat dressed in the latest style.

"The last four lines are the chorus and show the country boy stepping it up at a city dance. He is mockingly told to stamp away and be gallant to the ladies. The word 'dandy,' which first came into use about mid-eighteenth century, meant the same as 'macaroni.' "

Gonzalo said, "Okay, Manny, you win. It's not nonsense. But how does it help Sam's case?"

"I don't think it does," said Rubin. "Sorry, Sam, but Klotz sounds like a country boy making a fool of the city slicker and he can't help but think of the derisive song and how he's turning the tables on you."

Davenheim said, "I presume, Manny, that you think he must be a country boy because his name is Klotz. By that reasoning you must be a rube because your name is Rubin. Actually, Klotz was born and brought up in Philadelphia and I doubt that he's ever seen a farm. No country boy, he."

"All right," said Rubin, "then I might have been looking at the wrong end of the stick. *He's* the city slicker looking down on *you,* Sam."

"Because *I'm* a country boy? I was born in Stoneham, Massachusetts, and went through Harvard right up to my law degree. And he knows that, too. He has made enough roundabout references to it in his matador moments."

Drake said, "Doesn't your Massachusetts birth and upbringing make you a Yankee?"

"Not a Yankee Doodle," said Davenheim stubbornly.

"He might think so," said Drake.

Davenheim thought about that a while, then said, "Yes, I suppose he might. But if so, surely he would hum it openly, derisively. The point is, I think he's humming it unconsciously. It has a connection with something he's trying to hide, not something he's trying to show."

Halsted said, "Maybe he's looking forward to a future when he's going to be enriched by his crimes and when he'll be able to strut his way to town; when he can 'stick a feather in his cap' in other words."

Drake said, "Or maybe Klotz is thinking that his treatment of you is a feather in his cap."

Gonzalo said, "Maybe some particular word has significance. Suppose 'macaroni' means he's hooked up with the Mafia. Or suppose 'with the girls be handy' means that some Wac is involved. They still have Wacs in the army, don't they?"

It was at this point that Henry said, "I wonder, Mr. Avalon, if, as host, you will permit me to ask a few questions."

Avalon said, "Come on, Henry. You know you can at any time."

"Thank you, sir. Would the Colonel grant me the same permission?"

Davenheim looked surprised, but said, "Well, you're here, Henry, so you might as well."

Henry said, "Mr. Avalon recited eight lines of 'Yankee Doodle'—four lines of a verse followed by the four lines of the chorus. But verse and chorus have different tunes. Did Private Klotz hum all eight lines?"

Davenheim thought a moment. "No, of course not. He hummed—uh—" He closed his eyes, concentrated, and went "Dum-dum dum-dum dum-dum-dum, dum-dum dum-dum dum-du-u-um-dum. That's all. The first two lines."

"Of the verse?"

"That's right. 'Yankee Doodle went to town, A-riding on a pony.'"

"Always those two lines?"

"Yes, I think always."

Drake brushed some crumbs from the table. "Colonel, you say this humming took place when the questioning was particularly tense. Did you pay particular attention to exactly what was being discussed at those times?"

"Yes, of course, but I prefer not to go into detail."

"I understand, but perhaps you can tell me this. At those times, was it he himself who was under discussion or Sergeant Farber as well?"

"Generally," said Davenheim slowly, "the humming times came when he most emphatically protested innocence, but always on behalf of both. I'll give him that. He has never once tried to clear himself at the expense of the other. It was always that neither Farber nor he did thus-and-so or were responsible for this-and-that."

Henry said, "Colonel Davenheim, this is a long shot. If the answer is no, then I'll have nothing more to say. If, however, the answer is yes, it's just possible we may have something."

"What's the question, Henry?" asked Davenheim.

"At the same base where Sergeant Farber and Private

Klotz are stationed, Colonel, does there happen to be a Captain Gooden or Gooding or anything resembling that in sound?"

Davenheim had, until then, been looking at Henry with grave amusement. Now that vanished in a flash. His mouth closed tight and his face whitened visibly. Then his chair scraped as he shoved it back and rose.

"Yes," he said strenuously. "Captain Charles Goodwin. How the *hell* could you possibly have known that?"

"In that case, he may be your man. I'd forget about Klotz and Farber, sir, if I were you, and concentrate on the captain. That might be the one step upward that you wanted. And the captain may prove an easier nut to crack than Private Klotz has been."

Davenheim seemed to find no way to speak further and Trumbull said, "I wish you'd explain, Henry."

"It's the 'Yankee Doodle,' as the Colonel expected. The point is, though, that Private Klotz *hummed* it. We have to consider what words he was thinking when he hummed."

Gonzalo said, "The Colonel said he hummed the lines that go 'Yankee Doodle went to town, A-riding on a pony.'"

Henry shook his head. "The original poem 'Yankee Doodle' had some dozen verses and the macaroni lines were not among them. They arose later, though they're now the most familiar. The original poem tells of the visit of a young farmboy to the camp of Washington's Continental Army and his naïveté is made fun of, so I believe Mr. Rubin's interpretation of the nature of the song to be correct."

Rubin said, "Henry's right. I remember now. Washington is even mentioned, but as *Captain* Washington. The farmboy wasn't even aware of the nature of military rank."

"Yes," said Henry. "I don't know all the verses and I imagine very few people do. Perhaps Private Klotz didn't, either. But anyone who knows the poem at all knows the first verse or, at any rate, the first two lines, and that's what Private Klotz may have been humming. The first line, for instance—and it's the farmboy speaking—is 'Father and I went down to camp.' You see?"

"No," said Davenheim, shaking his head. "Not quite."

"It occurred to me that whenever you pressed hard on Private Klotz and might say, 'Farber and you did thus-and-so,' and he answered, 'Farber and I did *not* do thus-and-so,' the humming would start. You said, Colonel, that it was at the moment of denial that it tended to come and that he always denied on behalf of both Farber and himself. So when he said 'Farber and I,' it would trigger the line 'Farber and I went down to camp.'" Henry sang it in a soft tenor voice.

"Farber and he were in an army camp," said Avalon, "but, good God, that's stretching for it."

"If it stood alone, sir, yes," said Henry. "But that's why I asked about a Captain Gooden in the camp. If he were a third member of the conspiracy, the push to hum the tune might be irresistible. The first verse, which is the only one I know—"

But here Rubin interrupted. Standing up, he roared:

> *"Father and I went down to camp*
> *Along with Cap'n Good'n,*
> *And there we saw the men and boys*
> *As thick as hasty puddin'."*

"That's right," said Henry calmly, "Farber and I went down to camp along with Captain Goodwin."

"By God," said Davenheim. "That must be it. If not, it's the most extraordinary coincidence. . . . And it can't be. Henry, you've put your finger on it."

"I hope so. More coffee, Colonel?" said Henry.

Afterword

This story was the occasion of my making a great discovery. It came about this way:

I compose on the typewriter. Even first drafts get typewritten. It was my firm belief that it had to be so. If I dictated, I couldn't see what I was doing, and if I tried writing by hand, my fingers would get stiff and fall off halfway down the second page.

So on November 9, 1972, I found myself in a Rochester hotel room with a speech to give the next day. For that evening I had nothing to do and while driving to Rochester I had thought up the story you have just finished (unless you're skipping through the book just reading the afterwords). I was desperate. All I wanted to do was to write and I had not brought a typewriter with me.

Finally, I dug out some of the hotel stationery and decided to start the story by hand and keep on going till my fingers dropped off. It might kill a *little* time. So I wrote, and I wrote—and I wrote. Do you know I finished the entire story without lifting pen from paper and my fingers didn't hurt at all?

Now I need never take my typewriter. Since then I have handwritten several other items, while I was on board ship.

And you know what? While I was writing the story I discovered an odd thing. Writing by hand with pen and ink is *very silent*. That noise I always make writing isn't the writing; it's the *typewriter*. I thought you'd want to know that.

11

The Curious Omission

Roger Halsted was clearly suffused with a controlled glee when he arrived at the monthly banquet of the Black Widowers. He unwound his scarf (it was a cold evening with considerably more than a hint of snow in the air—since half an inch of it already lay on the ground) and said, "Have I got a guest for you!"

Emmanuel Rubin looked at him over his scotch and soda and said peevishly, "Where were you? Even Tom Trumbull beat you to the drinks and we thought you were welching on the host's responsibility."

Halsted looked hurt and his high forehead grew pink. He said, "I *called* the restaurant. Henry—"

Henry had adjusted the bread baskets and seen to it that the bran muffins affected by Geoffrey Avalon were in plain view. He said, "Yes, Mr. Halsted. The company has been informed that you would be a little late. I believe Mr. Rubin is merely amusing himself at your expense."

Trumbull said, "What guest?"

"That's why I'm late. I had to pick him up in White Plains and it's snowing harder up there. I had to call the restaurant from a gas station."

"So where is he?" asked Mario Gonzalo, more than usually nattily dressed in a maroon blazer, matching striped shirt, and matching patterned tie.

"Downstairs. Men's room. His name is Jeremy Atwood; he's about sixty-five; and he has a problem."

Avalon from his considerably better than six feet of height drew his thick and graying eyebrows together. "I've been thinking, gentlemen, of this very matter. The original purpose of the Black Widowers consisted of nothing more than dining and conversation. We have now reached the point where we never fail to have a problem to agitate us and disturb our digestion. What happens when we can't find one? Do we disband?"

Gonzalo said, "Then we're back to conversation without a purpose. There's always Manny."

Rubin said, his sparse beard lifting noticeably, "Nothing I say is without a purpose, Mario. Failing all else, there's the vague hope my words may serve to educate you. For one thing, I can show you why your latest painting is completely wrong."

"You said you liked it," said Mario, frowning and stepping into the trap.

"Only out of relief when you said it was your last painting and only until I found out you meant it was your latest."

But Halsted's guest was coming up the stairs now. He moved rather slowly and he seemed tired. Halsted helped him off with his overcoat, and when the guest removed his hat, he showed himself to be quite bald. Only a fringe of white hair remained.

Halsted said, "Gentlemen, this is my guest, Jeremy Atwood. I met him through the fact that one of his nephews is a fellow teacher. Mr. Atwood, let me present the company."

By the time the introductions were completed and a glass of dry sherry had been pressed into Atwood's hand, Henry had the first course on the table. Rubin stared at it suspiciously.

"No liver?" he asked.

"No liver, Mr. Rubin," said Henry. "Kidney slices are the base."

"Oh, Lord," said Rubin, "what's the soup?"

"Cream of leek, Mr. Rubin."

"Coming and going. They get you coming and going," he grumbled, and tackled the kidney with a gingerly probing fork.

Drake, with a glimmer in his small eyes which meant he thought he was on the track of a fellow chemist, said, "What does your nephew teach, Mr. Atwood?"

Atwood said, in a surprisingly musical tenor, "English

literature, I believe. I am not very well acquainted with him."

"I don't blame you," said Rubin at once. "Teachers of English literature have probably turned out more illiterates than have any other force of illegitimate culture in the world."

"You see, Mr. Atwood," said Gonzalo, striving for his own back, "Manny Rubin is a writer whose works have never been discussed by any teacher who was sober at the time."

Trumbull spoke at once to cut off Rubin's retort. "What's your own line of work, Mr. Atwood?"

"I'm retired now, but once upon a time I was a civil engineer," said Atwood.

Avalon said, "You do not have to answer any questions now, Mr. Atwood. That will come with the dessert."

It turned out to be unnecessary advice since Rubin had the bit in his teeth now and was off and running. With the soup, of which he had little, he developed the thesis that teachers of English generally and of English literature in particular had as their peculiar object the placing of the English language in chains and the making of literature a fossil in murky amber.

Over the main course, roast stuffed duck, Rubin proceeded to probe the motives of the English-teaching criminals and found it to consist of an embittered and hate-filled envy of those who could, past and present, use the English language as a tool.

"Like Emmanuel Rubin, of course," said Gonzalo in a stage whisper.

"Like me," said Rubin, unabashed. "I know more grammar than any so-called English teacher and have read more literature more closely than they can possibly have done, any of them. The thing is I don't let the grammar bind me or the literature force me."

"Anyone who writes ungrammatical twaddle can say the same," said Avalon.

"That means something, Jeff," said Rubin hotly, "only if you're prepared to say that I write ungrammatical twaddle."

Having disposed of his wild rice and somewhat neg-
lecting the stuffing, Rubin began an eloquent dissertation
on the damage done to young minds by those academic
delinquents and took on the other five members as each
raised objections until the *poire au vin* was served and the
coffee was poured.

"Can I have a glass of milk, instead?" said Atwood
apologetically.

Henry's assent was lost in Rubin's triumphant "There
you are. Any English teacher would have said, 'May I
have a glass of milk?' but Atwood knows he may. The
question is, does the restaurant *have* milk to serve?
Therefore, '*can*' he, not '*may*' he?"

Atwood said, "Actually, my grammar has always been
poor and maybe I should have said—"

Halsted rapped his spoon against the water glass and
said, "Enough grammar, Manny, enough. It's time for our
guest."

"And that's why," said Rubin in a parting shot, "I
don't collect reviews, because any English-lit type who
would waste his time writing reviews—"

"He collects only favorable ones," said Gonzalo. "I
know. He showed me his empty scrapbook."

Halsted's spoon kept up a series of chimes and finally
he said, "My friend Stuart—Mr. Atwood's nephew—
happened to mention, a couple of weeks ago, that Mr.
Atwood had a literary problem. Naturally, I was interested—for reasons we all understand—and inquired further.
It turned out Stu didn't know much about it. I got in
touch with Mr. Atwood and he told me enough to make
me think he would make an excellent guest for this meeting. Since I am hosting and he kindly consented to
come—"

Avalon harumphed stentoriously. "I trust Mr. Atwood
understands that he may be cross-examined rather—"

"I explained it all thoroughly, Jeff," said Halsted. "I
also explained to him that everything that goes on here is
confidential. As it happens, Mr. Atwood is rather interested in a solution to his problem, and is anxious to have
us help."

Trumbull's dark face lined into savage creases. "God damn it, Roger, you haven't guaranteed a solution, have you?"

"No, but we've got a fair record," said Halsted complacently.

"All right, then. Let's begin . . . Henry! Is the brandy on the way? . . . Who does the grilling, Roger?"

"Why, you, Tom."

The brandy was being poured neatly into the small glasses. Atwood raised his hand in a timid negative and Henry passed him. He turned his bright blue eyes toward Trumbull, "Am I to be grilled?"

"Only a manner of speaking, sir. We are interested in your literary problem. Would you care to tell us about it in whatever way you please? We will ask questions when that seems advisable, if you don't mind."

"Oh, I won't mind," said Atwood cheerfully. His eyes darted from one to the other. "I warn you that it isn't much of a mystery—except that I don't know what to make of it."

"Well, we might not know, either," said Gonzalo, touching his brandy to his lips.

Drake, who was nursing the remains of a cold and who had to cut down on his smoking in consequence, stubbed out a half-finished cigarette morosely, and said, "We'll never know if we don't hear what it is." He blew his nose into a bright red handkerchief and stuffed it into his jacket pocket.

"Won't you go on, Mr. Atwood?" said Trumbull. "And let's have some silence from the rest of you."

Atwood folded his hands on the edge of the table almost as though he were back in grade school, and a formal intonation colored his words. He was reciting.

"This all involves my friend Lyon Sanders, who was, like myself, a retired civil engineer. We had never actually worked together but we had been neighbors for a quarter-century and were very close. I am a bachelor; he was a childless widower; and we both led lives that might, superficially, have seemed lonely. Neither of us was, however, for we had each carved out a comfortable niche.

"I myself have written a text on civil engineering which has had some success and for some years I have been preparing a rather elaborate, if informal, tale of my experiences in the field. I doubt that it will ever be published but, of course, if it is—

"But that's beside the point. Sanders was a more aggressive person by far than ever I was; louder; more raucous; with a rather coarse sense of humor. He was a games person—"

Rubin interrupted. "A sports enthusiast?"

"No, no. Indoor games. I believe he knew and could play well every card game ever invented. He could play anything else, too, that used counters, pointers, dice boards, cups, anything. He was a master at Chinese checkers, parcheesi, backgammon, Monopoly, checkers, chess, go, three-dimensional ticktacktoe. I couldn't even tell you the names of most of the games he played.

"He read books on the subject and he invented games himself. Some were clever and I would suggest he patent them and place them on the market. But that was not what he wanted at all. It was only his own amusement that interested him. That was where I came in, you see. I was what he sharpened his analyses on."

Trumbull said, "In what way?"

"Well," said Atwood, "when I say he played those games, I do not mean in the ordinary sense of the word. He analyzed them carefully, almost as though they involved engineering principles—"

"They do," said Rubin suddenly. "Any decent game can be analyzed mathematically. There's a whole field of recreational mathematics."

"I know this," Atwood managed to interpose gently, "but I don't know that Sanders went at it in any orthodox manner. He never offered to explain it to me and I never bothered to ask.

"Our routine over the last twenty years was to spend the weekend at the games, applying what had been learned over the week, for often he would spend time teaching me. Not out of any urge to educate, you understand, but merely to make the game more interesting for himself by improving the opposition. We might play bridge ten weeks running, then switch to gin rummy, then to something in which I had to match numbers he thought of. Naturally, he almost always won."

Drake looked at an unlit cigarette as though he wished it would light itself and said, "Didn't that depress you?"

"Not really. It was fun trying to beat him and sometimes I did. I beat him just often enough to keep up my interest."

"Do you suppose he let you win?" said Gonzalo.

"I doubt it. My victories would always either enrage or chagrin him and they would send him into a fury of further analyses. I think he enjoyed it a little, too, for when he had too long a string of unbroken victories he would start educating me. It was a strange relationship but it worked. We were very fond of each other."

"Were?" asked Avalon.

"Yes," sighed Atwood. "He died six months ago. It was no great shock. We both saw it coming. Of course, I miss him dreadfully. The weekends are quite empty now. I even miss the rowdy way in which he poked fun at me. He bullied me constantly. He never wearied of making fun of me for being a teetotaler and he never stopped teasing me about my religion."

"He was an atheist?" asked Gonzalo.

"Not particularly. In fact, neither of us went to church often. It's just that he was brought up one brand of Protestant and I another. He called mine high-church and found nothing so humorous as to tease me over the elaborateness of the worship I skipped every Sunday in comparison to the simplicity of the worship he skipped every Sunday."

Trumbull frowned. "I should think that would annoy you. Didn't you ever feel like taking a poke at him?"

"Never. It was just his way," said Atwood. "Nor need you think that poor Lyon's death was in the least suspicious. You needn't search for any motives of that kind. He died at the age of sixty-eight of complications from a mild but long-standing case of diabetes.

"He had said that he was going to leave me something

in his will. He expected to die before I did, you see, and he said it was to compensate me for my patience in accepting defeat. Actually, I'm sure it was out of affection, but he would be the last to admit that.

"It was only in the last year before his death, when he knew he was failing, that this began to enter into our conversations. Naturally I protested that this was no fit subject for talk and that he merely made me uncomfortable. But he laughed one time and said, 'I won't make it easy for you, you genuflecting idol worshipper.' You see, just thinking about him makes me fall into his way of talking. I don't know that that's exactly what he called me at this time, but it was something. Anyway, leaving out the epithets, he said, 'I won't make it easy for you. We'll be playing games to the end.'

"He said that on what turned out to be his deathbed. I was all he had, except for the various hospital personnel that hovered about impersonally. He had distant relatives, but none of them visited. Then late in the evening, when I wondered if I ought to leave and return the next morning, he turned his head to me and said in a voice that seemed almost normal, 'The curious omission in Alice.'

"Naturally, I said, 'What?'

"But he laughed very weakly and said, 'That's all you get, old friend, all you get.' And his eyes closed, and he was dead."

Rubin said, "A dying hint!"

Avalon said, "You say his voice was clear?"

"Quite clear," said Atwood.

"And you heard him plainly?"

"Quite plainly," said Atwood.

"You sure he didn't say, 'The curious admission of Wallace'?"

Gonzalo said, "Or 'The furious decision in Dallas.' "

Atwood said, "Please, I haven't finished the story. I was at the reading of the will. I was asked to be. Also present were several of the distant relatives who hadn't visited poor Lyon. There were cousins and a young grand-niece. Lyon wasn't a really rich man, but he left bequests to each of them, and one to an old servant, and one to his school. I came last. I received ten thousand dollars which had been placed in a safe-deposit box for me and for which I would be given the key on request.

"When the will was read and done with, I asked the lawyer for the key to the safe-deposit box. There is no use denying that I can find perfectly good use for ten thousand dollars. The lawyer said that I must apply to the bank in which the box was to be found. If I failed to do so in one year from that date, the bequest was revoked and was to be otherwise disposed of.

"Naturally, I asked where the bank was located and the lawyer said that except for the fact that it was located somewhere in the United States he could not say. He had no further information except for one envelope which he had been instructed to hand to me and which he hoped would be useful. He had one other envelope for himself which was to be opened at the end of one year if I had not, by then, claimed the money.

"I accepted my envelope and found inside only the words I had heard from my friend's dying lips. 'The curious omission in Alice.' . . . And that's where the matter now stands."

Trumbull said, "You mean you haven't got your ten thousand dollars?"

"I mean I haven't located the bank. Six months have passed and I have six months more."

Gonzalo said, "The phrase might be an anagram. Maybe if you rearrange the letters you will get the name of the bank."

Atwood shrugged. "It's a possibility I've thought of. I can't remember Sanders ever playing anagrams, but I've tried that sort of thing. I haven't come up with anything hopeful."

Drake, who blew his nose again and looked as though he had no patience at the moment with careful reasoning, said, "Why don't you just go into every bank in White Plains and ask if there is a key to a safe-deposit box put away in your name?"

Avalon shook his head. "Scarcely playing the game, Jim," he said severely.

"Ten thousand dollars is no game," said Gonzalo.

Atwood said, "I admit that I would feel as though I were cheating if I simply tried to solve it by hit-or-miss, but I must also admit that I cheated. I tried the banks in several neighboring communities as well as in White Plains. I drew a blank. I'm not surprised at that, though. It's unlikely he would place it near home. He had the whole country to choose from."

"Did he make any trips out of town the last year of his life—during the time he started talking will to you?" asked Halsted.

"I don't think so," said Atwood. "But then he wouldn't have to. His lawyer could attend to that part."

"Well," said Trumbull, "let's try it this way. You've had six months to think about it. What conclusions have you come to?"

"Nothing on the message itself," said Atwood, "but I knew my friend well. He once told me that the best way to hide something was to make use of modern technology. Any document, any record, any set of directions could be converted into microfilm, and a tiny piece of material on which that was recorded could be hidden anywhere and never be uncovered by anything but blind luck. I suppose that the message tells me where to find the microfilm."

Rubin shrugged. "That only switches the focus of the problem. Instead of having the message tell us the location of the bank, it tells us the location of the microfilm. That still leaves us with the curious omission."

"I don't think it's quite the same," said Atwood thoughtfully. "The bank may be thousands of miles away, but the piece of microfilm, or just an ordinary piece of very thin paper, for all I know, might be close at hand. But no matter how close at hand, it might as well be a thousand miles away." He sighed. "Poor Lyon will win this game, too, I'm afraid."

Trumbull said, "If we tackled the problem for you, and managed to solve it, Mr. Atwood, would you feel you had been cheating?"

"Oh, yes," said Mr. Atwood, "but I would accept the ten thousand gladly just the same."

Halsted said curiously, "Have you got some idea as to the meaning of the message, Tom?"

"No," said Trumbull, "but if, as Mr. Atwood says, we're looking for a tiny message in a nearby and accessible place, and if we assumed that Mr. Sanders played fair, then maybe we could carry through some eliminations. . . . To whom did he leave his own house, Mr. Atwood?"

"To a cousin, who has since sold it."

"What was done to the contents? Surely Sanders had books, games of all sorts, furniture."

"Most of it was sold at auction."

"Did anything go to you?"

"The cousin was kind enough to offer me whatever I wanted of such material as was not intrinsically valuable. I didn't take anything. I am not the collecting type myself."

"Would your old friend have known this of you?"

"Oh, yes." Atwood stirred restlessly. "Gentlemen, I have had six months to think of this. I realize that Sanders would not have hidden the film in his own house since he left it to someone else and knew I would have no opportunity to search it. He had ample opportunity to hide it in my house, which he visited as often as I visited his, and it is in my house that I think it exists."

Trumbull said, "Not necessarily. He might have felt certain that there would be some favorite books, some certain memento, you would have asked for."

"No," said Atwood. "How could he be certain I would? He would have left such an item to me in his will."

"That would give it away," said Avalon. "Are you sure he never hinted that you ought to take something? Or that he didn't give you something casually?"

"No," said Atwood, smiling. "You have no idea how unlike Sanders that would be. . . . I tell you. I have thought that since he gave me a year to find it, he must have been pretty confident that it would stay in place for that length of time. It wouldn't be likely to be part of something I might throw away, sell, or easily lose."

There was a murmur of agreement.

Atwood said, "He might very likely have pasted it over the molding of a wall, somewhere on the undersurface of a heavy piece of furniture, inside the refrigerator—you see what I mean."

"Have you looked?" said Gonzalo.

"Oh, yes," said Atwood. "This little game has kept me busy. I've spent considerable spare time going over moldings and under-surfaces and drawers and various insides. I've even spent time in the cellar and the attic."

"Obviously," said Trumbull, "you haven't found anything or we wouldn't be talking about it now."

"No, I haven't—but that doesn't mean anything. The thing I'm after might be so small as to be barely visible. Probably is. I could look right at it and miss it, unless I knew I was in the right place and was somehow *prepared* to see it, if you know what I mean."

"Which brings us back," said Avalon heavily, "to the message. If you understood it, you would know where to look and you would see it."

"Ah," said Atwood, "*if* I understood."

"Well, it seems to me," said Avalon, "that the key word is 'Alice.' Does that name have any personal significance to you? Is it the name of someone you both knew? Is it the name of Sanders' dead wife, for instance? The nickname of some object? Some private joke you shared?"

"No. No to all of that."

Avalon smiled, showing his even teeth beneath his neatly trimmed, ever so slightly graying mustache. "Then I would say that 'Alice' must refer to far and away the most famous Alice in the minds of men—*Alice in Wonderland.*"

"Of *course*," said Atwood, in clear surprise. "That's what makes it a literary puzzle and that's why I turned to my nephew who teaches English literature. I assumed at the start it was a reference to the Lewis Carroll classic.

Sanders was an Alice enthusiast. He had a collection of various editions of the book, and he had reproductions of the Tenniel illustrations all over the house."

"You never told us that," said Avalon in hurt tones.

Atwood said, "Haven't I? I'm sorry. It's one of those things I know so well, I somehow expect everyone to know it."

"We might have expected it," said Trumbull, the corners of his mouth twisting down. "Alice involves herself with a deck of cards in the book."

"It always helps to have all pertinent information," said Avalon stiffly.

"Well, then," said Trumbull, "that brings us to the curious omission in *Alice in Wonderland*. . . . And what curious omission is that? Have you any thoughts in that direction, Mr. Atwood?"

"No," said Atwood. "I read *Alice* as a child and have never returned to it—until the bequest, of course. I must admit I've never seen its charm."

"Good Lord," muttered Drake under his breath.

Atwood heard him, for he turned his head sharply in Drake's direction. "I don't deny there may be charm for others but I have never seen the fun in word play. I'm not surprised Sanders enjoyed the book, though. His sense of humor was rather raucous and primitive. In any case, my dislike was compounded by my annoyance at having to detect an omission. I did not wish to have to study the book that closely. I hoped my nephew would help."

"A teacher of literature!" said Rubin derisively.

"Shut up, Manny," said Trumbull. "What did your nephew say, Mr. Atwood?"

"As it happens," said Atwood, "Mr. Rubin is right. My nephew was entirely at sea. He said there were a few passages in the original version of the story that Lewis Carroll had himself written in long hand that did not appear in the final published version. As it happens, an edition of the prepublished version is available now. I obtained a copy and checked through it. I found nothing that seemed significant to me."

Gonzalo said, "Listen! Where we go wrong, Henry always tells us, is in getting too damned complex. Why don't we look at the message? It says, 'The curious omission in Alice.' Maybe we don't have to look at the book. There is a curious omission in the message itself. The name of the book isn't *Alice*. It's *Alice in Wonderland*.

Avalon emerged from his wounded silence long enough to say, "It's *Alice's Adventures in Wonderland, if* you wish to be accurate."

"All right," said Gonzalo, "*Alice's Adventures in Wonderland*. Then we ought to concentrate on the rest of the title, which is *omitted* in the message. . . . Isn't that right, Henry?"

Henry, standing quietly by the sideboard, said, "It is certainly an interesting point, Mr. Gonzalo."

"Interesting, hell," said Trumbull. "What's curious about it? It's an omission of convenience. Lots of people would say *Alice*."

Halsted said, "Quite apart from that, I don't see what *Adventures in Wonderland* would *mean*. It's no more helpful than the original message. Here's my idea. *Alice in Wonderland*—beg pardon, Jeff, *Alice's Adventures in Wonderland*—contains verses, most of which are parodies of well-established poems of the day—"

"Poor ones," said Rubin.

"Beside the point," said Halsted. "They are not perfect parodies, however. Some verses are omitted. For instance, Alice recites a poem beginning 'How doth the little crocodile,' which is a parody of Isaac Watts's dreadful poem 'How doth the little busy bee,' though I don't think that's the actual title of the poem. Alice recites only two stanzas and I'm sure Watts's poem has at least four. Maybe the answer lies in the missing verses of the original."

"Is that a *curious* omission?" said Trumbull.

"I don't know. I don't remember the original version except for the first line, but it should be looked up. . . . The other originals to the parodies should be studied, too."

"I'll be glad to do so," said Atwood politely. "The point had not occurred to me."

Drake said, "I think that's a crock of crud. The message refers to a curious omission in *Alice*. I think it means in *Alice* as it now stands and not in some outside source."

"You can't know that," protested Halsted.

"Yes, but that's the point," said Trumbull. "It seems to me that if we get the right answer, we'll know at once it's right, and if we work out something that only uncovers a new layer of puzzle, that's just wrong."

Avalon said, "Well, nothing more occurs to me. Do we ask Henry?"

Atwood looked puzzled, and Avalon went on, "You have to understand, Mr. Atwood, that Henry, whose pleasure it seems to be to wait on us, has the faculty for seeing past complications."

Gonzalo said, "That's what *I* tried to do and you all ran me down. . . . Henry, isn't the answer in the full title of the book?"

Henry smiled regretfully and said, "Gentlemen, you must not put more on my shoulders than I can carry. I do not know the book very well, though I've read it, of course. If I'm to penetrate the meaning of the puzzle, it will have to be very simple."

"If it were very simple," said Atwood, "we would have seen it."

"Perhaps," said Henry, "yet it seems to me it must be simple. Surely, your friend, Mr. Sanders, wanted you to have the bequest. He put it in a game, and made a contest out of it, because that was his way, but he must have wanted you to win."

Atwood nodded. "I would think so."

"Then let's look for something very simple he felt you would surely see, but just subtle enough, perhaps, to make the game interesting. As I said, I don't know the book very well, so I'll have to ask questions."

"Very well, sir. Mr. Trumbull said *Alice in Wonderland* involved a deck of cards, and I do remember, from the Disney cartoon version more than from anything else, that the Queen of Hearts kept shouting 'Off with his head.' "

"Yes," said Avalon. "A female Henry VIII. The King of Hearts and the Knave of Hearts are also involved."

"Any other cards?"

"They're all mentioned," said Avalon. "The hearts are the royal family, the clubs are soldiers, the diamonds courtiers, the spades workmen. Three of the spades have speaking parts, the two, the five, and the nine. . . . Do you agree with me, Atwood?"

"Yes," said Atwood grimly. "It's fresh in my mind."

Trumbull said, "I suspect Henry is going to ask if any of the cards were omitted. Only a few are mentioned specifically—"

"The six I listed," said Avalon. "The King, Queen, and Knave of Hearts; the two, five, and nine of spades."

"But so what?" said Trumbull. "As many as necessary were mentioned and the rest were there in the background. There's nothing 'curious' about that. I insist on respecting the word 'curious.' "

Henry nodded, then said, "Are you an Episcopalian, Mr. Atwood?"

"I was brought up an Episcopalian. Why do you ask?"

"You said Mr. Sanders teased you about your high-church proclivities and you said you were a Protestant. Putting those together, I felt you might be an Episcopalian. . . . Do you have a chess set, Mr. Atwood?"

"Certainly!"

"Yours? Or was it a present from Mr. Sanders?"

"Oh, no, mine. A rather beautiful set that belonged to my father. Sanders and I played many a game on it."

Henry nodded. "I ask because it seems to me that we've all discussed *Alice in Wonderland* without mentioning that there was a sequel."

"*Through the Looking-Glass,*" said Avalon. "Yes, of course."

"Might that not be considered as included in the word *Alice?*"

Avalon nodded. "Certainly. As it happens, the full title is *Through the Looking-Glass and What Alice Found There,* so it surely bears as much right to be referred to as *Alice* as the other does."

"And isn't *Through the Looking-Glass* about chessmen?"

"Absolutely," said Avalon benevolently, his role as recognized expert having completely restored his good humor. "The Red and White Queens are important characters. The White King has a speaking role but the Red King just sleeps under a tree."

"And there are knights, too?"

Avalon nodded. "The White Knight has a battle with the Red Knight and then escorts Alice to the final square. He's the most amiable character in either book and the only one who seems to like Alice. He's usually considered a self-portrait by Carroll."

"Yes, yes," said Trumbull testily. "What are you getting at, Henry?"

"I'm looking for omissions. There is a reference to a white pawn at the start of the book, I think."

Avalon said, "I don't think you're as unknowledgeable about the books as you pretend, Henry. There *is* a mention of a white pawn named Lily in the first chapter. Alice herself plays the part of a white pawn, too, and is eventually promoted to a white queen."

"And rooks?" said Henry.

Avalon frowned in silence for a while, then shook his head.

Atwood interposed. "There's a reference to them. Take my word for it; I know the stupid books practically by heart. In Chapter 1, Alice enters the Looking-Glass house, sees chessmen moving about, and says to herself, 'and here are two Castles walking arm in arm.' The castles, of course, are also called rooks.

Henry said, "That accounts, then, for the King, Queen, Rook, Knight, and Pawn. But there is a sixth chesspiece, the Bishop. Does it play a role in the book or is it even mentioned?"

Avalon said, "No."

Atwood said, "Two bishops are shown in one of the illustrations to the first chapter."

"That's Tenniel's work," said Henry, "not Carroll's. Now isn't the total absence of the Bishop a curious omission?"

"I don't know," said Avalon slowly. "Lewis Carroll, a

thorough-going Victorian, probably feared giving offense to the Church."

"Isn't it curious to have him go so far in avoiding offense?"

"Well, supposing it is?" asked Halsted.

Henry said, "I think it possible that if Mr. Atwood checks the four bishops of his set, a set which Mr. Sanders knew Mr. Atwood cherished and would neither sell, give away, or lose, he will probably find the piece of film. If the head comes off, he should look inside. If the head doesn't come off, pull off the piece of felt it stands on."

There was an uncomfortable silence. "That's farfetched, Henry," said Trumbull.

"Perhaps not, sir," said Henry. "Mr. Sanders has more than once been described as having a raucous sense of humor. He teased Mr. Atwood constantly about his religion. Perhaps this final message is another way of continuing the joke. You are an Episcopalian, Mr. Atwood, and I suppose you know what the word means."

"It's from the Greek word for bishop," said Atwood, half choking.

"I imagine, then," said Henry, "Mr. Sanders might think it funny to hide the message in a bishop."

Atwood started to his feet. "I think I had better go home."

"I'll take you," said Halsted.

"I think the snow has stopped," said Henry, "but drive carefully."

Afterword

This, in a way, is a twice-told tale.

At a time before I had begun the Black Widowers series, I was asked by Union Carbide Corporation to write a short mystery without a solution for a contest they were running for their employees, who were to supply solutions, with myself making the final judgment on excellence.

Well, I wrote the short mystery, which was rather like the story you have just read. The contest was carried through successfully (two other writers also supplied short mysteries) and all was well.

However, I was made restless by the fact that the short mystery I wrote was never published—except on the book jacket of an edition of *The Adventures of Sherlock Holmes* which was given out to the contest applicants. That seemed a waste to me, and I abhor literary waste. It was especially annoying since the story appeared without my solution.

So I completely rewrote the story, lengthening it a good deal, placing it against the Black Widower background, and now I feel ever so much better. Especially since now my solution is included.

12

Out of Sight

The monthly banquet of the Black Widowers had reached
the point where little was left of the mixed grill save for
an occasional sausage and a markedly untouched piece of
liver on the plate of Emmanuel Rubin—and it was then
that voices rose in Homeric combat.

Rubin, undoubtedly infuriated by the presence of liver
at all, was saying, even more flatly than was usual for
him, "Poetry is *sound*. You don't *look* at poetry. I don't
care whether a culture emphasizes rhyme, alliteration,
repetition, balance, or cadence, it all comes down to
sound."

Roger Halsted never raised his voice, but one could always tell the state of his emotions by the color of his high
forehead. Right now, it was a deep pink, the color ex-
tending past the line that had once marked hair. He said,
"What's the use of making generalizations, Manny? No
generalization can hold generally without an airtight system of axiomatics to begin with. Literature—"

"If you're going to tell me about figurative verse," said
Rubin hotly, "save your breath. That's Victorian nonsense."

"What's figurative verse?" asked Mario Gonzalo lazily.
"Is he making that up, Jeff?" He added a touch to the
tousled hair in his careful caricature of the banquet guest,
Waldemar Long, who, since the dinner had begun, had
eaten in a somber silence, but was obviously following
every word.

"No," said Geoffrey Avalon judiciously, "though I
wouldn't put it past Manny to make something up if that
were the only way he could win an argument. Figurative

verse is verse in which the words or lines are arranged typographically in such a way as to produce a visual image that reinforces the sense. 'The Mouse's Tail' in *Alice in Wonderland* is the best-known example."

Halsted's soft voice was unequal to the free-for-all and he methodically beat his spoon against the water goblet till the decibels had simmered down.

He said, "Let's be reasonable. The subject under discussion is not poetry in general, but the limerick as a verse form. My point is this—I'll repeat it, Manny—that the worth of a limerick is not dictated by its subject matter. It's easier—"

James Drake stubbed out his cigarette, twitched his small grizzled mustache, and said in his hoarse voice, "Why do you call a dirty limerick dirty? The Supreme Court will get you."

Halsted said, "Because it's a two-syllable word with a meaning you all understand. What do you want me to say? Sexual-excretory-blasphemous-and-miscellaneous-generally-irreverent?"

Avalon said, "Go on, Roger. Go on. Make your point and don't let them needle you." And, from under his luxuriant eyebrows, he frowned austerely at the table generally. "Let him talk."

"Why?" said Rubin. "He has nothing to . . . Okay, Jeff. Talk, Roger."

"Thank you all," said Halsted, in the wounded tone of one who has finally succeeded in having his wrong recognized. "The worth of a limerick rests in the unpredictability of the last line and in the cleverness of the final rhyme. In fact, irreverent content may seem to have value in itself and require less cleverness—and produce a less worthwhile limerick, as limerick. Now it is possible to have the rhyme masked by the orthographical conventions."

"What?" said Gonzalo.

"Spelling," said Avalon.

"And then," said Halsted, "in seeing the spelling and having that instant of delay in getting the sound, you intensify the enjoyment. But under those conditions you have to *see* the limerick. If you just recite it, the excellence is lost."

"Suppose you give us an example," said Drake.

"I know what he means," said Rubin loudly. "He's going to rhyme M.A. and C.D.—Master of Arts and Caster of Darts."

"That's an exampe that's been used," admitted Halsted, "but it's extreme. It takes too long to catch on and amusement is drowned in irritation. As it happens, I've made up a limerick while we were having the argument—"

And now, for the first time, Thomas Trumbull entered this part of the discussion. His tanned and wrinkled face twisted into a dark scowl and he said, "The hell you did. You made it up yesterday and you engineered this whole silly nonsense so you could recite it. If it's one of your *Iliad* things, I'll personally kick you out of here."

"It's not the *Iliad*," said Halsted. "I haven't been working on that recently. It's no use my reciting this one, of course. I'll write it down and pass it around."

He wrote in dark block letters on an unused napkin:

> YOU CAN'T CALL THE BRITISH QUEEN MS.
> TAIN'T AS NICE AS ELIZABETH IS.
> BUT I THINK THAT THE QUEEN
> WOULD BE EVEN LESS KEEN
> TO HAVE HERSELF MENTIONED AS LS.

Gonzalo laughed aloud when it came too him. He said, "Sure, if you know that MS is pronounced Miz, then you pronounce LS as Liz."

"To me," said Drake scornfully, "LS would have to stand for 'lanuscript' if it's going to rhyme with MS."

Avalon pursed his lips and shook his head. "Using TAIN'T is a flaw. You ought to lose a syllable some other way. And to be perfectly consistent, shouldn't the rhyme word IS be spelled simply S?"

Halsted nodded eagerly. "You're quite right, and I thought of doing that, but it wouldn't be transparent

enough and the reader wouldn't get it fast enough to
laugh. Secondly, it would be the cleverest part of the limerick and would make the LS anticlimactic."

"Do you really have to waste all that fancy reasoning
on a piece of crap like this?" asked Trumbull.

"I think I've made my point," said Halsted. "The
humor can be visual."

Trumbull said, "Well, then, drop the subject. Since I'm
host this session, that's an order. . . . Henry, where's the
damned dessert?"

"It's here, sir," said Henry softly. Unmoved by Trumbull's tone, he deftly cleared the table and dealt out the
blueberry shortcake.

The coffee had already been poured and Trumbull's
guest said in a low voice, "May I have tea, please?"

The guest had a long upper lip and an equally long
chin. The hair on his head was shaggy but there was none
on his face and he had walked with a somewhat bearlike
stoop. When he was first introduced, only Rubin had reg-
istered any recognition.

He had said, "Aren't you with NASA?"

Waldemar Long had answered with a startled "Yes" as
though he had been disturbed out of a half-resentful resignation to anonymity. He had then frowned. He was
frowning now again as Henry poured the tea and melted
unobtrusively into the background.

Trumbull said, "I think the time has come for our guest
to enter the discussion and perhaps add some portion of
sense to what has been an unusually foolish evening."

"No, that's all right, Tom," said Long. "I don't mind
frivolity." He had a deep and rather beautiful voice that
had a definite note of sadness in it. He went on, "I have
no aptitude for badinage myself, but I enjoy listening to
it."

Halsted, still brooding over the matter of the limericks,
said, with sudden forcefulness, "I suggest Manny *not* be
the grill master on this occasion."

"No?" said Rubin, his sparse beard lifting belligerently.

"No. I put it to you, Tom. If Manny questions our

guest, he will surely bring up the space program since there's a NASA connection. Then we will go through the same darned argument we've had a hundred times. I'm sick of the whole subject of space and whether we ought to be on the moon."

"Not half as sick as I am," said Long, rather unexpectedly, "I'd just as soon not discuss any aspect of space exploration."

The heavy flatness of the remark seemed to dampen spirits all around. Even Halsted seemed momentarily at a loss for any other subject to introduce to someone connected with NASA.

Then Rubin stirred in his seat and said, "I take it, Dr. Long, that this is a recently developed attitude of yours."

Long's head turned suddenly toward Rubin. His eyes narrowed. "Why do you say that, Mr. Rubin?"

Rubin's small face came as close to a simper as it ever did. "Elementary, my dear Dr. Long. You were on the cruise that went down to see the Apollo shot last winter. I'd been invited as a literary representative of the intellectual community, but I couldn't go. However, I got the promotional literature and noticed you were along. You were going to lecture on some aspect of the space program, I forget which, and that was voluntary. So your disenchantment with the subject must have arisen in the six months since the cruise."

Long nodded his head very slightly a number of times and said, "I seem to be more heard of in that connection than in any other in my life. The damned cruise has made me famous, too."

"I'll go farther," said Rubin enthusiastically, "and suggest that something happened on the cruise that disenchanted you with space exploration, maybe to the point where you're thinking of leaving NASA and going into some other field of work altogether."

Long's stare was fixed now. He pointed a finger at Rubin, a long finger that showed no signs of tremor, and said, "Don't play games." Then, with a controlled anger, he rose from his chair and said, "I'm sorry, Tom. Thanks for the meal, but I'll go now."

Everyone rose at once, speaking simultaneously; all but Rubin, who remained sitting with a look of stunned astonishment on his face.

Trumbull's voice rose above the rest. "Now wait a while, Waldemar. God damn it, will all of you sit down? Waldemar, you too. What's the excitement about? Rubin, what *is* all this?"

Rubin looked down at his empty coffeecup and lifted it as though he wished there were coffee in it so that he could delay matters by taking a sip. "I was just demonstrating a chain of logic. After all, I write mysteries. I seem to have touched a nerve." Then, gratefully, he said, "Thanks, Henry," as the cup before him sparkled black to the brim.

"What chain of logic?" demanded Trumbull.

"Okay, here it is. Dr. Long said, 'The damned cruise has made me famous, too.' He said 'too' and emphasized the word. That means it did something else for him and since we were talking about his distaste for the whole subject of space exploration, I deduced that the something else it had done was to supply him with that distaste. From his bearing I guessed it was sharp enough to make him want to quit his job. That's all there is to it."

Long nodded his head again, in precisely the same slight and rapid way as before, and then settled back in his seat. "All right. I'm sorry, Mr. Rubin. I jumped too soon. The fact is I *will* be leaving NASA. To all intents and purposes, I *have* left it—and at the point of a shoe. That's all. . . . We'll change the subject. Tom, you said coming here would get me out of my dumps, but it hasn't worked that way. Rather, my mood has infected you all and I've cast a damper on the party. Forgive me, all of you."

Avalon put a finger to his neat, graying mustache and stroked it gently. He said, "Actually, sir, you have supplied us with something we all like above all things—the opportunity to exert our curiosity. May we question you on this matter?"

'It's not something I'm free to talk about," said Long, guardedly.

Trumbull said, "You can if you want to, Waldemar. You needn't mention sensitive details, but as far as anything else is concerned, everything said in this room is confidential. And, as I always add when I find it necessary to make that statement, the confidentiality includes our esteemed friend Henry."

Henry, who was standing at the sideboard, smiled briefly.

Long hesitated. Then he said, "Actually, your curiosity is easily satisfied and I suspect that Mr. Rubin, at least, with his aptitude for guessing, has already deduced the details. I'm suspected of having been indiscreet, either deliberately or carelessly, and, either way, I may find myself unofficially, but very effectively, blocked off from any future position in my field of competence."

"You mean you'll be blackballed?" said Drake.

"That's a word," said Long, "that's never used. But that's what it will amount to."

"I take it," said Drake, "you weren't indiscreet."

"On the contrary, I was." Long shook his head. "I haven't denied that. The trouble is they think the story is worse than I admit."

There was another pause and then Avalon, speaking in his most impressively austere tone, said, "Well, sir, *what* story? Is there anything you can tell us about it or must you leave it at no more than what you have already said?"

Long passed a hand over his face, then pushed his chair away from the table so that he could lean his head back against the wall.

He said, "It's so damned undramatic. I was on this cruise, as Mr. Rubin told you. I was going to give a talk on certain space projects, rather far-out ones, and planned on going into detail on exactly what was being done in certain fascinating directions. I can't give you *those* details. I found that out the hard way. Some of the stuff had been classified, but I had been told I could talk about it. Then, on the day before I was to give my lecture, I got a radiophone call saying it was all off. There was to be no declassification.

"I was furious. There's no use denying I have a temper and I also have very little gift for spontaneous lecturing. I had carefully written out the lecture and I had intended to read it. I know that's not a good way of giving a talk, but it's the best I can do. Now I had nothing left to give to a group of people who had paid considerable money to listen to me. It was a damned embarrassing position."

"What did you do?" asked Avalon.

Long shook his head. "I held a rather pathetic question-and-answer session the next day. It didn't go over at all well. It was worse than just not having a talk. By that time, you see, I knew I was in considerable trouble."

"In what way, sir?" said Avalon.

"If you want the fun story," said Long, "here it is. I'm not exactly talkative at meals, as you may perhaps have noticed, but when I went in to dinner after getting the call, I suppose I put on a passable imitation of a corpse that had died with an angry look on its face. The rest tried to draw me into the conversation, if only, I suppose, to keep me from poisoning the atmosphere. Finally one of them said, "Well, Dr. Long, what will you be talking about tomorrow?' And I blew up and said, 'Nothing! Nothing at all! I've got the paper all written out and it's sitting there on the desk in my cabin and I can't give it because I just found out the material is still classified.' "

"And then the paper was stolen?" said Gonzalo excitedly.

"No. Why steal anything these days? It was photographed."

"Are you sure?"

"I was sure at the time. When I got back to my cabin after dinner the door was not locked and the papers had been moved. Since then, it's become certain. We have proof that the information has leaked."

There was a rather depressed silence at that. Then Trumbull said, "Who could have done it? Who heard you?"

"Everyone at the table," said Long despondently.

Rubin said, "You have a strong voice, Dr. Long, and if you were as angry as I think you were, you spoke forcefully. Probably a number of the people at adjoining tables heard you."

"No," said Long, shaking his head. "I spoke through clenched teeth, not loudly. Besides, you don't realize what the cruise was like. The cruise was badly undersubscribed, you see—poor promotion, poor management. The ship was carrying only forty percent capacity and the shipping company is supposed to have lost a packet."

"In that case," said Avalon, "it must have been a dreary experience apart from your misadventure."

"On the contrary, up to that point it was very pleasant for me, and it continued to be very pleasant for all the rest, I imagine. The crew nearly outnumbered the passengers and the service was excellent. All the facilities were available without crowding. They scattered us through the dining room and gave us privacy. There were seven of us at our dining table. Lucky seven, someone said at the beginning." For a moment Long's look of grimness deepened. "None of the tables near us were occupied. I'm quite certain that nothing any of us said was heard anywhere but at our own table."

"Then there are seven suspects," said Gonzalo thoughtfully.

"Six, since you needn't count me," said Long. "I knew where the paper was and what it was. I didn't have to hear myself to know that."

"You're under suspicion, too. Or you implied that," said Gonzalo.

"Not to myself," said Long.

Trumbull said peevishly, "I wish you had come to me with this, Waldemar. I've been worrying over your obvious green-and-yellow attitude for months."

"What would you have done if I had told you?"

Trumbull considered. "Damn it, I'd have brought you here. . . . All right. Tell us about the six at the table. Who were they?"

"One was the ship's doctor; a good-looking Dutchman in an impressive uniform."

Rubin said, "He would be. The ship was one of the Holland-American liners, wasn't it?"

"Yes. The officers were Dutch and the crew—the waiters, stewards, and so on—were mostly Indonesian. They'd all had three-month cram courses in English, but we communicated mostly in sign language. I don't complain, though. They were pleasant and hard-working—and all the more efficient since there was considerably less than the ordinary complement of passengers."

"Any reason to suspect the Doctor?" asked Drake.

Long nodded. "I suspected them all. The Doctor was a silent man; he and I were the two silent ones. The other five made a continuous uproar, much as you do here at this table. He and I listened. What I've brooded about in connection with him was that it was he who asked me about my talk. Asking a personal question like that was uncharacteristic."

"He may have been worried about you medically," said Halsted. "He may have been trying to draw you out."

"Maybe," said Long indifferently. "I remember every detail of that dinner; I've gone over and over it in my mind. It was an ethnic dinner, so everyone was supplied with little Dutch hats made out of paper and special Indonesian dishes were supplied. I wore the hat but I hate curried food and the Doctor asked about my speech just as a small dish of curried lamb was put before me as an hors d'oeuvre. Between fuming over official stupidity and sickening over the smell of curry, I just burst out. If it hadn't been for the curry, perhaps—

"Anyway, after dinner I discovered that someone had been in my cabin. The contents of the paper weren't so important, classification or not, but what was important was that someone had taken action so quickly. Someone on the ship was part of a spy network and that was more important than the actual coup. Even if the present item were not important, the next might be. It was important to report the matter and, as a loyal citizen, I did."

Rubin said, "Isn't the Doctor the logical suspect? He asked the question and he would be listening to the answer. The others might not have. As an officer, he would be used to the ship, know how to get to your cabin quickly, perhaps have a duplicate key ready. Did he have an opportunity to get to your cabin before you did?"

"Yes, he did," said Long. "I thought of all that. The trouble is this. Everyone at the table heard me, because all the rest talked about the system of classification for a while. I kept quiet myself but I remember the matter of the Pentagon Papers came up. And everyone knew where my cabin was because I had given a small party in it for the table the day before. And those locks are easy to open for anyone with a little skill at it—though it was a mistake not to close it again on leaving, but whoever it was had to be in a hurry. And, as it happened, everyone at the table had a chance to get to the cabin during the course of the meal."

"Who were the others, then?" asked Halsted.

"Two married couples and a single woman. The single woman—call her Miss Robinson—was pretty, a little on the plump side, had a pleasant sense of humor, but had the bad habit of smoking during the meal. I rather think she liked the Doctor. She sat between us—we always had the same seats."

"When did she have a chance to reach your cabin?" asked Halsted.

"She left shortly after I made my remark. I was brooding too deeply to be aware of it at the time but of course I remembered it afterward. She came back before the fuss over the hot chocolate came up because I remember her trying to help."

"Where did she say she went?"

"Nobody asked her at the time. She was asked afterward and she said she had gone to her cabin to go to the bathroom. Maybe she did. But her cabin was reasonably near mine."

"No one saw her at all?"

"No one would. Everyone was in the dining room and to the Indonesians all Americans look alike."

Avalon said, "What's the fuss over the hot chocolate you referred to?"

Long said, "That's where one of the married couples

comes in. Call them the Smiths and the other one the Joneses, or the other way around. It doesn't matter. Mr. Smith was the raucous type. He reminded me, in fact, of—"

"Oh, Lord," said Rubin. "Don't say it."

"All right, I won't. He was one of the lecturers. In fact, both Smith and Jones were. Smith talked fast, laughed easily, turned everything into a double-entendre, and seemed to enjoy it all so much he had the rest of us doing it, too. He was a very odd person. The kind of fellow you can't help but take an instant dislike to and judge to be stupid. But then, as you get used to him, you find you like him after all and that under the surface nonsense, he's extremely intelligent. The first evening, I remember, the Doctor kept staring at him as if he were a mental specimen, but by the end of the cruise, he was clearly pleased with Smith.

"Jones was much quieter. He seemed horrified, at first, by Smith's outrageous comments but eventually he was matching him, I noticed—rather, I think, to Smith's discomfiture."

Avalon said, "What were their fields?"

"Smith was a sociologist and Jones a biologist. The idea was that space exploration was to be viewed in the light of many disciplines. It was a good concept but showed serious flaws in the execution. Some of the talks, though, were excellent. There was one on Mariner 9 and the new data on Mars that was superb, but that's beside the point.

"It was Mrs. Smith who created the confusion. She was a moderately tall, thin girl. Not very good-looking by the usual standards but with an extraordinarily attractive personality. She was soft-spoken and clearly went through life automatically thinking of others. I believe everyone quickly grew to feel quite affectionate to her and Smith himself seemed devoted. The evening I shot my mouth off, she ordered hot chocolate. It came in a tall glass, very top-heavy, and, of course, as a mistaken touch of elegance, it was brought on a tray.

"Smith, as usual, was talking animatedly and waving

his arms as he did so. He used all his muscles when he talked. The ship swayed, he swayed—well, anyway, the hot chocolate went into Mrs. Smith's lap.

"She jumped up. So did everyone else. Miss Robinson moved quickly toward her to help. I noticed that and that's how I know she was back by then. Mrs. Smith waved help away and left in a hurry. Smith, looking suddenly confused and upset, tore off the paper Dutch hat he was wearing and followed. Five minutes later he was back, talking earnestly to the head steward. Then he came to the table and said that Mrs. Smith had sent him down to assure the steward that she was wearing nothing that couldn't be washed, that she hadn't been hurt, that it wasn't anyone's fault, that no one was to be blamed.

"He wanted to assure us she was all right, too. He asked if we could stay at the table till his wife came back. She was changing clothes and wanted to join us again so that none of us would feel as though anything very terrible had happened. We agreed, of course. None of us were going anywhere."

Avalon said, "And that means she had time to get to your cabin."

Long nodded. "Yes, I suppose so. She didn't seem the type but I suppose in this game you disregard surface appearances."

"And you all waited?"

"Not the Doctor. He got up and said he would get some ointment from his office in case she needed it for burns, but he came back before she did by a minute or so."

Avalon said, tapping his finger on the table slowly to lend emphasis, "And he might have been at the cabin, too, then. And Miss Robinson might, when she left before the hot-chocolate incident."

Rubin said, "Where do the Joneses come in?"

Long said, "Let me go on. When Mrs. Smith came back she denied having been burned and the Doctor had no need to give her the ointment, so we can't say if he even went to get it. He might have been bluffing."

"What if she had asked for it?" said Halsted.

"Then he might have said he couldn't find what he had been looking for but if she came with him he'd do what he could. Who knows? In any case, we all sat for a while almost as though nothing had happened and then, finally, it broke up. By that time, we were the last occupied table. Everyone left, with Mrs. Jones and myself lingering behind for a while."

"Mrs. Jones?" asked Drake.

"I haven't told you about Mrs. Jones. Dark hair and eyes, very vivacious. Had a penchant for sharp cheeses, always taking a bit of each off the tray when it was brought round. She had a way of looking at you when you talk that had you convinced you were the only object she saw. I think Jones was rather a jealous type in his quiet way. At least, I never saw him more than two feet from her, except this one time. He got up and said he was going to the cabin and she said she would be there soon. Then she turned to me and said, 'Can you explain why those terraced icefields on Mars are significant? I've been meaning to ask you all during dinner and didn't get a chance.'

"It had been that day that we had had the magnificent talk on Mars and I was rather flattered that she turned to me instead of to the astronomer who had given the talk. It seemed as though she were taking it for granted I knew as much as he did. So I talked to her for a while and she kept saying, 'How interesting.' "

Avalon said, "And meanwhile, *Jones* could have been in your cabin."

"Could be. I thought of that afterward. It was certainly atypical behavior on both their parts."

Avalon said, "Let's summarize, then. There are four possibilities. Miss Robinson might have done it when she left before the hot-chocolate incident. The Smiths might have done it as a team, Mr. Smith deliberately spilling the hot chocolate, so that Mrs. Smith could do the dirty work. Or the Doctor could have done it while going for the ointment. Or the Joneses could have done it as a team, with Jones doing the dirty work while Mrs. Jones kept Dr. Long out of action."

Long nodded. "All this was considered and by the time the ship was back in New York, security agents had begun the process of checking the background of all six. You see, in cases like this, suspicion is all you need. The only way any secret agent can remain undetected is for him or her to remain unsuspected. Once the eye of counterintelligence is upon him, he must inevitably be unmasked. No cover can survive an investigation in depth."

Drake said, "Then which one did it prove to be?"

Long sighed. "That's where the trouble arose. None of them. All were clean. There was no way, I understand, of showing any of them to be anything other than what they seemed."

Rubin said, "Why do you say you 'understand.' Aren't you part of the investigation?"

"At the wrong end. The cleaner those six are, the dirtier I appear to be. I told the investigators—I *had* to tell them—that those six are the only ones who could possibly have done it, and if none of them did, they must suspect me of making up a story to hide something worse."

Trumbull said, "Oh, hell, Waldemar. They can't think that. What would you have to gain by reporting the incident if you were responsible?"

"That's what they don't know," said Long. "But the information did leak and if they can't pin it on any of the six, then they're going to pin it on me. And the more my motives puzzle them, the more they think those motives must be very disturbing indeed. So I'm in trouble."

Rubin said, "Are you sure those six are indeed the only possibilities. Are you sure you really didn't mention it to anyone else?"

"Quite sure," said Long dryly.

"You might not remember having done so," said Rubin. "It could have been something very casual. Can you be *sure* you didn't?"

"I can be sure I didn't. The radiophone call came not

long before dinner. There just wasn't time to tell anyone before dinner. And once I got away from the table, I was back in the cabin before I as much as said anything to anybody. Anything at all."

"Who heard you on the phone? Maybe there were eavesdroppers."

"There were ship's officers standing around, certainly. However, my boss expressed himself Aesopically. I knew what he meant, but no one else would have."

"Did you express *your*self Aesopically?" asked Halsted.

"I'll tell you exactly what I said. 'Hello, Dave.' Then I said, 'God damn it to hell.' Then I hung up. I said those seven words. No more."

Gonzalo brought his hands together in a sudden, enthusiastic clap. "Listen, I've been thinking. Why does the job have to be so planned? It could be spontaneous. After all, everybody knows there's this cruise and people connected with NASA are going to talk and there might be something interesting on. Someone—it could have been anyone—kept searching various rooms during the dinner hour each day and finally came across your paper—"

"No," said Long sharply. "It passes the bounds of plausibility to suppose that someone would, just by chance, find my paper just in the hour or two after I had announced that a classified lecture was sitting on my desk. Besides, there was nothing in the paper that would have given any indication of importance to the nonexpert. It was only my own remark that would have told anyone it was there and that it was important."

Avalon said thoughtfully, "Suppose one of the people at the table passed on the information, in perfect innocence. In the interval they were away from the table, they might have said to someone, 'Did you hear about poor Dr. Long? His paper was shot out from under him?' Then that someone, anyone, could have done the job."

Long shook his head. "I wish that could be so, but it can't. That would only happen if the particular individual at my table were innocent. If the Smiths were innocent when they left the table, the only thing on their minds would be the hot chocolate. They wouldn't stop to chat. The Doctor would be thinking only of getting the ointment. By the time Jones left the table, assuming he was innocent, he would have forgotten about the matter. If anything, he would talk about the hot chocolate, too."

Rubin said suddenly, voice rising, "All right. What about Miss Robinson? She left before the hot-chocolate incident. The only interesting thing in her mind would have been your dilemma. She might have said something."

"Might she?" said Long. "If she is innocent, then she was really doing what she said she was doing, going to the bathroom in her cabin. If she had to desert the dinner table to do so, there would have had to be urgency; and no one under those conditions stops for idle gossip."

There was silence all around the table.

Long said, "I'm sure investigation will continue and eventually the truth will come out and it will be clear that I'm guilty of no more than an unlucky indiscretion. By then, though, my career will be down the drain."

"Dr. Long?" said a soft voice. "May I ask a question?"

Long looked up, surprised. "A question?"

"I'm Henry, sir. The gentlemen of the Black Widowers organization occasionally allow me to participate—"

"Hell, yes, Henry," said Trumbull. "Do you see something the rest of us don't?"

"I'm not certain," said Henry. "I see quite plainly that Dr. Long believes only the six others at the table might possibly be involved, and those investigating the matter apparently agree with him—"

"There's no way not to," said Long.

"Well, then," said Henry. "I am wondering if Dr. Long mentioned his views on curry to the investigators."

Long said, "You mean that I didn't like curry?"

"Yes," said Henry. "Did that come up?"

Long spread his hands and then shook his head. "No, I don't think it did. Why should it? It's irrelevant. It's just an additional excuse for my talking like a jackass. I tell it to you here in order to collect sympathy, I suppose, but it would carry no weight with the investigators."

Henry remained silent for a moment, and Trumbull said, "Does the curry have meaning to you, Henry?"

"I think perhaps it does," said Henry. "I think we are in rather the position Mr. Halsted described earlier in the evening in connection with limericks. Some limericks to be effective must be seen; sound is not enough. And some scenes to be effective must be seen."

"I don't get that," said Long.

"Well, Dr. Long," said Henry. "You sat there in the ship's restaurant at a table with six other people and therefore only those six other people heard you. But if we could see the scene instead of having you describe it to us, would we see something clearly that you have omitted?"

"No, you wouldn't," said Long doggedly.

"Are you sure?" asked Henry. "You sit here with six other people at a table, too, just as you did on the ship. How many people hear your story?"

"Six—" began Long.

And then Gonzalo broke in, "Seven, counting you, Henry."

"And was there no one serving you at table, Dr. Long? You said the Doctor had asked you about the speech just as curried lamb was put before you and it was the smell of curry that annoyed you to the point where you burst out with your indiscretion. Surely, the curried lamb didn't place itself before you of its own accord. The fact is that at the moment you made your statement, there were six people at the table before you, and a seventh standing just behind you and out of sight."

"The waiter," said Long in a whisper.

Henry said, "There's a tendency never to notice a waiter unless he annoys you. An efficient waiter is invisible, and you mentioned the excellence of the service. Might it not have been the waiter who carefully engineered the spilling of the hot chocolate to create a diversion; or perhaps he who took advantage of the diversion, if it was an accident? With waiters many and diners few, it might not be too noticeable if he vanished for a while.

Or he could claim to have gone to the men's room if it were indeed noticed. He would know the location of the cabin as well as the Doctor did, and be as likely to have some sort of picklock."

Long said, "But he was an Indonesian. He couldn't speak English."

"Are you sure? He'd had a three-month cram course, you said. And he might have known English better than he pretended. You would be willing to conceive that Mrs. Smith was not as sweet and thoughtful underneath as on the surface, and that Mrs. Jones's vivacity was pretense, and the Doctor's respectability and Smith's liveliness and Jones's devotion and Miss Robinson's need to go to the bathroom. Might not the waiter's ignorance of English also be pretense?"

"By God," said Long, looking at his watch. "If it weren't so late, I'd call Washington now."

Trumbull said, "If you know some home phone numbers, *do* call now. It's your career. Tell them the waiter ought to be investigated, and for heaven's sake, don't tell them you got the notion from someone else."

"You mean, tell them I just thought of it? They'll ask why I didn't think of that before."

"Ask them why *they* didn't. Why didn't *they* think a waiter goes with a table?"

Henry said softly, "No reason for anyone to think of it. Only very few are as interested in waiters as I am."

Afterword

This story appeared in the December 1973 issue of *Ellery Queen's Mystery Magazine* under the title "The Six Suspects." Again, I prefer my own title.

The inspiration here arose out of the fact that I was on a cruise like the one described in the story. Some of the events even happened but, I hasten to say, there were no scientific secrets on board as far as I know and no mystery.

One last word. Based on past experience, I am going to get a lot of letters asking me if I intend to write more Black Widowers stories. Let me answer that with a firm and definite: Yes. That, perhaps, will abort the letters.

As a matter of fact, I have at the moment of this writing, completed and sold six more Black Widowers, five to *Ellery Queen's Mystery Magazine* and one to *The Magazine of Fantasy and Science Fiction*. You see, then, that it is quite possible that eventually you will be asked to read something entitled *More Tales of The Black Widowers*.

I hope so, because its' fun writing these stories—and thank you all for reading them.